Morris Automated Informati...

P9-DKD-947

0 1029 0420117 7

FICTION   Dunmore, Helen,
DUNMORE   1952-

             Mourning Ruby.

DATE			

Parsippany-Troy Hills Public Library
Parsippany Branch
292 Parsippany Road
Parsippany, NJ 07054

MAR 2 2 2004   BAKER & TAYLOR

Mourning Ruby

By the Same Author

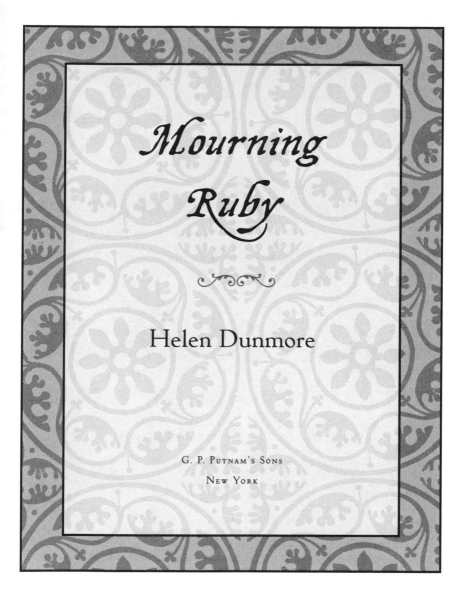

Mourning Ruby

Helen Dunmore

G. P. Putnam's Sons

New York

This is a work of fiction. Names, characters, places, and incidents either
are the product of the author's imagination or are used fictitiously,
and any resemblance to actual persons, living or dead, business
establishments, events, or locales is entirely coincidental.

∎P

G. P. Putnam's Sons
Publishers Since 1838
a member of
Penguin Group (USA) Inc.
375 Hudson Street
New York, NY 10014

Copyright © 2004 by Helen Dunmore
All rights reserved. This book, or parts thereof, may not
be reproduced in any form without permission.

A list of credits can be found on pages 277–78.

Library of Congress Cataloging-in-Publication Data

Dunmore, Helen, date.
Mourning Ruby / Helen Dunmore.
p.   cm.
ISBN 0-399-15148-6
1. Children—Death—Fiction.   2. Friendship—Fiction.
3. Grief—Fiction.   I. Title.
PR6054.U528M68   2004   2003054812
823'.914—dc21

Printed in the United States of America
1   3   5   7   9   10   8   6   4   2

This book is printed on acid-free paper. ∞

Book design by Meighan Cavanaugh

Mourning Ruby

Prologue

A car comes up, with lamps full-glare,
    That flash upon a tree:
    It has nothing to do with me
And whangs along in a world of its own,
    Leaving a blacker air.

We're on the coast road to Zennor from St. Just. The sun set half an hour ago and the western sky is hung with rags of light. Dark is gaining fast.

Ruby and I are walking northward. We keep to the road, with Ruby's hand in mine. Not a single car has passed us.

If we were in a house now, looking from a window, we would see only black. But when you are out in the living dark it takes a hundred shapes and shades.

We are safe. Soon night will fold around us as we walk on, but even before the moon rises there'll be enough starlight to see the pale stripe of the road. And Ruby's a good walker.

On our left, below the cliffs, the vast Atlantic breathes.

A basking shark came in close around the Island last summer. Dolphins played off Gwithian and people went out to visit them in boats.

The seals will be feeding their pups now, on the ledges they've chosen. The mother seal's fat melts from her as she pours calories into her pup. The equation is that by the time she needs to roam free and feed, the pup will survive without her. It doesn't always work, that goes without saying.

Ruby knows if she sees a seal pup alone in one of the coves, she mustn't go near, still less touch. The spoor of her humanity would drive the mother seal away forever.

It hasn't been abandoned, Ruby. The mother's probably watching you now.

It's dark. We hear the distant pull of the sea, the cry of the last gulls heading out of land. Ruby asks me how far it is and instead of telling her I sing a song she knows.

How many miles to Babylon?
Four score miles and ten.
Will we get there by candlelight?
Yes, and back again.

If your heels are nimble and light
We may get there by candlelight.

"Are my heels nimble and light?" Ruby asks.

⁓

We walk on. I hold her warm, soft hand more tightly. We can keep up this pace for hours if we have to. It's easier walking by day than by night. If she gets too tired I'll hoist her on my back.

"Do whales go to sleep?"

"Everything has to sleep."

"Does the sea sleep?"

"I don't think so."

Are witches real and why do animals eat other animals? Why is it that we fear our own kind more than any other creature we might meet on these lonely roads at night? It's not the vixen's cough or the cliff's drop that makes me prickle. It's those headlights, far off, sweeping the granite hedges.

Those headlights, too fast. They come full on and the black safe night ruptures round us.

I sweep Ruby onto the verge. I push her into the wetness of long grass. She yelps protest but I smother it with my body which shields her so that if anything's hit it'll be me and never Ruby.

We are held in white oncoming light. I don't even hear the car engine. Too close, spitting up stones, the car sweeps past.

It's gone. I wind Ruby out of the folds of my coat. On our left, below the cliffs, the vast Atlantic breathes. Ruby and I walk on.

I would sleep forever if it would give me dreams like this.

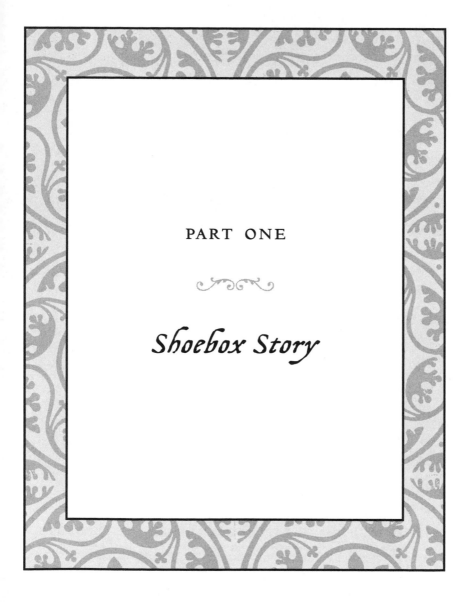

PART ONE

Shoebox Story

Foundling

She was a good-looking girl, too; where did she come from?

She dodged into the yard with me in her arms, tucked up in a shoe-box. Or, to be exact, a box that once held a pair of men's size eleven mid-tan calf-leather shoes.

The cardboard's worn now, but there's still a picture of the shoes on the side. They look very manly. I expect this is why I've always loved the smell of leather.

"Goodbye, baby," she said, as she put me down by the warm, gusty ventilator at the back of Vittorio's. I reckon she would have reckoned someone would be out soon. Kitchen staff are always taking a break in the backyard. You see them out there, sucking on a fag as if they're doing mouth-to-mouth on themselves.

She didn't think of rats. I've thought of them, and I've shivered for myself in that shoebox, all alone and crying for someone.

I didn't cry. That's clear from Lucia's story. That story, along with the shoebox, is my inheritance. And as inheritances go, it has turned out more substantial than you'd think.

"Goodbye, baby," my mother whispered. Or maybe she called me by the name she'd given me. But I don't know what that was. I don't know who I was in those hours before my story began, the hours when I was my mother's child. She didn't pin a note onto my clothes, for me to read when I was grown up.

I'm glad of it. She understood that she had no rights in the future of a baby she was about to give away. She wanted me to start with a clean sheet.

She backed out of the yard, tripping over something that made a clang and scared the rats off for those vital first minutes. It must have frightened my mother too. She hurried away down the street, in her too-tight black skirt, with her pink sweater stretched over big, pearly breasts.

How do I know that? I can't believe that I ever tasted those breasts. Could she have let me taste her, and then left me?

⁓

The kitchen door opened in a gush of steam, and Lucia hurled an onion into the darkness of the yard. It hit the side of my box and I began to scream. It was the Madonna who told Lucia to throw that onion, and if she hadn't done so there is no doubt that I would have been eaten by a rat before the night was out. So Lucia told me. She was slicing onions from a net sack when she came upon the third bad one. It was firm to the touch, but when she sliced it she saw the gray fust in its seams. Usually she'd have slung it into the bin under the counter, but this time la Madonna had picked Lucia for action.

Holding the fusty onion, Lucia kicked open the kitchen door. She was packed with the aggressive pleasure that builds up, night after night, from working well at a job that is below your capacity. Cursing the supplier who had tried to make an imbecile of her, she hurled the onion into the night with all her strength. But it wasn't just Lucia's own strength that threw the onion. La Madonna took Lucia's arm, flexed her muscles and filled them with the power of a shot-putter.

In Lucia's second version, given after we had drunk another cup of coffee together, the onion was perfectly healthy. What happened was that Lucia had the door open as usual, and she heard the clang of metal as my mother tripped on leaving the yard. She hurled the onion at the cat she thought my mother was. But even so, it was a virgin's strength that powered her arm.

◦❦◦

I think that these were my mother's calculations when she decided to abandon me by a ventilation shaft in the backyard of an Italian restaurant:

- that I would be warm,
- that there would be food nearby,
- that Italians love babies.

Lucia did not love babies. She knew far too much about them for that. She had loved her own three babies, born to her in her early twenties and already grown at the time of my birth. All of them had given and were still giving her pain. Giancarlo, little Vittorio, and Stefania. These were Lucia's babies, now hidden in adult flesh. She would never be unfaithful to them with anyone else's child, but at the sight of a shoebox full of baby Lucia became practical.

She scooped me out of the box and I dangled like a baby cat. She held me up in her two hands, her strong fingers supporting the back of my neck, and assessed me for what I was and what I might become.

"*Femmina,*" she pronounced to herself, taking in the bright pink ribbons on my nightdress. Cheap rubbish, *la poverina*. My purple feet were bare.

Once inside with me, she placed my shoebox on a shelf and phoned for the police. Not for a second did it occur to Lucia to keep me. She made no fuss, she didn't cry out, and service continued as usual in the restaurant. Big Vittorio knew nothing about it until a chunky police-woman bustled through the restaurant, closely followed by a police-man who looked embarrassed, as if someone might accuse him of being the baby's father. He was only young.

"How old is it?" he asked, as Lucia demonstrated the real, live baby.

"Two days, three days," she shrugged. "The cord is still there." And she whipped up my nightdress to show the cord stump, which had not yet shriveled and fallen off. Neither had it been carefully attended with powder and wipes, as ordered in maternity hospitals. My cord stump was bare and raw. The policeman looked away.

"So it's a boy," he said stupidly.

"Is a baby girl, *naturalmente,*" said Lucia to the policewoman. And so I was.

Lucia held on to this part of my story and gave it to me when I came looking for it. By then I no longer kept the shoebox with me. It was somewhere in the house I'd left along with my marriage. Compared to other things that had happened, the shoebox seemed of minor impor-tance now. I needed the story, not the object.

The restaurant no longer existed, and Big Vittorio was dead. Little Vittorio, now over fifty, was an insurance broker. I visited Lucia in her garden flat. We sat all one hot afternoon in the tiny garden which Lucia had packed with explosions of flower, and she told me what she knew. Sometimes she reached out to touch my bare brown knee.

She was an old woman with knots of vein in her legs. I looked at the hands which had taken me out of my box. I listened to the voice that had pronounced me female, more surely than any midwife.

Lucia, you didn't pretend to have forgotten my story when I came to find you. You told me as much as you knew. I think you wondered why I hadn't come to find you earlier, but you said nothing about that. The truth is that it was only possible for me to come and find you when I was no longer in search of my mother at all.

Naturally I have often wondered about the shoebox. Did my mother go into a shop and ask them if they had a large one, this big, big enough to put a baby in? If the shoe-shop assistant was exceptionally helpful, she may even have clambered up a ladder to the very top of her stack of boxes, to find the treasure my mother required.

My mother, down on solid earth, holding her hands apart, this far. Big, shapely hands. She stares up, and her face is wan in the gloom of the shoe-shop stockroom.

"No, bigger than that. Try the next size."

Alternatively, the shoebox may have held shoes bought by my father. This gives me more to work on. If he wore size eleven shoes, then he was a tall man—or else he was stocky, with exceptional feet and hands. (He might have grown tall, had he not been ill-fed in his childhood. In fact, he might have become an athlete . . .)

These shoes, these precious shoes of calf leather. My father had been saving for weeks. He snuffed the smell of new leather and loved it, just as I do. He wore the shoes, but never threw away the box. It was too big and useful, and besides it had the price of the shoes on its side, proud evidence of what he had spent.

It's hard to throw away a box like that. It might come in handy. But my mother did take the price off. I can see where the price label was, and I like her for the delicacy that made her refuse to place her baby inside a box marked £10 10s. Or ten guineas, as they would have said in the expensive shop where my father bought the shoes.

(But she neglected to take out the price slip inside the box. It must have lain there safe beneath my head.)

Ten pounds ten shillings was a lot of money for a pair of men's shoes in 1965. I've done my research on this, and it suggests three possibilities.

My father was rich.

My father lived above his means.

My father preferred shoes to babies.

There are no such things as guineas anymore, but I'm glad they existed when I was born. A girl for ten guineas has a ring to it.

Lucia might simply have handed over the baby, and kept the box. But she gave it to the policeman, while the policewoman took charge of my damp, furious self, and so my history was preserved. These days they might be able to take my mother's DNA off the cardboard, from the marks made by her sweating fingers. Maybe there was saliva on the box from the kiss she gave me as she set me down. But it's too late for all that. And besides, my mother committed no crime.

How far off was my mother by the time the policewoman took charge of me? She escaped. She hurried away, turning corner after corner. She would have been bleeding still, after my birth.

Inquiries were made. A man walking his dog (or so he said) remembered seeing a woman hurry away from Vittorio's backyard. She was almost running, and she was not wearing a coat on that late-September evening. He saw her clearly in the light of a street lamp. So what did she look like, this woman?

The man made a quick shape with his hands to show my mother's curves. Out, in, out. Yet this was a woman who had only two or three days earlier given birth to the *femmina* in the shoebox. How could she be so shapely?

She could. We're like that in my family, to go by what evidence I have: that one sighting of my mother, and the sight of myself in the mirror when Ruby was two days old. We are women who snap back into shape after giving birth. I possess that glimpse of my mother in late-September lamplight: out, in, out. Breasts straining her pink jersey. A too-tight black skirt. I compare it to my own figure in the hospital mirror. While the other women in the post-natal corridors pulled helplessly at handfuls of leak and flobber, I snapped back into shape. My strong, curved peasant body was born to be back at work within the day.

A tight dark skirt and a sweater that stretched over her breasts. That's what the man glimpsed when he was walking his dog.

Yeah, tight. You know. You could see everything. Out, in, out.

Lucia's eyes were half shut, as she told me her part of the story. Behind her, ranks of geraniums, lobelia and nasturtiums rioted. Lucia had done her duty. She had preserved me from a yard full of rats and shadows. She had handed me over to authority, raw, screeching, but unharmed.

2

Baby Aeroplanes

the wife wants a child
the wife wants a child
ee ay ee ay
the wife wants a child

I mistrust sensitive people. In my experience what they are chiefly sensitive to is themselves. My adoptive mother had nerves as rare as orchids, and I was on them most of my life.

In her bedroom's smelly darkness she lay flat with an airline eye-mask over her eyes. In the back lane I ranged with my cap-gun, ambushing witches. Out of the side of my mouth I told myself the count. Ten shot to death that day already. When metal touches a witch they just melt into nothing, and my cap-gun was bronze. I held the barrel close to my nose to breathe in that wild gun smoke.

It was not so hard to adopt a baby in the mid-sixties. Twenty years later I'd have been a rarity, even a treasure, but I was common enough then. A healthy newborn female infant in search of a home. My adoptive parents never struck me as frivolous people, but there was something frivolous in their decision to adopt. They can't ever have let loose the whole energy of their thought on the question. Did they really want a child? Did they like children, or know what they were like?

A baby. My adoptive mother must have hypnotized herself with those two words. *A little baby.* Once, when I was eight, I dug out from the bottom of the sideboard a bag full of baby clothes: cobweb cardigans, silky romper suits, a white dress with coral embroidery. Folded, new, untouched.

"Oh well," said my adoptive mother, a touch of embarrassment in her manner as she took the bag back and folded it shut again. "There was no point putting you in these. You were sick all the time."

A baby. A little baby. They had planned to adopt a little boy next, once I had settled, my adoptive mother often told me reproachfully. But I was such a difficult baby that it put them off. I wouldn't sleep. When she tried to give me my Cow & Gate I twisted aside from the teat and screamed, and milk would spurt over both of us. She would ram the bottle back in because she was afraid I would starve, and I would choke on the milk.

"You'd have thought I was trying to torture you, not feed you!"

I had eczema and colic and I rubbed my mother raw. She could not face the whole thing again and so I deprived her of the son she would have loved, and who would have loved her. The big, sunny baby who would have understood her and slept through the night from birth. *Her real child.*

⌒〰⌒

I used to plot my way back into the past so I could change it. If my real mother had kept me, I could have danced in the street to make money for us both. My twinkling feet would have captured the hearts of strangers and charmed the cash from their pockets so that we could buy fish and chips and furniture. Nothing would have stopped me. I'd have danced until my feet bled.

Everyone knows that mothers want to sacrifice themselves for their children, but there are also children who would give blood to have their parents appear to them, just once, on the battlements of their lives.

You know those women in shawls with babies wrapped up like sausages who walk the length of Tube trains asking for cash? Sometimes the baby has a label pinned onto its clothing:

—I am refuge searching money for HOMELESS.

The woman has written out the label in spiky writing, or maybe it's one shared label that gets passed from woman with sausage baby to woman with sausage baby. This kind of babywork commands my respect. I'm not criticizing my mother for leaving me in a restaurant backyard, but it's a pity she didn't think of pinning a label on me and taking me down the Tube. I would have been with her all the way. Fat tears would have squeezed themselves between my lashes, but I wouldn't have made a sound. I'd have known that in the confined spaces of a Tube carriage a baby's screams would produce only irritation, not cash.

(If I'd been an inch prettier, or a mile less mouthy, I'd have done a lot better with both my mothers. If only a newborn baby possessed a strategy.)

At first people mostly gave money to these women with their labeled sausage babies, but now there's a consensus that times have changed and it's all right to act tough on this issue, even if you are sensitive inside. No matter how much money you give to one poor person, there is always another. It's almost as if they are breeding— perhaps with the help of the money you've given them. And here comes another one, dragging the baby round the underground while she is probably getting hundreds of pounds in benefit which we are paying for.

As the woman with baby comes yodeling up the Tube carriage, I get out as big a note as I've got in my purse and fold it into the baby's wrappings. Quick as a knife, the woman vanishes the money. She doesn't want the rest of the carriage seeing how much she's got from me, in case it dries up their wallets and purses.

She needn't worry. Their wallets and purses were dry to begin with. They turn their faces from her, mute and stubborn.

("What right have *you* got to be so critical?" my adoptive father used to say. "What's so wonderful about *you?*"

My cap-gun, I thought to myself. In my mind I caressed it and smelled its bitter smoke.

"Take that look off your face," said my adoptive father.)

In my opinion it would be good if everyone on the Tube had a descriptive label pinned to their clothes, as these women do. It could be as truthful or untruthful as they liked.

> *I am highly skilled pickpocket, reformed mugger*
> *wanting YOUR MONEY but don't worry, no violence*
> *I am not here. Only my body is here.*
> *I am drunk and I enjoy violence if there are*
> *enough of me*

It's true that I'm favoring the less cheerful possibilities. Some labels could well be shorter and sweeter.

> *I had a good day*
> *I like the look of you*
> *I'm happy*

But who was it said that happiness writes white?

⁘

Like the interior of an aeroplane, the inside of a Tube train has strict rules. We don't cry, scream or let ourselves do more than stiffen as the brakes squeeze shut in the deepest passages. I know that logic well. Control yourself, and the world will reward you by controlling its terrors. I watch the mothers with labels pinned onto their babies. I listen as they put back their heads and yell out folk songs from the poorer regions of countries no one wants to hear about. Their faces split in song, as if they are giving birth.

The Russian poet Mandelstam once wrote about baby aeroplanes. He wrote about an aeroplane in full flight giving birth to another aeroplane which immediately flies off and gives birth to its own baby...
It's a metaphor, Joe taught me, as he taught me so much else.

I can see Joe now. We were in the kitchen of our shared flat, and hard rain was spattering the windows. It was late. Joe had worked until he was so lit up he couldn't sleep. In our separate rooms our separate beds waited, but we didn't go to them.

"A metaphor? So you mean Russian aeroplanes can't really give birth?"

"Rebecca."

"OK then, tell me about it."

"It's a metaphor for the way he worked. For the way things came alive in his head."

"Only in his head?"

My words echoed. Too much happened in the head between me and my flatmate Joe. I added up all the brilliance and generosity and sharp wit in Joe's face and still couldn't make them come to what I wanted. I didn't like to think about what he added up when he looked at me.

"In his head," said Joe, "and on paper. The point is that he set it down on paper, or we'd know nothing about it."

Our conversation didn't go far. Joe wanted to read me the poems in Russian, but I was tired. I went to bed. In the morning I gave him a long wool and cashmere overcoat I'd found in a charity shop and had cleaned for him. Joe put it on immediately, and he wore it every day that winter.

But since then I've never been able to stop looking for those baby aeroplanes. They must be on the tarmac somewhere, butting their mothers' sides, sucking at the fuel line, pretending to be big enough to fly.

"Mandelstam never wrote about baby Tube trains," Joe told me another time. "Maybe because he was killed before they built the Leningrad metro. Imagine the metaphors he would have made out of that. He would have liked the way the trains stop with their doors matching exactly to the holes in the walls. You don't wander up and down the platforms choosing your carriage. You step right in and you are swallowed."

This is the full story of the metaphor, as given to me by Joe. *Someone asked Mandelstam what poetry was like, and he said that it was like an aeroplane flying along which gives birth to a baby aeroplane which immediately begins to fly with its full strength and its own life, and gives birth to its own baby aeroplane. All this happens without any of the aeroplanes missing a beat. All this happens within one poem. Mandelstam's baby aeroplanes never nuzzle and butt around their mothers' bellies. Immediately they are born they fly off, with their own life.*

It took me a long time to learn to love Mandelstam. At first he belonged too much to Joe. But I love him now. He was murdered by Stalin and no one knows where he is buried. He was last seen picking over a rubbish heap in a transit camp at Vladivostock.

Before that, in Voronezh, standing in the ruins of his own life, he wrote about a woman limping over the empty earth. He wrote of her beautiful, uneven footsteps. Stalin had not yet murdered him, but he was, let's say, in the process of murdering him. The decision was already made in some playful, trivial corner of the Stalin brain. All it had to do was take the trouble to enact itself.

I believe that Mandelstam was right about those baby aeroplanes.

He'd given the whole of his life in order to understand them. Although I haven't yet seen them, I believe that they are there. So I look out for the moment when a cigar tube of sterile metal gives birth, whilst flying at full strength.

But in my experience, we cannot always fly at full strength.

3

An Engine Has Failed

When you fly at full strength you cannot fall. Once I watched a TV program which aimed to show scared flyers why they were wrong. The program was made for flying phobics, and it worked so well they thought we should all have a chance to see it.

In the TV diagrams the gray metal body of the plane was borne aloft by cushions of force and thrust. The diagrams proved that no aeroplane could ever shrug its metal shoulders, stop pretending that it's possible to defy gravity and plummet out of the air. Not only was the aeroplane incapable of such a wish, but natural forces would not permit it.

Once, when I was flying to meet Adam in Hong Kong, where he was taking part in a conference, I woke at dawn and walked to the back of the plane. A man had lifted the window shutter and was staring down.

I joined him. Thirty-three thousand feet below us were the mountains of Mongolia, red as the mountains of the moon.

"We wouldn't last a minute down there," said the man, in a cold determined voice. "What takes you to Hong Kong?"

"I'm meeting my husband. He's at a conference."

"What's he do?"

"He's a neonatologist."

"Neonatologist, hey?" said the man, regarding me with his boiled blue eyes.

"Yes. He works with newborn babies. Premature babies."

"I know what the word means," said the man. "You got any babies yourself?"

Adam and I had been married twelve months. I remember the moment I answered that man. The clarity and sureness with which I said, "No. Not yet," and the way he said, "All the fun still to come, eh?" in a lubricious voice as if he was thinking of the sex we would have to conceive the child.

The mountains beneath us were Mongolia, yet I could reach out my hand for a paper cup of iced water. I went back to my seat and shut my eyes as the plane began to buck through clear-air turbulence. I said to myself what I always say at these times: *Rocked in the cradle of the deep. Rocked in the cradle of the deep.* I don't know where it comes from or why it helps, but it does. Around us the deep held our plane on the palm of its hand, tossed it up, let it fall.

When an engine fails there's no preparation. It was years later that I found this out. I was on my way back from New York to London. A work trip. I'd done everything I was sent to do. Sidney House would open in five weeks and my employer, Mr. Damiano, would probably bring me back with him for the opening. I had been sorting out all the last-minute glitches. Snagging.

I thought Mr. Damiano was pushing it with the name he'd chosen for the new hotel. It wasn't a name with any style. Mr. Damiano disagreed. He said that Sidney had a nice feel to it. It was a good name to give to a cabdriver. What he really meant is that we've got people to the point where any name we give will work. I hoped I wouldn't find out that Sidney was the name of the dog Mr. Damiano had when he was a boy, rather than that of the minor English poet whose work he'd given me to read.

We have Sidney, we have Lampedusa (*Where're you staying? Oh, the Lamp Post. Naturalmente.*), we have Villon (*Village*), Langland, Sorescu, Cavafy, Sexton and Bishop. Mr. Damiano is an educated man and right from the start, as each hotel was named, he would give me what he considered the finest work of the author. After a week or two he would talk to me about it, as if the writer were as important as the bar, the quality of the wet-room tiling, the reputation of the chef. Lampedusa is the only prose writer. Mr. Damiano says there is no reason for this, but that he also intends to name a hotel after F. Scott Fitzgerald one day, so I'm reading *The Last Tycoon*.

Mr. Damiano has educated me, as Joe did. Adam, no. Adam changed me. We changed each other. That's something different.

It's nice on a plane when your work's all done. We were already out of land and the big dark swell of the Atlantic was moving under us. I flicked on the flight map and watched our plane, as big as New York State, push its way northeastward. The flight attendant brought the dinner I'd ordered, but I didn't feel like eating it. I drank my wine and watched the sky darken. More than an hour of the flight was already gone. The air was so smooth that my drink lay still in its glass.

"Ladies and gentlemen, this is Captain Willis again," came the light Surrey voice that had already told us about the fine weather, the tailwind that would get us to London ahead of schedule, and the fact that he hoped we would enjoy our flight with him, "I'm afraid that one of our engines has failed and so we are not able to proceed to Heathrow, but shall be returning to Kennedy instead."

I was surprised that he didn't put it better. *We have a problem with one of our engines,* maybe. *A minor problem.*

I looked around. The flight attendants, smiling pleasantly, immediately began to collect the dinner plates. The man behind me protested that he had not even begun on his fillet steak. "It's just a routine procedure, sir," said the girl, whipping his steak out of sight. A dark-haired, confidential, heartbreakingly handsome steward came and sat beside me.

"As you are sitting by the emergency exit, madam," he said, "you'll be aware that we'll be carrying out certain special procedures on landing, to ensure the safety and well-being of all our passengers."

"What?"

"I'll be preparing the exit for an emergency landing," he said, with a wink. "And you'll be in the front row."

"Is that good?"

"It's not bad," he said consideringly. "Not one of the worst places to be sat, I'd say."

The man behind me leaned around my seat and asked if I thought the engine noise sounded different. I listened but I couldn't tell. He put his lips together in a smile and asked if I'd like to see a picture of his little girl. He passed me a plump blondey baby with a smiling face and I held out a photo of Ruby, but without letting go of it.

"She's beautiful," he said immediately, before he could have had time to take in how beautiful she was. I said that his baby was beautiful too.

"I've never been on a plane when they've pulled one like this," said the man. I told him I had, and it had all been fine. They had done an emergency landing and everything had worked out.

"Oh, OK," said the man, nodding firmly. "I'm glad to know that." Then he asked me where it had been.

"Moscow," I said, thinking it through.

"Jesus," said the man. "You wouldn't get me on one of those Russian planes. Don't you know their air traffic control is all shot to hell?"

I shut my eyes. *Rocked in the cradle of the deep. Rocked in the cradle of the deep.* I could hear a change in the engine noise and I wondered if we were still over the Atlantic Ocean. Joe had told me once where the continental shelf began, but I couldn't remember. If we were over land maybe someone was looking up at this moment. Maybe they could hear the change in our engine sound. They would listen and be glad that their feet were planted on solid earth.

The man behind me tapped my arm.

"I've been watching that girl over there." He indicated the flight attendant who was checking the overhead lockers. "She looks pretty upset to me. When the crew gets scared, I get scared." He said it as if this was a rule of life he'd always abided by.

"She split up with her boyfriend last night," I said. "She was telling me about it when she brought the wine."

"Girl stuff, huh," he said. "You'd think she'd have something better to worry about than her boyfriend right now."

The hour passed slowly, but the two times the man tapped my arm again I pretended to be sleeping. I was afraid he'd wake me to say, "Sleeping, huh. Think you'd have something better to do than sleep," but after a couple of taps he rang for the flight attendant and started telling her that everyone gets bad knocks in life but they are part of growing into the person God means you to be.

"We're following a routine procedure for the benefit of customer welfare and safety, sir," she replied. "After our landing in Kennedy you will be transferred to the next available flight with the minimum of wait."

The plane was going down fast. Suddenly the lights of New York shocked into view. My ears hurt, and the handsome steward came to take his seat directly opposite me.

"Soon be down," he said, and winked again. He leaned forward braced like a runner, with his hand gripping the emergency handle. The plane whooshed upward, then steadied itself.

"We're coming in to land."

The plane went down with a bang but held steady as it hurtled down the runway. What I hadn't thought of were the fire-trucks and other emergency vehicles with flashing lights that raced with us parallel to our runway. We were down. We were on the runway. We were not on fire. The handsome steward relaxed his grip on the emergency handle.

"You won't get your chance to go down the chute today," he said. The plane slowed until it was a solid thing again on solid land.

"No way are they getting me up in one of these things again. No way," said the man behind me. But I knew they would.

Mr. Damiano's Dream

So there I was on the tarmac, waiting for someone to shepherd me. The air was thick and warm and wind blew in gusts from the hurricane tail that had passed through New York two days before.

I already knew how disappointed in me Mr. Damiano would be. I was going to go back to London and tell him that I was leaving his employment. I wouldn't be caught up into his bright new future. My momentum had stalled. I no longer wanted to sit in business class in the hope of sitting in first class one day.

No way are you getting me up in one of these things again.

I would never tell Mr. Damiano the true reason. Mr. Damiano has given me everything he knows about life. Not many employers would share their dream as he does. How you have to be tough, and how you can put the name of a minor English poet on everyone's lips. In his heart he's a fairground man. He picked me up out of the mud and cleaned the dirt off me. He put me up on the trapeze with a plume of light on me. I swooped from continent to continent, I dealt with men who wanted to cheat him, I cached a thousand details in my memory and reported them to him. There we were, the hotels and all of us who worked in them, spangled with the dream Mr. Damiano carried. He gave me a job.

But Mr. Damiano could never see what I saw as our big gray aeroplane turned solid and hit the ground and churned into the tarmac with all its force and thrust. The fire-trucks raced alongside us with their flashing lights and the wall of foam they'd made for us. Ruby was riding up front, in the cabin of the very first truck. She had a fireman's helmet crammed onto her dark red curls and she was staring straight ahead with her lips parted. I think she was saying something but I couldn't hear it through all the metal, and the thunder of engines. She didn't look at me but I could tell she knew I was here. She had come for me.

❦

I'm on the tarmac, Mr. Damiano. Everything was going sweetly on the route you made for me, but now the engine has failed, and I've had to turn back.

I know you would come to get me if I asked. I know you'd pick me up and shake me and make something of me again. I am your personal assistant, and I know that you value me.

These past three years you could have lain me on two planks and sawn me in half if you'd wanted. I trusted you that much, and I still do. You taught me the business and said that working with me gave you a nice feeling, and so we kept on. Three years between us now.

(Mr. Damiano, I don't like those olives from I Promessi Sposi that I ordered for the Moon Bar. They look like washed-out baby aubergines in the lighting we've chosen. And beautifully darned linen napkins aren't going to work in New York. Not unless you put the seamstress in the corner to darn very slowly all the while that the people are dining, so they see how much time and skill it costs and how much more luxurious it is than buying new.)

I love your business more than anything in my life now. It was you who taught me that there doesn't have to be a minibar and a glaze-eyed man in a braided coat springing to open the door and say, "Welcome home!" every time a guest steps into the lobby, and a ten-dollar charge to wash a shirt. There don't have to be ill-paid women coming in to turn down the beds at night, for cash on the pillow. Hotels don't have to smell of sealed windows, central heating and flower-scented cleaning products.

You got rid of all the comfortless clichés of luxury. You filled toy boxes to bring along to guests' rooms when they had their children with them, and before the guests arrived you invited some of the staff children in to play with the toys, to take the newness off them. "Kids playing with toys puts life into them." You paid the best wages in the business and wouldn't allow tipping. You told me that true luxury was an emotion. When people feel it, they know what it is.

I saw Ruby for one second. I thought that this time she had come for me. For once I had not been waiting for her, but she had come all the same. My body melted and I waited for the aeroplane to splinter. I waited for one of those gray metal splinters to hurl me on its spear through the window to where Ruby was.

It must have been a child-sized fireman's helmet that Ruby was wearing, because an adult one would have slipped over her face and hidden it. I saw her face quite clearly. She was pale and excited and her lips were parted.

I thought she'd come for me. The tears that started from my eyes at that moment have grown sticky on my skin.

⌘

We waited on the tarmac in the dark while the warm wind blew. Soon someone would come to shepherd us to the buses which were driving out from the terminal to meet us. There would be another aeroplane for us soon. Just like the man behind me, I would have to get on it.

I turned and saw the man who had been sitting behind me. He was blowing into his hands as if he felt cold. Just like me, he had fallen out of his life for a while. The air reeked of jet fuel and from the way people were looking around you could tell it was making them nervous.

As soon as I'm back in London, I thought, I'll go to Mr. Damiano. He's always working, night and day. I'll push open the door of his office. (He doesn't like me to knock. When someone comes in without knocking, he already knows that it's me.)

"You're a little later than I thought you would be, Rebecca," he'll say. Not because he's annoyed in any way, but because he's got a mind that can keep far more inside it, easily and comfortably, than most minds I know. The time of my projected arrival would be as clear in his mind as a clock on the wall, no matter how deep he was in his work.

"But you're back. Good."

This is where I'll have to explain to him that I'm not back, in any sense that he means. I won't tell him that I saw Ruby in the fire-truck, but I'll tell him that I've got to go away for a while, and that he's perfectly right not to trust me anymore, not to want me back. I'm abandoning him just before Sidney House opens.

I'll tell him about the olives and the napkins.

The Death of Stalin's Wife

When I say that my husband had red hair, you'll probably imagine a pale man, freckled, with washed-out blue eyes. But Adam's eyes were brown, and his hair was the same dark red as Ruby's. Adam's hair was cut close, in tight-sprung coils that pushed against your fingers. Ruby's curls were looser, silkier. There was a blue shine on the red of her hair.

The first night I saw Adam was the night Joe jumped out of the window.

I was in the kitchen of our attic flat, rolling pieces of chicken in seasoned flour, when Adam came up the stairs with Joe. I had shared the flat with Joe for three years. It was the kind of love that keeps you safe, and sex never entered it. We knew too well what other things would have flown out of the box then. Fear, disappointment, rage. *Just friends*, as people say, lingering stickily on what they touch. But in my view friendship can be rarer and tenderer than love.

We knew each other in our dailiness. The rush of water into a kettle, the heap of tangled washing in a blue plastic laundry basket, the smell of each other's bedrooms. Joe didn't ask me to take care of him, because he already knew how to take care of himself. He was as handy as a sailor when it came to keeping the place as it should be. I remember the time I saw Joe pour washing soda down our kitchen sink, and follow it with a kettleful of water, and smile at my surprise.

"You get a buildup of grease in the U-bend otherwise," he said.

Joe and I were a family. We weren't born into it, or adopted into it, but we made it together like a nest from what everyone else considers rubbish.

We shared our shopping, our phone bills, our colds, our friends and our festivals. Joe would buy a little Christmas tree and wedge it in the crook of the parapet gully and run a cable out to it. Five floors up, our tree shone with steady light.

Joe's mother came to visit us every six months. She would clamber the flights of stairs to our flat, bracing herself before the last, steep, twisting climb up the servants' staircase. She would fetch up at our kitchen table with a flag of purplish-red flying in each cheek. She climbed those stairs as if they were the mountain of her love for Joe. When she'd recovered, Iris would drink tea from a rose-spattered cup and saucer which we kept for her, and bring a packet of Jaffa Cakes out of her stout mock-leather shopping bag.

They'd grown up alone together, a woman who'd never thought she'd have a child at all, and the child whose intelligence glittered like sparks of light from a faster and more daring planet.

"He gets it from his father," Iris would say to me, remembering how Joe's father would play correspondence chess on paper in those days before computers, and how he answered the questions on TV quizzes before the contestants could get a word out. She used to tell him that he could make their fortune if he chose. But he would never go on TV. He was too . . .

Shy? Nervous?

No, that wasn't it. Iris cast about for the right form of words. "He wouldn't want to use his gifts in that way," she said at last. "He was a man of principle."

He died of an asthma attack when Joe was two, and then Iris was on her own, forty-five, four-square, and probably more afraid than I'd ever understand. Joe's father didn't even suffer from asthma. He was a strong man. He had been in the RAF and passed a stringent medical.

His death came out of the blue.

"She used to bike me to school," Joe told me. He described the tough, black, upright bike with its carrier seat and wicker basket. When it rained she wrapped a yellow plastic cape and hood around him so that nothing of him showed but a strip of his face. He remembered the broadness of her back and the way the bike surged boldly alongside the buses and lorries, with a ring of its bell to warn drivers. He was proud of her. She never socialized at the school—the other mothers were girls, to her—but she read every note that came home, found out about every chance that could be Joe's, and watched tirelessly to see what the other children wore and what equipment they carried, so that Joe could have the same. The teachers frayed her nerves but she made herself learn their language and do her son justice at parents' evenings.

She had a little job, lunchtimes at the local pub, which fitted in nicely with school hours. In the holidays six-year-old Joe sat on a bar stool while she cleaned, and she would buy him lemonade as his reward. Iris had her widow's pension, and her widowed mother's allowance. She never spoke to Joe of money.

Once, stupidly, I mentioned the size of a phone bill that had just come in. Iris frowned but said nothing. After she had gone Joe found an envelope propped behind the coffee jar. There were four twenty-pound notes in it. *Towards your bills, I know how heavy they get this time of year.*

I blushed when I saw those notes. Iris had never dared debt, or lived sloppily. "What we never had," she said to me once, talking of her own childhood, "we never asked for." Now Joe and I and everyone else under thirty had got into a different world, but Iris didn't trust it. If she had known about Joe's overdraft she'd have tried to post her twenty-pound notes into the mouth of that, too.

She liked me and I liked her. She never spoke the questions in her head. Two separate rooms, two beds plump with pillows and duvets. She wanted more to happen, she wanted Joe to be happy. I was a nice girl. But she knew, because her instincts were good, where our limitations lay. Our flat, to her, smelled of compromise.

She was squarer than ever now, well past seventy, broken veins in her cheeks and hair whipped into blue-white curls by a local girl who was ever so good and would come to the house. But she'd loved and she'd been loved and she knew what there wasn't between us, even if what there was still puzzled her.

Adam was the new consultant neonatologist at The Stephen Maternity Hospital. Joe had met him a couple of months before, one Friday chess night at the Volunteer. Someone else had brought Adam to play chess.

News of Adam came to me like a flag in front of a rare new engine. He'd been at Bart's, doing work on apnea of prematurity.

It's all a long time ago now. I don't remember the difference between what I knew then and what I know now. I probably didn't even know what a neonatologist was, let alone apnea of prematurity. Living with someone, you can't help absorbing what they do. You get the language around you and you start to use it yourself, without thinking. Maybe that's what makes people pretend to be doctors when they're not: it's so easy to absorb the language to yourself.

Adam was thirty-eight, Joe was thirty, and I was twenty-six.

Adam used to say that not many doctors were good scientists, and at first I couldn't understand what he meant. What else were they, if not scientists?

"They have a gift for doctoring," said Adam. "All they need is enough science to back it up. They want to know which pages to look up in the book, or on the website."

But Adam wanted to write new pages in the book. He had the open-mindedness, the fluidity matched with precision, the playfulness which lets you dance on the edge of what's known. He was clever. He was good. He was working on surfactant, the stuff that coats the lungs and lets you live.

In neonatology, clinical practice changes week by week. Ten years ago was another world. Different technology, different drug protocols: a whole different world. Adam lived all those changes minute by minute. He knew who was doing what, how the clinical trials were going, when the fresh ground would take his weight.

I don't believe they even had artificial surfactant then. I'd have to check it. More babies died, and more babies lived on with crippled lungs.

Joe and Adam started to play chess together on other days. They became friends. The private room at the Volunteer was only available on Fridays, so they'd go to the flat Adam was renting while he looked for a house. Both of them worked late most nights, and Adam lived alone. Adam must have talked about his work, and Joe probably talked about his, because for both of them work was what they were.

Joe has the fastest, most powerful mind I've ever known. He needs five hours of sleep, I need eight or more. If I woke in the night there was always a line of light under his door. The computer would be on. Books and papers lay thick on the floor around his desk, gutted, absorbed, discarded. A heap of papers waiting for translation lay in a box file on the right side of the desk.

Joe, like Adam, was dancing on the edge of what's known. He wanted to build a whole new ballroom out over that space. He was working on what would become his first book, about the death of Stalin's second wife, Nadezhda Alliluyeva. With this book, Joe would leave the deep quiet backwaters of research and catch the wave of commerce, as history flooded into TV programs and bookshops.

Joe had done an intensive course in Russian and while he still had to have a lot of material translated, he was beginning to make his own versions, and to tease out the layers of meaning packed into a verb or an idiom. He taught me a few words but they clogged on my tongue and I didn't like them.

But I loved the way Joe talked when he told me about Nadezhda Alliluyeva. She died in 1932, when she was only thirty-one years old. The official cause of death was appendicitis. It was suicide, say the history books, but you can also find almost any version of her death that you want.

She drank a glass of poisoned wine intended for her husband.

She did not shoot herself, but was shot.

She died because she had been naïve, like millions of other idealistic young women at the heart of the Party. She thought that if Stalin were given the full facts about the murderous impact of collectivization, the policy would change. Like that. Immediately. He was the leader but he did not know what was being done in his name.

"Imagine if it happened this way, Rebecca," said Joe one chilly Sunday afternoon as we sat drinking beer in the kitchen. "Where's Stalin? He's in the heart of the Kremlin as usual, behind his desk, working unceasingly for the good of the Soviet people. It's two A.M. and he's still not gone to bed."

"Like you."

"Precisely. So Nadya gives up waiting for him. She steps into the heart of his power, the lamplight by that desk. She stands before him with her hands clasped and her eyes on his face. She begins to tell him what he needs to know in order that he can change everything about the policy that doesn't work and is wrecking people's lives, and make it all right again.

"If this is what she did do, it doesn't mean that she was exceptionally stupid. There were thousands of people all over the Soviet Union who thought that way. *If Comrade Stalin knew, he'd put a stop to this. It's the officials who are to blame for hiding what's going on from him.* Russians have been believing that for centuries. *The Tsar doesn't know what's being done in his name, he's our little father. It's the officials and bureaucrats who have got between him and us. Let's send a petition to the Tsar, let's beg him to meet us so that we can present him with our petition."*

"But she was his wife," I argued. "She must have known what he was like."

"It's just a version, Rebecca. So, she tells him. He doesn't greet the information with gratitude and surprise, however. He flies into a rage and wipes her out. He's got no choice, he's got to get rid of her. What she represents can't coexist with what he is becoming. She's the past and she's got to be liquidated because liquidating someone doesn't mean the same as killing them, it means expunging what they are and what they represent, and then behaving as if they never existed. And soon it's as if they have never existed."

"What's the other version?"

"She marries him at seventeen. Her name's Nadezhda, that means hope. She is full of hope and zeal and revolutionary fervor. She loves Stalin. He's older and stronger and he's enormously powerful, and the wonderful thing is that he loves her back. He wants her. He's her leader as well as her husband. She idealizes him.

"He loves her too, that's important. He treats her brutally. He crushes her and the children and she knows there is no way she can possibly escape him. If she hadn't loved him and he hadn't loved her it wouldn't matter so much—or at least it'd be a different kind of tragedy. She kills herself out of knowledge of what he is and what she's become."

"Do you think that's what really happened?"

"There's another possibility. She kills herself in revenge. She knows what it will do to him, and he knows what she's intended to do to him. She has wanted to punish him, and she's succeeded, and he can't bear the idea that anyone's had that degree of power over him. From now on, he'll never run that risk again. Once she's dead, he changes and becomes more and more isolated. He's suspicious of everyone. Friendship and family are finished—he'll be sentimental to his daughter but he'll never let anyone get close to him again.

"Before Nadya was buried, he took note of who came and who didn't come to view her body. He stayed there for hours, marking them all down, making certain that they'd pay for it if they hadn't behaved right.

"It's what they said that interests me, the two of them, before she died."

"Does anyone know?"

"No. But she left a letter. He read it and immediately destroyed it."

Joe lifted his beer bottle and drank.

"It was a key event," he said.

Key events were what Joe searched for. He would ask me to analyze my own life in terms of key events.

"No, no," he would say impatiently, when I told him about the shoebox again. "That's not what I mean. The shoebox is what you were *meant* to know about. But what weren't you meant to know about?"

"I don't know what you mean."

"There was a case in the paper. Some people who owned a house with a large garden sold off part of the land for development. When the builders uprooted a pear tree they found the bones of a newborn baby under it. In the end, the story was that a mother and daughter had lived together. An old woman and a middle-aged woman. But the daughter had become pregnant, God knows how or by whom. She was thirty-eight, but her mother kept her in the house for months and took the baby the night it was born, smothered it and buried it under the pear tree. Then she pretended it had never existed."

"What did the daughter do?"

"She went along with it, it seems. But what if she hadn't? What if she'd suspected her mother might harm the child, and she'd dragged herself off her bed immediately after the child was born, and put the child in an old shoebox, and crept out of the house to leave it in the backyard of an Italian restaurant, so that it would survive?"

"That's not what happened," I said. His words rasped me. Story was all I had and I wasn't having anyone else retelling it. Not even Joe, not then.

"You're right," said Joe. He rose to get another beer. "It's not what happened, but sometimes the real story doesn't tell you the truth. If I were telling your story—or mine—" He bent down to look inside the fridge, and his voice was muffled. "If I were telling your story, I'd tell it from an angle. You wouldn't necessarily know at the outset that it was your story at all. The facts wouldn't seem to fit at first.

"'Where's my shoebox?' you'd ask. '*There isn't any shoebox in this story so it can't be mine.*'"

I laughed. Joe spun round, waving a bottle of beer. His face glowed with excitement. "But then you'd read on, Rebecca. You'd start to recognize things. You would know where you were, because the pattern inside the story fitted the shapes inside your life."

"But think how well you'd have to know someone, to do that."

"Do you think I don't know you well enough?"

We were silent, looking at each other, until Joe glanced down at the beer in his hand.

"Do I want this?" he asked.

"Yes, you do. Pass me one, Joe."

He bent down again to rummage in the back of the fridge.

"Yes, I do," I said quietly, but he heard me, turned and looked up at me with an expression on his face I hadn't seen before.

"You do what, Rebecca?"

"Believe you know me well enough," I said.

⁂

A few months earlier Joe had showed a colleague a draft of the chapter which described the midnight conversation between Stalin and Nadezhda Alliluyeva. It was chaotic, his colleague said. It leapt about and had no objectivity. It read like a novel, not the work of a historian.

Joe wasn't too bothered. He was building his ballroom of the past, where there'd been empty air before. The floor of his ballroom was waxen and silken. Joe's mind hummed. Of course the dancers would come. How could they bear not to?

6

A Jump Five Floors Up

For the sword outwears its sheath,
And the soul wears out the breast,
And the heart must pause to breathe,
And Love itself have rest.

I've never liked to think too much about breathing. It's safer not to imagine the labor of it, life-long. If you know too much detail, you might not be able to go on. At school they taught us the wonders of what our bodies were doing as if they were especially rich and powerful engines which we had been given by our parents. We sat and observed them from the bright-lit chamber of our brain. We were never truly implicated in what our kidneys did, or our hearts. At the same time, in another lesson, Byron told us that the heart must pause to breathe. I believe that he was right.

So, we'll go no more a—roving
So late into the night,
Though the heart be still as loving,
And the moon be still as bright . . .

It was Mr. Damiano who got me to learn that poem. He told me that I should learn poems by heart and then I would always carry them with me. There would be many, many times when I would think I had nothing, and then discover that I still had the poems.

Byron was right about the heart. Whether he was right about the soul I don't know, but I like the way he puts it. The soul grows strong and fierce and it needs to be let out. The body effaces itself, as the cervix effaces itself at birth.

Adam came bounding up the narrow stairs to our flat. I turned and saw the close, fierce pelt of his red curls. I looked away quickly and flipped the chicken pieces over in the seasoned flour.

"You must be Rebecca," said Adam.

"Yes," I replied. "I must."

He had red hair but dark brown eyes. It seemed to me that his face was deeply lined, but then he was thirty-eight and I was twenty-six. His face was scored and I wanted to read what was written there.

"What are you cooking?" he asked, drawing up a chair and sitting down at the table opposite me.

"Chicken stew. It's for later."

"It looks good."

I stared at the naked chicken pieces. Their flour coating hadn't done much for them yet. I knew they would soon turn gold in the hissing oil, but it was better for guests not to see the pallid, uncooked meat. The pieces which I hadn't yet rolled in flour lay in their bowl. They looked blue and babyish in their translucency.

"It'll be ready at eight," I said. "But maybe you don't want to wait that long."

"I'm happy to wait," said Adam.

Joe poured wine for us, and I peeled shallots while the two of them sank into talk. It was getting dark outside the windows, and there was the city far below, the slope of it falling away from the tall thin terrace where we perched five floors up. I looked out and saw car headlights moving over the dual carriageway. An ambulance went by with its blue light flashing. The siren reached us and I wondered if Adam would turn to it, but he didn't. The sky had turned lilac, from the mixture of orange street light and rain-sodden dusk. It was a beautiful color and I thought about how natural things are not always the most beautiful.

Adam got up and went to stand by the window, with his back to us. I could watch the shape of his body without him seeing. His outline was strong against the lilac that was changing minute by minute into a more ordinary darkness.

"It's starting to rain," said Adam. "The windows in the next room are wide open. Is it part of your flat?"

"It's Joe's room," I said. "He always leaves them open. He wakes up and finds rain in a pool on the floor."

I fried the chicken in oil, added stock and wine and the vegetables. The pan spat and a plume of savory steam went up to the low ceiling. It was Joe who'd taught me to cook. I only knew about beans on toast, pizza and toasted sandwiches before I met him.

Joe had watched me eat my usual food without comment, for the first few weeks. He never criticized it, but he brought me into the pleasure world step by step. He'd taught himself everything and then he taught me. I'd been living with half nothing, believing I was lucky if I had a cheese roll for lunch and the hot water didn't run out before I had my bath. Joe taught me to go into shops I'd walked past automatically all my life. I went inside and bought wine and flowers and books and music.

One day, to make Joe smile, I wrote out the menus which my adoptive mother fed to us on a two-weekly rotation. I remembered every meal by heart.

Week One, Monday: Corned beef, tinned peas and tinned new potatoes. Strawberry Angel Delight.

Each morning we measured out our cornflakes with an off-white melamine cup. To drink there was hot Ribena, or hot Bovril, or good fresh water from the tap.

The glory of my adoptive mother's housekeeping was that she was never hostage to the seasons. They filled the boot of their Mazda with tins and packets once a month. She was particular about where the tins came from. Corned beef from Argentina was no good even if it was on special offer. To buy Heinz baked beans was to spend money for the sake of spending money. Only fools bought instant mashed potato, which had no food value compared to the tinned variety.

She taught me that potatoes were waxen and slippery and came ready-peeled, carrots grew in cubes and corned beef had to be warmed under the hot tap to loosen its coat of fat so that it would glop out of the tin. At Christmas we had a Plumrose Ham from a bigger tin. The strip of metal that wound onto the key-opener was so long that it sometimes broke under the tension, slashing a thumb.

Day by day, Joe undid my good housekeeping. I got soil on my fingers, and I sliced up meat which bled. I learned to check the eyes of fish before I bought them, to see if they were full and bright, and then not to look into them again. We picked shot out of pheasants, and I learned that hares, like horses, have saddles.

We were in the middle of all this life when Adam came.

"I'll put on some music," said Joe. He had installed a sound system throughout the flat. There were speakers in the kitchen, his room, my room, the big square landing which was big enough for a sofa where Joe would lie late at night, punch-drunk with work, while Blind Willie Johnson sang "I Know His Blood Can Make Me Whole."

Joe should have gone out of the kitchen door, across the landing and into his room. But he passed behind me, brushing against my body so that I turned. Adam moved aside as Joe pushed open both kitchen windows, pressed his hands down on the sill and vaulted into the gully outside. The parapet was maybe eighteen inches high. It ran the length of the terrace, and a low wall divided the gully outside the kitchen from the gully outside Joe's room.

Joe sprang into the gully. He balanced himself, and turned to face left. There he was, printed on my eyes against the darkness. He rose up, outlined against the lights of the city that dropped away beneath us. If he made a mistake the next surface he would hit was a stone terrace, five floors down.

He stepped back two or three paces. I did not know what he was doing, but then I saw he needed to take a run so he could jump the low wall that divided the gullies. He ran past and I heard his breathing and then the thud as he did it, he jumped over the wall and landed outside his bedroom window. I wasn't afraid to move now. I ran to the kitchen window and watched him as he put both his hands on the sill of his own room, vaulted it and disappeared inside.

When he'd gone the whole risk of it hit me. The back of my knees stung with fear. The gully was shining wet, and so was the surface of the low wall. The parapet was too low to save a child, and Joe had been drinking as we sat in the kitchen. If he had caught his foot on the wall nothing would have held him. I heard again his heavy breath and the thud of his feet as he ran and took the low wall in the dark and rain, five floors up.

A gust of wind blew rain over me and I shut the window as "Crossroad Blues" flooded the room. I thought of Robert Johnson selling his soul to the devil at the crossroads, and wondered if it was true that anyone could do that. Well, Robert Johnson had found out soon enough if the devil was real or not. He was my age when he died. To me no music was worth any part of you belonging to anyone else.

"Do you go out on that parapet?" Adam asked me.

"In the summer sometimes. I sunbathe on the wall."

"I wish you wouldn't," he said, and it sounded like the closest thing anyone had ever said to me.

Adam sat opposite me at the kitchen table and ate my chicken stew. Joe sat at our side, quietly drinking and slipping layer after layer of skin off the shallots until there was nothing left but a heap of pearly cores.

Adam wrote a letter to Joe late that night, after he'd gone home, and delivered it by hand the next morning. He wrote that he would

not come to the flat again. He didn't know the nature of the relationship between Joe and me but he did not want to damage something he
could not repair.

Joe showed me the letter. His eyes were puffy with hangover. "He
thinks I'm your father. Or your lover."

It was a shabby gray morning but the flat glowed. I'd got up early,
gone out for fresh bread, made coffee, bought a bunch of early nar-
cissi. I'd lit a fire in the small iron grate in my room and the flames
were as bright as petals. If you'd looked in through the window it
would have been any orphan's dream of home.

It was my dream of home. Why would I jump out of the window
into the dark and the rain?

7

Fall or Fly

"I don't want him to come again," I said. Joe blinked, rubbed his eyes and said nothing. His eyelids were permanently reddened from too much reading and working at the computer screen.

"I mean Adam," I said. "It's better if he doesn't come again."

"I knew who you meant," said Joe, and he took two oranges from the yellow bowl on the table. "I've been seeing someone," he added.

A wave of heat swept across me.

"Who?"

Joe took a third orange from the bowl. He held two oranges in his right hand and one in his left. He tossed up the left-hand orange and began to juggle. He couldn't look at me while he was juggling. His eyes followed the oranges as they swung into rhythm and his eye movements were like a shoal of fish darting to safety. But his hands were sure and the oranges flew swift and even.

"She's called Daniela. Dani."

"How long have you been seeing her? Why didn't you tell me?"

"I thought it was best to wait until we saw how things went. Between me and Dani."

Faster and faster he whipped the oranges into the air from the cup of his hands. They blurred, and I stopped looking at them.

"You've been practicing again," I said.

"Yeah, I practice when I get stuck. It clears my mind."

No one I'd ever known used their mind as Joe did. I wondered then if he would ever wear out, but now I know that when he sat there juggling the oranges he was only at the beginning, feeling the ease with which he was coasting past what he was doing even six months earlier, beginning to sense how far acceleration might take him.

"When Hitler attacked the Soviet Union," said Joe, "Stalin went into a state of fugue. He retreated to his dacha. He fell in on himself. No one knew why he'd gone or whether he'd come back again."

I knew that "fugue" was a musical term. I thought of aeroplanes dive-bombing, and German parachutists landing like dandelion clocks all over Europe. What had that got to do with music or Stalin? Maybe he was one of those dictators who imagine they are a creator, and play clumsily on grand pianos while their cowed intimates applaud. I imagined a row of Stalins in a hall lined with mirrors, playing on the black-and-white keys with pudgy fingers while above him a chandelier shivered from the bombardment.

"Did Stalin play a musical instrument?" I asked. I never felt foolish asking Joe any question I wanted, no matter how ignorant.

"By fugue here, I meant flight," said Joe.

"You mean he ran away?"

"The dacha was outside Moscow. So he went to the forest, which is what a north European would naturally do when he was at his wits' end. A man from Finland or Sweden, say.

" 'How long shall I stay in the forest?—Until my heart is healed of its sickness,' " sang Joe.

When he sang he had a dramatic projection that you never heard in his speaking voice. He stopped singing and grinned at me.

"But Stalin wasn't a northern European. He was a Georgian. Think about it," he went on, letting the oranges fall, catching them. "It's June. There are birch trees growing around the dacha and it's warm. The German army's advancing, he ought to have known it was going to advance. He's the leader. He's the heir of Lenin, the father of the nation, the guardian of the revolution. And now he's let this happen. He and Hitler go and make a gentleman's agreement between dictators and Hitler doesn't keep it. Just like Stalin's never kept an agreement in his life, unless it suits him. So there he is, outmaneuvered by the most obvious thing in the world. Everyone's been trying to tell him what's going to happen, and he's ignored them. The outcome is that he's been fucked by the man he'd hoped to screw."

"Why are you so interested?"

"Don't you see how crucial it is? It's a key event. Stalin went to his dacha and no one knew what to do. What would any of them have dared do? Think of how he treated the whole crew of them. Mandelstam called them a gang, a rabble.

"Stalin used to make them dance after dinner. They had to keep drinking, because he watched them to see how many glasses they had. He wanted them drunk and incapable. If they dared, they'd ask the servants to bring them red water instead of red wine. He wanted them drunk, so that they would humiliate themselves and know that they'd humiliated themselves.

"When they were drunk enough, they had to dance. He'd get them up on their hind legs. He made Khrushchev dance a Cossack folk dance."

Joe's face was lit. He leaned toward me.

"If only we knew about all these things while they were still happening. Think how different the world would be."

"We wouldn't need historians," I said.

"Imagine if we'd known about the Politburo dancing like bears on chains, or John Kennedy fucking everything that had a heartbeat."

"I don't want to know."

"You do."

"I don't. It scares me. It seems as if there's no pattern in anything. Just people stumbling over themselves into nowhere."

"Listen, Rebecca. It's 1941. Anything could have happened. What if Stalin had stayed at the dacha? What if he'd never come back to Moscow? They'd have had to get rid of him eventually. No matter how terrified they were they'd have done it, and history would have got going again. But a different history."

"We'd still have won," I said vaguely. I didn't know enough about the war.

"I don't think so," said Joe. "Fugue. You take a flight inside yourself when reality becomes unbearable."

"Did he go back to Moscow?"

"Of course he did," said Joe. "Otherwise we wouldn't be sitting here."

"So we're in this flat thanks to Stalin."

Joe got up and went to the window. He leaned forward gently with his palms on the sill.

"I thought you were crazy when you chose this color for the walls," he said.

Our kitchen walls were the clear color of crushed red cherries.

"But you were right," he added.

I remembered how I hadn't been sure about the color, but Joe had said so firmly, "Yes, that'll look good, Rebecca," that I had believed him.

"It's a beautiful color," Joe said. Very gently, he stroked the wall as if it were a living thing, then he turned to the window. He stood looking over the city to the southwest, where the weather came from.

"Time to leave the dacha," he said. "I've been offered a job in the States."

"Where?"

"Princeton. I'm going to take it."

"But what about——?"

Joe turned. His eyes were on me, fully mine.

"What about what, Rebecca?"

"What about Dani? Daniela?"

Joe stared at me blankly and I knew he'd been lying. He was lying. He was heroic. My eager, greedy heart wanted him for the first time. *You can have them both*, it whispered to me, but Joe knew better.

"No, Rebecca," he said to me, his voice low and toneless. "No, no, no. I don't want that."

A Yellow Cardigan

Joe was the first person to visit me when Ruby was born. He came when she was eight hours old and I was washed and stitched and adrift in the holy feeling that the pain was over. Adam had gone to catch the shops before they shut. (He came back with white freesias, chocolate, a heap of January peaches, a patchwork cushion to support Ruby while she fed, a pot of jasmine trained around a wooden hoop, a cherry-colored cashmere shawl. Adam hadn't a mean bone in him. To him money really was what we all pretend to believe it is—a means, never an end. He would stand in the flower shop, staring at the big zinc buckets. He would taste the cold sweetness of the air and ask the girl for all the white freesias she had. He let money spray and splash and then if he wanted nothing he spent nothing.)

It was coming dark outside the windows. When they changed shift the new midwife leaned over the bed and I felt the cold air on her.

"It's trying to snow," she said.

The baby smelled of birth. There were little clots of blood in the wisps of her hair, weighing it down. She hadn't stirred when Adam laid her down in the plastic cot, and I saw how skillfully he handled her, as if he already knew her.

Joe had cut his hair short. The back of his neck looked exposed, raw. There was gray at his temples, and he looked older than he was. He leaned over Ruby's cot and touched her cheek with the back of his index finger. Her lips mambled and she pressed toward him.

"You look so well," he said to me.

"I could pick her up and walk straight out now," I said. "But I have to wait. We're all going home tomorrow."

They'd given me a room of my own because I was married to Adam. Ruby's cot was a little way farther from the bed than it should have been, and I reached out and pulled it close. Less than a month before, while I was waiting for the birth, a woman had dressed up as a nurse and gone into a maternity hospital in Birmingham and stolen a day-old boy called Billy Joe. It had taken them two weeks to find him. He was living in a new four-bedroom estate house with a happy couple who had bought off-plan and confided to the estate agent when they moved in that their baby was due in three months' time. And that maybe they'd be looking for a bigger house soon!

How many months had they been preparing for that baby? While Billy Joe's mother dreamed of his birth, their plans were ripening. Her baby was already their kidnap. I did not dare shut my eyes until Adam was in the hospital room with me. Then I'd sleep, while he watched Ruby.

What if one of the nurses was a fake, biding her time until I slept and she could take my baby from her cot like a pea from a pod? I was in a room on my own. No one would see. Even if I woke up maybe I wouldn't have the strength to fight her, and no one would hear if I called. I wished myself in a ward with other women, with only a floral curtain between us. We could watch out for each other and sleep in turns. I knew they would be thinking of the stolen baby, as I was.

My mother put me in a shoebox and we were parted forever. I knew that the time that surrounded birth was dangerous. I wouldn't be safe until Ruby knew who she was, and how to get back to me if we were ever parted. And even then—

"My mother sent you this," said Joe, giving me a rose-sprinkled parcel. I opened it. It had a dry floral scent, like potpourri. There was a little cardigan, chick yellow and meltingly soft, with tiny mother-of-pearl buttons.

Who would have believed that Iris's red, raw fingers could make something like this? But I felt the old panicky flash of guilt toward her.

"She thought yellow would be right, whatever," said Joe. "If you had a boy or a girl."

"Yes."

"But if you don't like it, put it in a drawer. The baby doesn't have to wear it."

"I do like it. It's beautiful."

I stroked the wool. The texture was as tough and fine as cobweb, and the color so true it looked as if it would come off on my fingers. I imagined myself dressing Ruby in it.

"I'll write to Iris," I said. "I'll send her a photo of Ruby wearing the cardigan."

"She'd like that." Joe smoothed and folded the wrapping paper, looking down. Then he smiled at me. "I'm going away soon, Rebecca."

"But you've been away. You've only been back a few months."

"I'm going to Moscow," said Joe. "I'm researching my next book."

My eyes filled with tears. It was the sight of that cardigan, which Iris had made for a different baby, a baby that would never be born.

"You're always going to Moscow."

"I need to stay there for a while. There's a lot of stuff I can only do out there."

There was Moscow, thick with history. I'd never seen it but I imagined Joe there, stamping his feet on the packed snow, talking Russian and buying chicken feet from a stall off one of the main streets. It was Joe who had told me about an old woman counting out her coins to buy two hundred grams of chicken feet. She was short of fifty kopeks and he'd offered her coins but she had looked at him with suspicion and had refused to take them.

Here was Ruby, washed up on the shore of my body and knowing no better. It was only eight hours since I'd turned into a mother, but I would never be good enough for her.

"I'm afraid I won't know what to do with her," I said.

"Of course you'll know," said Joe.

He touched my hand. We were two separate people, touching. My concerns were not his and we were not a family anymore. It was right and natural and only what I could expect, but I wanted more. I was greedy and selfish, wanting him to feel for me what it wasn't good for him to feel. I was a glutton for intimacy.

"Why do you think you won't know?" asked Joe.

"Because I can't remember what anyone did for me. I can't remember my childhood at all."

"Look at her," said Joe. Ruby was wrapped in sleep, her closed eyes a thin, sealed line. Her hospital nightgown had slipped off one shoulder, and her skin was mottled, purple and pink.

"She's got furry shoulders," I said. Suddenly I couldn't bear her to be in that plastic cot any longer. I lifted her awkwardly and the hospital blanket fell off so that her frail purplish legs dangled naked. She was hot. I laid her beside me and she moved in close, burrowing her way back toward the smell of my skin and the flesh she'd lived in all her life until eight hours ago. One of her eyes opened. I'd been told that babies couldn't focus, but she was looking at me. Then her eyelid fell shut again and she slept.

"Did you know she was a girl?"

"Yes."

My girl, my daughter. I hadn't thieved this love, though I was still fearful that someone would come in and denounce me for taking a baby that didn't belong to me. The midwives called her my daughter straightaway and I wondered how they dared, how they could be so certain.

"Oh, she's lovely, your little girl," said the midwife who'd delivered her, wrapping Ruby up in a sure way that made a parcel of her. "She's like a little doll." Ruby was my little girl and there would never be any need to explain her. For the first time, I was tied to someone by blood.

"You could bring her to see me in Moscow," Joe said. "There's enough room in the apartment for all of you to stay."

The door opened and there was Adam with snow on his hair and his arms full of flowers and carrier bags. Joe stood up and the two men faced each other, oddly squared up to each other like boxers or dancers. But Adam dropped the flowers and bags on the bed and took hold of Joe. They embraced, crushed close. I wished I had once held Joe like that.

"Isn't she beautiful?" asked Adam. He knelt by the bed and a drop of snow fell, dissolving in the heat that Ruby and I made. Adam's face was ablaze and tender and I knew that he was like me, not safely himself anymore, but lost in Ruby. We'd made her and in doing so we'd lost ourselves.

I remembered the night she'd been conceived. No one had ever told me I'd know the moment it happened. I'd expected to be surprised one day by a blue line in a pregnancy test in a public toilet.

We were going down and down in the dark, locked together. We didn't speak or move or seem to breathe. In the deepest of those circles of bliss I felt Ruby's touch.

One day I'd tell her about it.

"You can't have known," she'd say.

"I did know."

"You can't have done."

Or maybe I'd say nothing. Ruby must have her own life, right from the beginning.

"Yes," said Joe. "She's beautiful."

First Christmas

I have mislaid the key. I sniff the spray,
And think of nothing. I see and hear nothing;
Yet seem too, to be listening, lying in wait
For what I should, yet never can, remember:
No garden appears, no path, no hoar-green bush
Of Lad's-love, or Old Man, no child beside,
Neither father nor mother, nor any playmate;
Only an avenue, dark, nameless, without end.

We were walking down a long, gray street of terraced houses. It was Christmas Day, and three in the afternoon. Adam had just come back from the hospital.

A baby had died that morning. A boy called Nicholas, born at thirty weeks. He'd died following a hemorrhage into the lungs, six days after birth.

Nicholas had been born after years of fertility treatment. Labor had started at twenty-five weeks; they'd stopped it but there were still problems and Jess had delivered by cesarean at thirty weeks. The baby had moderately severe respiratory disease but he was being managed on a ventilator and Adam thought he was stabilizing.

Adam got a call at ten P.M., went into the hospital and stayed most of the night. He came home for a shower and breakfast, and then went back. We didn't say any Christmas things to each other.

Ruby was eleven months old. Sometime we'd have to decide whether we would celebrate Christmas with her or not, but this year it wasn't necessary. Adam was irreligious in a Jewish way, and I was irreligious in a Christian way. What kind of way Ruby would be irreligious, we didn't yet know.

We walked along the street, which was stripped of people, as if a war had taken place rather than a festival.

People think that doctors become callous. They think that a man like Adam must keep a membrane around his work so that it won't get into his life. Maybe it would be better that way. But Adam knew them so closely in those hours and days and weeks, mother and father and child, the holy trinity of the maternity hospital that gets made and remade and remade, day after day after day.

He'd first seen Jess when she'd been brought in with contractions, panicky, knowing much too much already about all the things that can go wrong. She'd been trying to have this child for years. He'd explained to her what would happen if her labor could not be stopped, how the baby would be cared for, what a twenty-five-week baby looks like, how big he would be, what to expect. Jess and Ian knew already that the child was a boy, and they had named him. And then for five weeks Jess had been in the hospital, on a drip, holding on to each hour and day. When the baby couldn't be held back any longer, Adam was in the operating theater, and Nicholas was delivered into his hands. Adam was responsible for Nicholas's care until he died.

Adam did something I can't fathom, to absorb that experience into him time after time without flinching, and yet be ready to begin again, by another bedside, with another phone call, with another baby born so early it couldn't cry.

I knew that Adam was going back, in his head, over everything that had been done for Nicholas. He would evaluate it all. There were things to be learned, even if all you learned was more about unpredictability and your own limitations. These were the worst times, when it had looked as if a baby would make it and then it didn't.

Nicholas was chill and stiff. The nurses would have made a print from the palms of his hands, and a print from the soles of his feet, and photographed him in death as they'd photographed him in life. If the parents could not bear these things now, they might ask for them later.

We had our living baby in her all-in-one winter suit, in her sheepskin pushchair liner. I stopped pushing and knelt to look at her. Her cheeks were lit with a flush of sleep, and I leaned close to feel her breath, so much stronger now than when she was newborn.

"Is she warm enough?" Adam asked. He came round and tucked her hands inside the sheepskin. Ruby would never wear mittens. I knew how big she would seem to him, and solid, with her skin like a fortress compared to the veiny, dark, translucent skin of the prem babies in their incubators.

Already, I thought, Nicholas knows all the mystery of life.

⁓

Adam put his arm around me. He took the left handle of the pushchair and I took the right. We walked awkwardly, bumping hips through the bulk of our winter coats.

That night we would put Ruby into the deep cot where she seemed to swim herself to sleep. We would leave on the little light beside her. We would prop her door open, and prop our door open. We would take hold of each other. We would sink into each other.

We voyaged on in the dark, going farther each night. In the day, no matter what, I felt the waves of it beating in me, moving me. Soon Adam would come home. Soon we would walk upstairs. Soon we would turn on the little light, prop the doors, begin. We would fall asleep, still deep in each other's bodies, locked, going down. In the morning Adam would get up first for Ruby and put her into bed beside me while I still slept. I would wake and see her face rising like the sun.

Damiano's Dreamworld

But never met this Fellow
Attended, or alone
Without a tighter breathing
And Zero at the Bone—

Before he went into the hotel business, Mr. Damiano ran a fairground. It was a place of dreams, both tawdry and bright. When I met him, his fairground days were long gone, but the more I knew him, the more I thought that one day he'd disappear and go back there. He would vanish from his empire of hotels and if you looked for him you might find him in a little traveling fair touring Linz and Melk and the outskirts of Vienna. He would be back in his booth in the middle of the fair, holding the strings that made a thousand dreams move. He would have shrugged off his beautiful suits and he'd be wearing embroidered waistcoats, white shirts and leather boots so soft they made you want to bite into them.

But then he'd be an old man. Mr. Damiano, like anyone else, would accelerate into age. His power would be gone.

I could not believe it would happen. He appeared immune from death and sickness. You couldn't see Mr. Damiano without sensing that this was a man in his prime, at the height of his powers and knowing it. It was a prime that had nothing to do with youth. No, it was a climate which he had created, and in which he lived. By sheer force of what he was, he was borne through a high, sunny air in which things happened faster and more brilliantly than they did on earth.

He had rescued me. He had thought it was only a job interview, the time we first met. How could he know that when I answered his questions my lips creaked open because for weeks I had talked to no one? I had lain in my rented room day after day, watching the money go. I'd unlearned all Joe's lessons of pleasure, all Adam's knowledge of love. I'd learned again what I'd known in childhood: the habit of nothing. It was the icy truth on which I holed myself, and sank down.

To eat becomes troublesome.

To choose a T-shirt or a pair of jeans becomes a mountain of weariness.

The phone rang until it stopped, waited ten minutes, rang again. I listened as if I was hearing church bells for services I would never attend.

I did not bath or wash my hair or look in the mirror. If I had done what I wanted I would have torn out my hair and dressed in rags and ashes. Rags and ashes would have comforted me, as the sharp, rank stink of my flesh and my dirty hair comforted me.

I was effaced. For a while, in the years I'd shared with Joe and then with Adam, I'd forgotten what it felt like to be nothing. I'd believed the life I'd lived was really mine, that I possessed it and was safe at last.

With Adam I'd become the woman I'd once glimpsed at the door of lighted houses, and envied. A young woman in an old narrow house with a porch light that spilled yellow on the steps at homecoming. Behind her was the sound of children playing, water running for a bath, footsteps in another part of the house. A young woman who hurried downstairs with a baby on her hip when a delivery man rang the doorbell. She gave the signature that was needed, took the package, smiled a smile that had nothing to do with the delivery man and went back inside her house.

I was home, at home, like her.

Those gray streets where we'd walked arm in arm, those gray streets where we had wheeled Ruby in her pushchair and smiled at passersby who smiled at our smiles. That bed where we'd lost ourselves. Those knotted, tangled, sweat-stained sheets. The key in the door, the phone call when one of us was running late, the reassurance, the details which we shared and which were of no interest to anyone else. The way I would shape the things that happened in my days with Ruby into news for Adam.

Ruby's heat. The living heat of Ruby that you sensed as you walked into the room where she slept.

I pushed her to the baby clinic feeling an impostor, because my joy was so great. I liked the health visitor, because she never doubted that the dailiness of Ruby was really mine. It was my job to look after her. Ruby's hearing test, her vaccinations, her difficulty in moving on to solids, her weight gain. With the other mothers I clucked and deprecated babylife, but I knew that like me they must be masking the joy they felt so that no one would sense it and steal it from them.

When Mr. Damiano called me into his employment I was like Lazarus, sunk in the grave of myself. I'd learned that story at school and always hated it. Imagine going through the pain and fear of dying, and then being brought back to life, and knowing that you had to go through it all again.

God knows, Mr. Damiano wasn't Jesus. He treated me better than that. He didn't think that he was resurrecting me, but he gave me a job. He became my employer, paid me a wage and filled my days with a life I could never have imagined. He believed in my capabilities. He wanted to know where I was and what I was doing. My opinions and my information mattered. He sent me zigzagging on aeroplanes from continent to continent. Once he sent me up in an air balloon because he wanted to find out if such a trip might give pleasure to our guests.

I told him I was afraid of falling. I told him I was afraid I would jump out if there was only the edge of a basket between me and a hundred-mile map of where I might drop.

"They won't let you jump," Mr. Damiano told me. "They will have thought of that. I hope they have, because among our guests there will be some with a tendency to fall. We are not fixing up these hotels for superhumans, always remember that."

⤳

Sometimes, after a long day's work, we would drink a glass of wine together. Mr. Damiano would tell me about his fairground days.

"Everyone who worked for me was an artiste. Did you never see my advertisements?"

His eyes searched my face seriously. There was a quality of innocence in his vanity which made me want to laugh aloud as I used to laugh when Ruby made a hat from a plastic saucepan out of her toy oven, and danced for me. Mr. Damiano's hair was not yet gray. Sometimes, every six weeks or so, it would begin to seem gray, but then it would blacken again.

"You will have seen my advertisements, Rebecca," said Mr. Damiano, "even if you don't remember them."

He used to hire light aircraft. He sent them flying along the length of summer beaches, then back again, trailing their banners.

"Come to Damiano's Dreamworld," the banners read.

Yes, I had seen them. Suddenly I was sure I had seen them. I remembered a windy day at Southend, with the sea miles out and my adoptive mother beside me, handing me an egg sandwich. The wind blew. There was grit in my teeth. We sat in a row, my adoptive parents and I, with the car blanket on our knees, a flask of tea, a bottle of 7UP for me and a little packet of Twiglets which I sucked until all the Marmite was off them. I let my saliva wash the twigs into mush. I counted how many seconds each Twiglet took to dissolve.

They promised that the sea would come back, and then we would

swim. They had timed it wrong and I know she was disappointed, after
the effort and the long drive, that the sea had shrunk to a pencil line
at the horizon.

"It's all right," I said. "I didn't want to swim anyway."

"Of course you wanted to swim. What else do you come to the sea-
side for?" asked my adoptive father.

The sound of the plane flared in our ears. We all looked up, rows of
families on the broad beach, as the plane swooped low trailing its banner with blue writing on it. *Come to Damiano's Dreamworld*, it said. I
picked the words out aloud.

"Wherever the hell that may be," said my adoptive father. I believed
he was big enough to pull the aeroplane out of the sky and crush the
glad message in one fist.

I hear him now. *Wherever the hell that may be.* Those were his exact
words, and they had an elegance of phrasing I don't associate with him.

He's here with his stewed tea and his daughter with her head bowed
and the hair sliding across her face. With her right hand, the one he
can't see, she's secretly burying her egg sandwich.

He wanted a bouncy girl, a daddy's girl, a girl who'd race to the
door at the scratch of his key and drag him in, hanging on his hand. A
rosy, noisy, curly-haired caution who would pour out nonsense to
make him grin.

"What did you do at school today, Rebecca?"

"Nothing."

The plane flies back along the beach. The banner swirls then
straightens and I read it aloud for the second time, proud of the way I
manage the difficult name.

Wherever the hell that may be, he whispers to me, one adult to
another now. My adoptive father is forty-four, and I am thirty-six. We
are on the level. I don't need to bury my egg sandwiches anymore, I
can simply hand them back to him.

"I don't like this."

And he's free too. He can tell me what he really thought of his
hunched wife and child, of the blank beach and the aeroplane that

went away with its message that stirred his senses and would never satisfy them. *I don't like this*, he might say too, and with justification. He wanted something and he didn't get it. He made himself safe by pretending to want nothing.

Mr. Damiano liked to fly with the pilot. He liked to hear the snap of the banner as the plane turned, and the noise it made as it flowed behind them like a sail. Maybe he once saw my face among all those upturned faces.

He restored scarlet and gold horses for the merry-go-rounds. They were the size of beast a full-grown man could ride on. Their nostrils flared as the music began and they rose and fell, faster and faster, their silver stirrups glinting in the fairground lights. Each of them had a name, like a horse of flesh.

They came from far places. Mr. Damiano got word of them and they arrived after long journeys by strange, circuitous routes. A neat brown pair from Hungary, a single plumed horse from Vienna, a ruined nag from a German fair that needed paint and leather and metal and a new mane and tail of real horsehair. Mr. Damiano took the flotsam of a dozen carousels and prepared them to face the music again. Their saddles creaked, their bridles clinked, slowly they began to rise and fall against the dark blue fairground night. They were made to take the weight of a full-grown man, and a woman too, the pair of them crushed together, gripping the pole, joined at breast and hip and thigh. When the ride was over and the couple stepped off they would stagger, and catch hold of each other again before they wandered, dazed, into the crowd.

He hired jugglers and fire-eaters by the season. The clairvoyant had predicted the death of Kennedy, and in the supper-tent roast pigs were sliced and served up with crackling on plates of bread.

There were tumblers and a dance band, tight-rope walkers, barrel-organs. There were clowns and conjurors and a man who could free himself when bound with chains at the bottom of a dull-green glass tank. There was a girl who had trained a poodle to pick out words from an alphabet board, at her direction. There were men in rags who magicked them into tailcoats, and a woman who could hang by her teeth from a rope suspended thirty feet above the crowd. Behind the hall of mirrors a mind reader practiced, and one year a real mermaid told fortunes.

"A dugong," said Mr. Damiano.

"What made you go into hotels?" I asked Mr. Damiano when he interviewed me. He was telling me about the bears that still dance in Russia, and I didn't say that I had seen them. He was looking at me too closely. I thought he would see the cracks in my smooth face.

"How old are you?" he asked back.

"Thirty-three."

"Have you children?"

"No."

"A husband?"

"No."

Mr. Damiano looked at me. His back was to the window and his face was hard to read. His big shoulders rested peacefully inside the most beautiful suit I had ever seen. The room was pale and still, lit only by a jar of tulips. In the outer offices there were telephones and computers. In here, nothing.

"They are similar businesses," Mr. Damiano answered me. "A man who succeeds in the fairground business will do well in hotels if he puts his mind to it. People do not visit my hotels to sleep and to be fed. They visit them to discover that I have already found out what will give them the greatest pleasure. If you want the job, it is as simple as that. That's all we are trying to do."

"Yes," I said. "I want it."

He looked at me closely to check that it was true, and then he nodded.

Moscow

Adam and I first took Ruby to Moscow when she was two years old. By then Joe had a Russian girlfriend called Olya. There'd be no problem with the baby, he said when we phoned to arrange the details. Olya knew where to buy all the things babies need. She had a sister who would babysit for Ruby while the four of us went out. Joe hadn't seen Ruby for nine months. He kept a baby in his mind who no longer existed.

"She's out of nappies," I said. "She sleeps in a proper bed now."

I was always moving Ruby on. To me, a red, hot lump in Ruby's mouth was already a tooth. She could nearly crawl, nearly stand alone, nearly walk. It took me a long time to understand that it was only the day itself that mattered, not what the sum of Ruby's days might one day bring.

"She'll be fine in Moscow," said Joe. He thought I was hesitating because of Ruby. "Russians love babies. Make sure you bring enough warm clothes for her, or the babushkas will stop you in the street and tell you to dress her properly."

It surprised me when Joe said *Russians love babies.* It wasn't like him to make a generalization. He'd told me a thousand things about Russia, but all of them were specific and they all sounded real, except for this.

Russians love babies. What did that mean? I looked at where Ruby was playing. She held a book of nursery rhymes and she was singing songs from memory, turning the pages randomly in the middle of a line. Her face was bland and pearly and I knew that there was another game going on inside the singing game. She was pretending to be someone else: me, perhaps. Noticing me, she glanced up with a faint, warning frown. She did not want to be interrupted. A kiss now would affront her.

"We're going to Russia, Rubes," I said. My voice sounded odd in the kitchen silence. Outside, the sky was white. There was so much time in these long days with Ruby that sometimes I would see the big hand quiver as it came to rest at the end of another minute. That was the way I used to watch the clock at school. I learned to tell the time early and other children would ask me in whispers, *How long till play time? How long till dinner time? How long till home time?* I had time in a bag on my lap, a substance that I owned and gave out when I chose.

Adam wanted me to go out more. Ruby could play with other children at groups in church halls. I could take picnics and share them with other mothers and babies in parks.

Three nights a week, I worked in a bar in town. The hourly wage barely covered Ruby's babysitter, but the tips were good. We wore black dresses and I pulled my hair back tight and put on lipstick. It wasn't a place people drank to get drunk, though there were drunks sometimes. It was a warm, dark, secretive bar with a regular clientele. I liked working there. I liked the bloom on people's faces when they felt well looked after, and the things they would say to me that I felt sure they wouldn't say to anyone else. (But I knew that if any of the other girls went to the table it would be the same warm look in the eyes, the same tips, the identical bloom and confidences, or at most only a little different. Maybe that was what I liked.) If customers were out of order it was easy to let them know it. It wasn't the kind of bar where you could behave as you liked. If you wanted that there was the whole Strip to go to. We were different.

The money I earned, I kept for Ruby. We didn't need it, although often I wished we had needed it, and that it was because of my tips that Ruby would have new shoes and holidays. Adam's money came so thick and fast that our joint bank account brimmed. We had direct debits and never had to worry when the bills came in. Adam had even begun to overpay our mortgage so that we would be free of it sooner. But I was wary of that joint account. It still seemed to me like stealing when I wrote a check on it, unless it was for gas or electricity.

I thought that maybe one day Ruby would like to travel, or buy herself a piano, and then I'd say to her out of the blue that she had her own account with thousands in it, saved up for her so that she wouldn't have to ask anyone for money, not even me.

⁍

Joe met us at Sheremetyevo airport. He got a taxi with a driver who thought he spoke English and who drove very fast, with a strange loose acceleration as if the car wasn't in gear or properly touching the road. He kept turning fully round to talk to us. His eyes were beautiful, pale blue, washed out. Drunkard's eyes, and there were bottles of beer in the passenger glove compartment. I pressed Adam's arm and showed him where the bottles were.

"Tell him to slow down," Adam said to Joe. "Ruby isn't secured." The car braked sharply and I let out my breath and made myself believe it was all right to have brought Ruby here.

"I told him you wanted to look at the sights," said Joe.

Outside the window the flat, soiled snow stretched away, the same color as the sky. In the distance there were tower blocks, pylons and black, prickling stands of trees which looked as small as weeds against the bulk of the blocks. The way the land was used reminded me of New Jersey. Russians and Americans could afford to waste their countryside. They could have as much ugliness as they chose. They knew they had thousands of miles of prairie, mountain ranges, forests, and lakes as wide as inland seas. It was hard to understand, if you came from a small country.

The taxi hit a pothole and made Ruby bounce on the fake leather seat. She liked the feeling and she made herself bounce again. Her eyes flashed at us, bad and bold, and Adam and I smiled at each other. A thousand times a day, we saw things in her which no one else would ever see.

"It's minus seven," said Joe. "It was down to minus fifteen last week. Seven's not bad, as long as there's no wind."

But all the same Ruby's breath squeaked as I lifted her out of the car and she turned her face into my shoulder to hide it from the cold.

Olya had thick black hair. It sprang strongly from her hairline, which was like the point of a valentine heart. Olya wasn't beautiful. She was tall, shapely and forceful, and when I first saw her she had her back to me. Her hips were wide, her legs braced, her feet planted. She was at the stove in the small apartment kitchen, frying little meat patties. As we crowded in she turned, and pushed back her hair. Broad face, matte, thick skin, dark eyes. Maybe she was plain, but she was the kind of woman I liked to look at. Her smile was spacious and kind and she went on frying the patties without haste, as if it was as important as anything else a person might do.

It was three in the afternoon. We ate the meat patties with beetroot, pickled cucumbers and potatoes. Olya had made dill sauce and there was cranberry relish. Afterward we had a jar of preserved pears, and ice cream. The pears were whole, with their stalks still on, and their cheeks had been stained red with cochineal. Olya had preserved them herself, she told us, when a friend had given her six kilos of pears last September.

"They're excellent," said Adam. "You must give us the recipe."

"No, you must take the jar home!" said Olya. "I wrap it up in newspaper, and it won't break when you fly."

"On the flight," said Joe.

"Was there vanilla in them?" I asked.

"You noticed it! It's so nice cooking for people who notice what they are eating. Now Joe could eat the newspaper instead of the pears and if I ask him he says, 'Very nice, Olya.'"

I stared at her. Was she talking about Joe, who'd taught me most of what I knew about food?

"Luckily Olya does all the cooking," said Joe. He looked at me, deadpan.

"Yes, that's lucky," I said.

Olya would not let us touch the duty-free whiskey. We began with pepper vodka, continued with champagne, then returned to vodka. Since I'd had Ruby, I was out of the habit of drinking. I put my hand over my glass when the bottle came round to me.

"Do you know what vodka means, Rebecca?" asked Olya. "Voda is water. Vodka is little water. You take a little water for your health. It's good for your blood movement."

"Circulation," said Joe.

Olya gestured at the window. "You see what winter is like here," she said.

Outside, the same pallor of sky, thickening now. Heaps of dirty snow, packed ice on the pavements. We were on the fourth floor. The wind was rising and people walked with their heads down. There was a desultory, numb look to the street life, as if it had no money to make it stir.

"Did you see the man lying on the ground, by the airport access road?" I asked.

"Drunk," said Joe.

"Won't he freeze?"

"He'll get picked up by the airport police."

"Some freeze, every winter," Olya corrected him. "They are too drunk to know how cold they are, and so they die. If they are lucky they can sleep on a ventilation shaft where there is warm air, but often the police pull them off."

Adam lifted his glass of vodka and looked through it. It had the faintest yellow sheen in it, though it was perfectly clear. Ruby was curled on his knee, drowsy, sucking the piece of muslin nappy which she took to bed. Her eyes were still open but they were glazing. Her faith in us clenched my heart. As long as we were with her, she did not mind where she was.

"Let's drink a toast to Ruby," said Joe, but Ruby was past stirring, even at the sound of her own name. All through the flight she had perched on my lap, or Adam's, watching everything.

"To Ruby," said Adam. He smiled down at her, his face naked and tender. A drop of vodka fell on her hair.

"To Ruby."

"To Ruby."

Olya said something in Russian and Joe told us it meant health and long life. Olya's words seemed to have weight to them, as if her wishes were true gifts. Maybe it was only because they were said in a foreign language.

"And good dreams," said Olya.

"So, how's the new book going, Joe?" Adam asked.

"I'll tell you about it," said Joe, filling our glasses again.

Thanks to Stalin

Life has become better, Comrades,
life has become more cheerful!

"So here we are in this flat thanks to Stalin," said Joe. The words stung
in my head.

"Don't you remember?" asked Joe.

"No."

"It was something you said to me once."

But I still couldn't remember. Olya rose, and went to make tea.

"I'm tracking the bastard down," said Joe. "But he's slippery."

"What are you writing about?"

"If you can call it writing. I sit for three hours and when I get up
there are two words on the screen. Ask Olya."

"What are you not writing about, then?"

"The same old thing. Stalin's fugue. What a man does when he's in
charge of everything and the world still goes wrong. What was he
doing? What did he think he was doing?"

"You tell me," said Adam suddenly, surprising us both.

"All right," said Joe.

⁓

He explained the problems. Closed archives, archives that open for a while then close again, archives that can be accessed briefly, with an official standing at your side, newspaper files with months of issues missing, people who were too afraid to write anything down, people who are dead, people who falsified their sources when they wrote their histories, and made sure the water they left behind them was full of mud. Fear, the best censor of all.

"Not still fear, after all this time," said Adam. "Surely. Everything's different now."

"It can't be different," said Joe. "The present here is what the past has made it, just like anywhere else. Only here, it's more difficult to uncover the roots of the past and find out where the behavior of the present comes from. People hide things and they don't want to talk about them. It's ours, they say. Even if they do talk, they don't trust outsiders to make the right kind of sense out of them.

"Imagine telling someone from outside, like me, how you sat still as a bird when you heard your neighbor being taken away. You didn't breathe, you didn't move. You edited yourself and fitted in and survived."

"Why do you want to make them talk?" asked Adam.

Joe smiled. "I'm writing a book."

"Is that a good enough reason?"

"It has to be. It's the only reason I've got. I'm not going to include all these personal stories, anyway. When people say to me, 'You won't put that in your book, will you?' I'm not lying when I say that I won't, it's between them and me. Their personal stories are all-important but they're not usable. I need to know them. I need to understand what I can about what it was like to live then. I need to be able to go into those rooms of the past and walk around in the dark without bumping into the furniture.

"I've got to get to where he was. The person at the heart of all that terror. Terror was the dominant emotion of the twentieth century and we don't understand it.

"I talked to a man whose mother was taken away when he was six. She was a minor Party official. When Stalin, Molotov and Yezhov made their speeches to the Central Committee at the plenary in February 1937, it became clear that it was people like her who were the targets now. The Party itself was going to be turned inside out and gutted. No Party member was safe."

He stood up, went to the window and stood there looking out. Olya had come in with glasses of tea which she placed on the low varnished table. I lifted my glass of tea, and drank.

"She sleeps well," said Olya, nodding at Ruby. Both of us looked at Ruby in Adam's arms, her closed, pearly eyelids with the faint blue veins, her pale cheeks, the curl of dark red hair that clung to her forehead, damp with sweat. It was very hot in the apartment.

Olya leaned over, unfastened the cardigan Ruby was wearing and very carefully slid first one arm and then the other out of its sleeves. Her thick dark hair fell forward, touching Ruby's cheeks, touching Adam's clothes. Neither of them stirred. Olya slipped the cardigan off, and folded it neatly.

"Olya likes babies," said Joe. He had turned away from the window and was watching us all. I couldn't tell from his voice if he was praising Olya, or blaming her.

"Yes, I like babies," said Olya. "They have something which other people don't have anymore." But she said it very quietly, as if she had to say the words but did not expect him to listen to them.

"The man I spoke to," Joe continued, "he didn't know anything about the speech to the Central Committee, or the beginning of the Yezhov terror. He was a child of six. What he knew was this. His mother lost her job. Suddenly she was at home in the apartment all the time. He knew something was wrong because of the terror that clung round her like a smell. She kept saying that things were fine, there was nothing the matter. He remembers being angry with her and asking why she didn't go to work as usual. He remembers that she was sorting out his clothes, putting away his winter clothes and mending his summer ones, and she got out a pair of shorts he didn't like and said it would do for another summer, and he was angry.

"Then one day, quite early, she woke him up by kissing him. The smell of terror was stronger than ever. She kissed him and held him tight and he would like to remember that he kissed her back and clung to her but he knows that he didn't. He said, 'I want to go back to sleep, Mama, leave me alone,' and he turned over in the bed, away from her. He knew that she was still there bending over him, but he kept his eyes squeezed shut.

"You already know what I'm going to say. That was the last time he saw her. They didn't come for her in the night, they asked her to go in and answer a few questions, clarify a few points. She went on her own two legs, not taking anything with her.

"She was too afraid to listen to the truth of that smell of terror that surrounded her and told her to put on her warmest underwear, take her spare glasses, stitch a photo of little Volodya into her knickers.

"She went and she didn't come back.

"There he was, six years old. His father survived for the time being—he died later, in the war. But Volodya wasn't sent to an orphanage, he kept his identity, he knew who he was. His grandmother took him, because his father thought he would be safer there.

"Volodya blames himself. He has never stopped blaming himself for being bad-tempered with his mother that morning, for saying that he wanted to sleep. For not embracing her. For not looking up when she remained there, bending over his bed. For hearing the door close behind her, and turning over in his bed, back into the warmth of it, and going to sleep again. A child of six cannot forgive himself.

"So, this is the furniture that's got to be in the room when I write about Stalin's fugue."

"He told you all those things," said Olya, "and yet you're not going to put them in your book."

"I've told you why."

"What happened to his mother will disappear, also," said Olya. "No one will remember it."

We were all silent for a while. I thought of Ruby in her bed, and the way I liked to sit beside her, when Adam was working and she was asleep. I thought of old gravestones and how they sometimes mark the deaths of children, one after another in the same family with the same first name, dying in their infancy. I thought about how we try to believe that parents then suffered less than we do, because they were accustomed to loss.

But it isn't so. We think it to comfort ourselves, but in thinking it we belittle them.

Ruby stirred and gave a catlike triangular yawn. Adam smiled and stroked her hair. I saw how he caught Olya's eye. He had liked the way she noticed that Ruby was sweating, and the sure and gentle way she'd taken off Ruby's cardigan. I looked at Olya and Adam and thought that they were similar people. They might belong together, in another world.

But they did not belong together. It was Adam who could make me ache and feel the rich darkness unfold to let us down into it. It was my child he had on his lap.

"So," said Joe. "Here we have him. It's a beautiful summer day and he's out at the dacha. The German army is advancing into Soviet territory at fantastic, unexpected speed.

"Unexpected, that is, unless you are Stalin and you've had accurate, detailed intelligence about German troop movements, weaponry concentrations, overflights of Soviet territory and plans for invasion after the spring planting. For months and months you've been getting warnings from the highest levels. Some of them have come direct from the German military itself.

"You've ignored it all, and that looks like the act of a fool. But you're not a fool. You are Stalin. You are a cunning, manipulative, highly skilled strategist. You grasp situations and you act: that's why you are where you are, and why you've stayed there, at the top.

"So let's say that you were trying to gain time. You thought that you could stave off the German attack for a few vital months, by pretending to believe it was not imminent, by not allowing yourself to be provoked into action.

"But you didn't prepare. You didn't do what was necessary. Or maybe you'd won so many battles that you simply could not believe that this time you would lose, and that Hitler would be even more cunning, more ruthless, more manipulative than you. That he would succeed, and you would fail.

"Khrushchev says that when the invasion came you cried out: '*All that Lenin created we have lost forever.*'

"Did you really say that? Or was Khrushchev remembering those nights when he had to dance a Cossack dance with his buttocks almost touching the floor? *All that Lenin created we have lost forever.*"

I could see that Olya didn't like it when Joe talked like that, as if Stalin was still here with us and might answer him. Even to me it seemed like bad luck. The bones of some men don't lie as still as they should.

"Too many questions," said Olya. "People read histories in order to hear answers."

"You're wrong, Olya," said Joe passionately. "You are completely wrong and you don't understand why I am writing this book. People will read it in order to know what the right questions are. They'll read it in order to go into those rooms and know where the light switch is, even though it's dark."

"Maybe I'm wrong," said Olya. "But it's my history you're writing about."

"A man like Stalin belongs to all of us," said Joe. "He couldn't have been what he was without the permission of the whole world. Think of the Yalta Conference."

"Oh my God," said Olya, getting up again. "Why should I think about the Yalta Conference, or about any of it? I don't have to think about any of it anymore, don't you understand? Nobody can make me learn those parts of the history books if I don't want to. Why should I give such a man space inside my head?"

"He's there already," said Joe. "He's in all our heads. He's colonized our minds. We haven't begun to understand Stalin yet, or Hitler. We're still reacting to the blows, that's all. We are still staggering from them."

Adam was drinking more vodka. Away from the hospital, relaxed, holding Ruby, he was letting himself drink far more than usual. His face was smudged and softened. Maybe he was listening to Joe, maybe he wasn't. He and Ruby together, her skin like his for all its baby pearliness. Mine was darker. His red curls, her red curls with their blue shine. There was a touch of sun in the afternoon light and it shone through the dirty double windows and onto their hair. They were beautiful together.

"No phone," I said aloud.

"Of course there is a phone," said Olya quickly and a bit indignantly.

"No. I meant no phone that will ring for Adam. No calls from the hospital."

He'll be at peace, I meant. No one can touch us here.

Adam smiled, and held out his hand to me, from far away. I leaned across the sofa and touched his fingers, but they were soft and unresponsive. He was a little drunk, and happy. Now Olya was watching him, too.

"A man who was afraid of poison," said Joe. "He'd lost a lot of weight and looked skinny and shaky and old. A man who would go on the radio for the first time early in July, nearly two weeks after the invasion, speaking with marked hesitation, loudly drinking water in the pauses. He would sound shaky. A man whose hands sweated, so that when he handled documents he left oily marks on them. Maybe one day I'll be holding a document and I'll see those oily traces and I'll know who read it before me, who put his mark on it.

"But a clever man. Never, never to be underestimated. What I'm interested in is why he lost himself during those few days, and where he went. What he ate, who he talked to, where he walked, what he knew and what he didn't know. What he thought about. What he believed would happen, now that the German army was on the move, with its superior equipment and the element of surprise on its side.

"But Stalin hadn't been surprised. He'd been shocked, that's something else. He'd seen the surprise coming miles off, but the shock was that Hitler had dared to rouse him, as no one for years had dared to rouse him.

"You have to think of a cunning man, a fanatically suspicious man, as suspicious of being fed false information as he was of being fed poisoned food. A man whose wife had killed herself and left a letter which scorched his spirit for the rest of his life.

"Was Stalin really cornered when he went out to the dacha and disappeared from public life? No, I'm not sure. Maybe it was more like a body in crisis. The way the body can shut down most of its functions so that the vital ones are preserved. So that it keeps on living. Maybe, with most of his life shut down, Stalin could think at triple speed—"

"My God," said Olya, "my God, Joe, you are making my head hurt."

"I'm sorry, Olyenka," said Joe, and he passed his hand over her thick black hair. The touch made it clear to me that there would be no babies for Olya from Joe. He stroked her hair as if it were beautiful fur.

It was almost dark. I wanted to take Ruby on my lap, to feel the warmth and weight of her pinning me down.

I thought of the little boy whose mother had gone. Volodya. Six years old. Maybe he went back to sleep again, after the door closed behind his mother. When he woke, the daylight was strong. He sat bolt upright in bed, completely awake. He listened for her footsteps, but they didn't come.

"Give Ruby to me," I said to Adam. He stood up carefully, so as not to wake her. He laid her down on my lap, inside the shape of my arms. Ruby stiffened, then relaxed.

"My two darlings," said Adam. His voice was so quiet no one else in the room would have heard it. My whole body flooded with happiness and I looked down so that he wouldn't see the tears in my eyes. I thought that this was why we had come to Moscow, though we hadn't known it. We had come to be loosened from ourselves, to hear of griefs that were larger than our own, to be able to say those sweet words that so often stuck on our tongues.

Barnoon Is Heaven

beautiful today the surf on Porthkidney sands
and the standing out of the lighthouse, sheer
because of the rain past, the rain to come, the rain

Adam's gran was a girl from St. Ives. Her daughter married Adam's father, who was Jewish and gave Adam the red hair that darkened into Ruby's curls. Adam's parents met in London, during the war. Everyone was leaving their homes then and the old links were broken. They came together in a rented flat in Primrose Hill.

His gran is buried in Barnoon Cemetery, overlooking the sea. We found her grave and stood beside it, reading the lettering. It had long ago lost the raw look of death. It was settled into the earth and the wind and light played around it in a jewel-like way I had never seen in any other graveyard. Most graveyards collect darkness, but this one collected light.

Adam's father was irreligious in a Jewish way, like Adam. Adam's mother had been brought up a Methodist, but after she was twenty she had no time for it.

"But she never told my gran that," said Adam. "She didn't want to upset her. My gran had a hard life and the chapel kept her going."

I liked to hear of all these things being carried on in the bloodstream. Adam reached so easily into his past, and pulled down handfuls of history. My gran, my great-granddad, he said. He knew them on both sides, back and back. He had documents as well as stories, he had buildings where they'd lived, and gravestones. Adam had told Joe those stories once, and Joe had listened intently. I watched Joe soaking them up in the way he absorbed material he might one day use. Joe saw me looking, he saw me frowning maybe, warning him off. But he only smiled, a faint, sweet smile. *You know me, Rebecca. You know how I am.*

Adam's ancestors would be Ruby's, too. She would pass through my historyless body and come into her inheritance. When she could speak, she would be able to say, *My gran. My great-granddad.*

"The baby will have cousins all over Cornwall," said Adam, when I was pregnant and we came to St. Ives. "God knows how many."

We stood in Barnoon Cemetery, by his grandmother's grave. It was November and I was seven months pregnant. The wind blew and the sky was pale and torn with cloud. We'd come in from Trevail where we were staying in a cottage which had no running water. Adam lit the fires, pumped the water, made me stay in bed until the rooms were warm.

I bent down, balancing myself, and touched the stone of his grandmother's grave. I thought of the years she had been there with the smell of salt on the springy turf, and the sea sounding, and the boats sailing around the Island and out to the fishing grounds. Her grave was tended, with white pebbles on it and a little bush that was bare now but might have flowers in the spring.

"One of my cousins looks after the grave," said Adam.

"I'd like to be buried here," I said.

"Lots of people want that," said Adam. "There's competition." He helped me up and clasped me close so that my belly bumped against him. "Don't think about it now."

Ruby jumped inside me and I felt how alive I was, packed with life. "I could belong here," I said. "I wouldn't feel lonely here."

The wind whipped hair into my eyes and I turned my face aside, but Adam made a frame for my face with his hands and turned me to look at him.

"Are you lonely?"

"No, of course I'm not."

Adam opened his coat and wrapped it so that we were all inside it, the three of us, him and me and the baby who would be our daughter. Ruby.

"Let's keep you both warm," he said.

We went into town and the wind pushed us in and out of the salt, intricate streets. It was a white gale, with no rain in it. Adam tapped the smart paint on a cottage door as we went by.

"The town's changing," he said. "London money coming down."

The wind raced and roared and I wanted to run with it. Ruby was excited too. She turned inside me like a fish and thudded against my flesh. I wondered if she knew where she was, and felt that she belonged here.

We went into a hotel and a slow, tired man served us coffee. I lifted the cup and tasted its sour taste and I was flooded from head to foot with happiness.

You can write about memory forever. You can do it to avoid writing about what happened. It's one way out of it. Tell a story, tell another story. Stories falling as thick as snow to bury what happened. But it won't work anymore.

So, this is what happened.

It was a warm evening in August. Adam was home, and so for once I didn't need the babysitter when I went out to work. I had to be at the bar at seven, and usually I'd have bathed Ruby first, but it was such a beautiful evening that Adam thought he'd take Ruby to the park after they'd eaten. It would be light until eight-thirty. Ruby wanted to ride her bike. She'd just started to ride it without stabilizers, which was good for a five-year-old. Adam always made her wear a bike helmet.

They were still eating when I left. They were sitting together at the table, eating macaroni and cheese.

"Have some of your lettuce, Rubes," I said. I was standing at the mirror, tying back my hair into its tight knot. I put on lipstick, and blotted my mouth. In the summer we wore sleeveless black dresses and after months of sun my arms were a smooth even brown. I was pleased with the way I looked, even though I knew it didn't much please Adam when I walked out of the door on my way to the bar. There was no need for me to work there. Why did I hang on to the job? He would have understood if I had been taking an evening class, or working as a nurse. But what value is there in going to a bar and serving drinks and listening to people's stories of their lives?

"I'm going to work now, Ruby," I said, as I always did.

"Have you got to?" she asked, as she always did.

"I'll come in and give you a kiss when you're asleep," I said.

"Even if I'm fast asleep?"

"Even if you're fast asleep. I'll tiptoe in. I won't wake you up."

We said the same words every time. They had no meaning except to satisfy Ruby. I straightened up, and smoothed down my dress. I kissed Adam too and then I started looking for my keys and couldn't find them, so I was late and I think I forgot to call goodbye.

But when I got to work there was a problem. Anna had changed shift, because her babysitter couldn't come in the next day. Pauline was supposed to have told me this already, but she'd been off sick and she'd forgotten. There was a new girl being trained, and we had too many staff that night and not enough the next. So...

I was in a good mood. I told Anna I'd do her shift the next night and I made sure it was all written down on the rota so there wouldn't be any mess-up over pay, and I walked back out into the sunshine with everybody happy.

Ruby would be so pleased. I wouldn't tell her I was working tomorrow. Today was what mattered with Ruby. I'd walk up to the park and meet them, and maybe we'd go for a drink at the Silk Garden. It was such a beautiful evening and they lit the lamps around the garden when it went dark. Ruby loved those lamps.

I was going to go straight up to the park and meet them, but then I thought I'd change first. The house had that quiet sunlit feeling and I knew straightaway that it was empty. I changed quickly because I wanted to get up to the park before they left. I put on my white T-shirt with the embroidered daisies that Ruby liked, and my jeans. As I was going out of the house I remembered that my hair was still pulled back for work. I unpinned it, shook it out and combed my fingers through it. It took about a minute in front of the mirror.

It was ten to eight as I went out of the door and locked it. I ran down the steps and turned left, walking east. The sun was on my back, the air thick and golden as syrup. The sun was going down and the light was beautiful after the stale whiteness of the day. I noticed a few plane leaves on the pavement, dry and brown. I thought of the thick fallen leaves of autumn and how Ruby liked to jump and stamp in them. I was walking fast, hoping to get to the park, up its long green slopes and into the children's play area while Ruby was still there, high up on a swing maybe, her heels in the blue air, her red curls tipped back. She was always yelling at me to push her higher and I was always holding back, not wanting her to go too high.

I was coming down the road, looking down toward the end. I had a clear view. The main road was ahead of me, cutting across, and opposite was the road that led downhill from the park. And there was Ruby.

The sun was full on her face and she didn't see me. She was running down the pavement and Adam was behind, bent over the bike to push it, one hand on its saddle, the other on the handlebars. Ruby's bike helmet was strapped to the handlebars.

She wasn't far ahead of him. Two cars went along the main road, hiding her. Then there she was again, racing downhill. The gap between her and Adam was wider now. She was running faster than he could keep up with, because of the bike—

she always stops at roads
she's never run into a road
but look how fast she's going
Adam
she's too far ahead
the gap between them
stop Ruby stop Ruby stop
Rubystop

"Ruby!" I shouted. "Ruby, stop there!"

Ruby heard me. She looked up as she ran, squinting through the sun which was behind me and full in her face. Ruby saw me. She didn't stop. She took off, racing for me with the wildness that she knew was safe because my arms were there. She would spring through the air that divided us, thud into my body and I would break her fall.

I saw things in a jigsaw all at once and very clear.

Adam dropped the bike. He was off the ground, he was tearing for Ruby in great leaps. A dark blue car flashed round the bend in the main road.

"Adam!"

He was behind her. He was fast but the gap was too big. I was running and Ruby was running for me, full tilt into the dazzle of the setting sun. I don't think she even saw the main road.

The blue car skidded. The brakes screamed and the wheels tore at the road. I saw the blue car go sideways past me with Ruby on its bonnet. The driver's mouth was wide open. Then the car hit the side of a plane tree, and Ruby was thrown off. I watched her fall on her back, on the back of her head. Her body convulsed.

She was moving. She was alive. She was trying to get up. I was on my knees in the gravel.

"Don't touch her, don't touch her, don't touch her," said Adam. She arched again as if the road was shocking her. Then she went still. She went small. Adam had his mouth over her mouth, trying to find her breath.

There were people pressing round us. I looked up at them from all fours, like a dog. "I rang on my mobile," said a man. "They're sending an ambulance."

"He's a doctor," I said. "Her father's a doctor."

I could barely see Ruby. I bowed down so my face was almost touching her foot in its dirty trainer. Ruby's trainers were never dirty like that. I always put them in the washing machine every week. Her pink jeans too, they had stuff all over them. I lay on the road and stroked her ankle inside the thick trainer. Adam was still crouched over Ruby, but he wasn't breathing into her anymore. He had stopped. He wanted me to look after her now. I lifted my head and saw Ruby's face, shocked sideways and covered in muck. I knew I would have some wipes in my bag. I always carried them, for when Ruby ate ice cream or there wasn't any paper in public toilets. I would clean her face, and then I'd put her jeans in the washing machine, and her trainers. I would come back and wash the road with a bucket of water and Ruby would help me swoosh it over the gravel. She would like that.

⁓

Barnoon is heaven. We wanted somewhere for Ruby where she would be safe.

It was possible to open Adam's grandmother's grave and put Ruby there with her. Adam wouldn't have a heavy coffin for Ruby. We didn't want her to feel locked in. The coffin was made of a special kind of cardboard and it was so light that Adam carried Ruby in his arms, by himself.

"Give her to me a minute," I said. I held the box and I could feel Ruby. She was heavy and I had to brace myself to take her weight.

You're getting to be a big girl now, Rubes. You get down now. I can't carry you anymore.

We Are as We Are

After great pain, a formal feeling comes—
The Nerves sit ceremonious, like Tombs—

One evening that November Adam was reading a research paper. The room was quiet. I'd lit a candle, which I did every night now, because candles give life to a room. Each night there was a different candle. Sometimes they were fat and stubby, sometimes they were tall and soaring like church candles. The tall ones wound their way down swiftly. I bought scented candles and decorated candles. There was a shop I used to go to in those months, kept by a young woman who had begun her business by making all the candles herself, in her bathroom. She liked to talk about the atmosphere which a particular candle would bring to a room.

Tonight's candle was the blue of polar ice. It burned steadily, without a flicker, and was scentless. I watched a gob of wax make its way down the candle stem.

Adam let his papers fall to the floor. They slithered down off his knee and the movement of the paper disturbed the candle so that its flame fluttered, then stood upright again.

"I can't make sense of this," said Adam. His eyes were wide open, blank. "I read it and as soon as I read it I lose it. My memory's fucked."

"Can't you leave it?"

"I could let it go. It's only one paper. But—"

"But you remember when you're at work? You remember things at work?"

Adam's fists were clenched. He bumped them on the table, very, very gently, very restrained. "It's different at work," he said.

"That's good," I said.

He had split his life in two. In the compartment of work, the lights were still on. It was warm and there were voices and footsteps, comings and goings, even little family jokes of the kind people have when they work together night and day. Minute by minute Adam was there, concentrating, frowning, smiling, changing with every change in the babies, noting every detail of a drug protocol. He didn't let go. He wouldn't let go. More and more, work was drawing him in. He was becoming involved in an international project on HIV and prematurity. There was going to be a lot of travel. There'd be overseas conferences and I could come with him.

Adam had to stay later and later at the hospital, because he couldn't work at home. He couldn't concentrate. Our house was full of grief, packed solid with this thing that kept changing shape and seizing us in new ways. It had moved in like a crowd of strangers: animal, vegetable, mineral. At one moment it was a picture book, the next it became a scuffed place under the swing. It sat at Adam's desk, it would not let us sit at the kitchen table, it pounced as next-door's cat squirmed in the autumn sun. It trod everywhere. In the shower water hit me like rods of iron and I gasped at its weight. It filled the garden and shriveled the nerine lilies and bronze chrysanthemums. It got into birdsong and the sound of sirens. It lay between us in bed like a sword.

There was no room for anything else. Adam couldn't use the computer. He could barely use the phone. People would call us at home and say, "Adam, are you all right? You sound different."

We learned that it only took two or three months after Ruby's death for people to begin asking us if we were all right.

I gave up the bar. I tried to go once, but when I saw my short black dress hanging in the wardrobe, my head began to drum.

If Anna's babysitter hadn't let her down. If I had told Adam it was too late for Ruby to go to the park. She gets silly when she's tired. When they're tired or when they're hungry, that's when accidents happen.

You might leave the front door open while you fetch the shopping in. Suddenly she's out of the house. You run down the steps and catch her as she races into the road. You grab her, shake her. She starts to cry and you yell, *Don't you ever, ever, ever do that again.* You both go back in the house and shut the door and your heart's still pumping while she bawls and howls and clings to your waist scrubbing her tears and snot into your jeans. And you sit down together on the hall floor and she burrows into you, and you comfort each other.

⁊

If I had gone straight to the park in my work clothes instead of going home to change. If I'd left my hair as it was. That minute I'd spent shaking out my hair and combing it with my fingers. The minute ticked through my head again. I'd been looking at myself in the mirror.

I turned away from the mirror. I opened the front door, found the keys in the side pocket of my bag. I locked the door, came down the steps. I felt the August heat on my arms.

Better put her pink jeans in the wash tonight, she wants to wear them all the time.

⁊

Another November evening. Adam was back so late these days that I knew I had plenty of time. I would light my candle, and read Joe's letter again. It was an email, but I'd printed it out and put it in an envelope to keep.

He didn't write about our feelings, or about his own. He wrote about Ruby. He wrote about her yellow cardigan, and the day she was born, and the visits we'd made to Moscow, and how when Ruby was four Olya had taught her how to say "Do you want to be my friend?" in Russian because this was what Ruby said to everyone she met. And then Olya had invited her niece to play with Ruby. They'd played together, not seeming to notice that they weren't speaking the same language. Ruby and Sveta both fell over in the park and both wanted Disney plasters on their almost invisible grazes when they came back to the apartment. And Sveta liked the plasters so much that Ruby secretly put a handful of them in her jacket pocket so Sveta would find them when she got home. Joe remembered everything, in a way I thought no one else would remember.

I think of you both constantly, he wrote at the end of the letter. I believed him. Joe was constant. It seemed to me when I held the letter that his thoughts flowed toward me, strong and sure, over thousands of miles. It was true even though he had never touched the paper, because I had printed out his email. It bore no marks of his sweat, and there was no envelope which might have his saliva on the seal.

I think of you both constantly. He was thinking of Ruby like that, remembering the Disney plasters and the yellow cardigan. He remembered the way Ruby would balance in his arms, lightly, with a straight back and frowning slightly at first. And then breaking into a smile, petal after petal of it, her eyelids, her cheeks, her lips—

Joe didn't tell me to turn my mind away, to forget, to make things bearable, to heal myself. He did not write about the stages of grief.

Winter was coming. The trees and bushes were losing their leaves. Soon they'd be dry and brown, stiff and scratchy, and to all outward appearances dead. But inside, if the frost didn't burn it away entirely, there was the quick of the plant. It was barely green but if you put your lips to it you could feel that it was moist. How I dreaded the thought that inside my shriveled self there was something that wanted to come back to life.

I folded Joe's letter, and put it away. I blew out the candle, and turned off the lights. The house was so familiar that I could find my way around in the dark. I put on my nightdress and my dressing gown. I walked around the rooms, checking that the lights were off in all of them, the TV unplugged, and everything safe.

I came to Ruby's room in the dark. I hadn't changed her sheets, or washed her pajamas. The smell of Ruby clung to them.

I always promised her I would come in and kiss her goodnight after I came back from work. Even if I'm asleep? Ruby asked. Even if you're asleep, I repeated. I like the smell when you come back from work, she said. Sometimes I forgot, but the next morning I always told her I'd done it. I told her about how she was all curled up and I tucked the duvet round her, and you know what, Ruby, you were snoring. Like this. That made her laugh.

The thing was to stay in her room. The dark and the Ruby smell melted into me and I hung in time. There were no minutes anymore. I didn't have to hold on.

"I'm here, Ruby," I said. "Go back to sleep. You had a bad dream."

I thought that Adam had come home too, and slipped into the house without telling me. He was waiting in bed, feeling the empty space where I belonged. He knew that I'd come soon, when I'd settled Ruby down.

I didn't try to touch Ruby, not even to stroke her cheek. She knew I was there.

"Go to sleep, Rubes," I said.

⁂

The days were nothing anymore. I had to get through them and I understood why Ruby wasn't there in them. I would look at my watch as the day drew on and know it was only a few hours now, and then I would be with her again.

One night the phone kept ringing. It rang for twenty rings and then it stopped, but after a brief pause it began to ring again. I couldn't answer it. When you're settling a child down you can't always get to the phone in time. People understand that.

Ruby's bedroom was dark and warm. Water sucked and gurgled in her radiator. I must find the key and bleed it, I thought. The noise was loud enough to keep Ruby awake.

"It's only your radiator, Rubes," I said, in case she thought it was something bad. I moved my chair closer to her bed. I didn't need to touch her. She could always tell when I was there. She felt my presence just as I felt hers.

"I'm here. Go back to sleep," I said. "You don't want to be tired and grumpy in the morning."

Ruby was restless. I knew she wanted me to sing to her.

How many miles to Babylon?
Four score miles and ten.
Will we get there by candlelight?
Yes, and back again.

If your heels are nimble and light
We may get there by candlelight.

"My heels are nimble and light," said Ruby.
"I know they are."
"Are yours?"
"Not as light as yours. But we'll get there, Rubes."

The light crashed on. It was Adam standing there in his coat. He came across to me and the cold air of outside touched me.

"I heard you talking," he said. "Rebecca, you've got to stop this."

Everything shriveled and went. In front of me there was a flat bed, a lamp and a toy reindeer. On my lap there was a limp pair of pajamas.

"She's gone," I said.

"Yes," said Adam.

"She's—"

"Yes."

"Why didn't you let me keep her?"

"For Christ's sake, Rebecca. For Christ's Christ's sake."

"I'm sorry, Adam," I said. "I'm sorry, I'm so sorry, I'm so sorry, I'm so sorry, Ruby, I'm so sorry, I'm so sorry—"

It was the heart of the night. Our best time, the time we always returned to ourselves. We could dissolve the day's quarrels in a moment. I checked the illuminated face of the alarm clock. Twenty past one. Adam had fallen asleep. He was breathing shallowly, fighting the current of sleep as it tried to carry him into deeper waters. I wondered who was in his dream.

He must sleep. He must recover himself. He needed eight hours' sleep, or he wouldn't be able to work.

He had to work. When I'd first met him and loved him I'd loved his work too without knowing it, because it was in every part of him, twisted into his fibers. His sureness, his attentiveness, his boldness. His lack of fear when he touched a baby who was little bigger than his hand, and had been startled into life months too soon. I would have shrunk back. I would have been too scared of causing more pain. I would not have dared do anything for fear of doing harm. But Adam wasn't afraid. He didn't shrink back and he trusted that what he did would be of use. He held together in his head the whole complex thing, and acted simply. He always talked to the babies, wouldn't do anything to them without telling them what he was doing.

He must sleep. I thought of his hands which I knew so well I seemed to know them from the bones outward. Robust hands, and practical and tender. It was too dark for me to see if his hands were still clenched into fists.

❦

So often I'd thought that our bed was a ship and we were voyaging in it together. I would roll over in the bed and imagine the waves leaping around us, and the fathomless water. Everything that was in us made up the voyage. Our body heat, our dreams, the taste of Adam's sweat, the juice of sex, the pang of Ruby's conception. We would go on and on, pushed where the waves took us. We would die in that bed, I believed.

Nothing in Adam was alien to me. There were unknown things, but nothing alien.

He groaned, and heaved himself over. Now his back was turned to me.

The wind was getting up. I'd left the window open and it sucked at the curtain, drawing it in and then letting it belly outward. I always left our bedroom door open and I couldn't stop doing it. The door creaked, and moved. Its catch tapped against the frame.

I must close the door. I must close the window so that the wind doesn't come in.

I pushed back the bedclothes and slid out of bed. I went over to the window and the curtain blew into my face. I fumbled between the folds of cloth, found the parting of the curtains and drew them back.

There was the tree-lined street. The plane trees were tanned orange by the street lights, and they had lost their leaves. Wind was moving in the big, bare branches. The street was blank and still.

The cold wind made me shiver but I pulled the sash up a little higher.

On the first day that Ruby came home, we wrapped her cherry-colored shawl around her in the car seat. We carried her swiftly from the car to the house, and shut the door, and turned the heating up. We would not have let a drop of rain fall on her.

When it was a cold day but we weren't sure if it would rain or not, we would stand in the hall and debate which coat she should wear. Her waterproof was not as warm as her fleece-lined coat. And we'd tie on her scarf, even though she didn't like it. *It'll keep you warm, Rubes.* Ruby always spread her fingers out wrong for her gloves. She would have three fingers crammed into one woollen finger, and half the glove limp.

Ruby, stand still. You are not going out without your gloves.

When there was frost I would turn her radiator up and creep into her room before we went to bed to check that she hadn't thrown off her covers. Outside, the frost burned its way into the Turkey fig Adam had planted, and killed it. Inside the house, in her warm room, in the nest of her bed, was Ruby.

I stood at the window now, and watched the sterile, flickering shadows that the wind made out of bare twigs and branches. She would never be in her bedroom again. The line was cut. I could go into the bedroom and sit beside her bed in the dark but I would not feel her or smell her. The bed would remain blank and her soft toys would slowly lose their characters. She was out there, in the wind and cold. I knew she couldn't feel it but I flinched at the rain spattering on the windows.

Put on your boots, Ruby. No, not your fleece, you'll need your waterproof today. Let's put your hood up.

The rain spattered. We couldn't shelter her. We had failed.

"Ruby," I said, but even as the word left my mouth I knew how thin it would sound. There would never be an answer.

The house was nothing anymore. It was a shell, booming where the weather struck it. It meant nothing.

I must close the window, I thought. But I couldn't bring myself to shut the window when Ruby was still outside. I wanted the rain to come in, and the wind. I wanted the house to dissolve.

Reproaches

We wove a web in childhood,
  A web of sunny air,
We dug a spring in infancy,
  Of water pure and fair:

We sowed in youth a mustard seed,
  We cut an almond rod . . .

"You reproach yourself," said Mr. Damiano, when I had finished speaking. I nodded. I had told him everything and now it was quite dark. I hadn't gone to my flat or showered or unpacked. I had gone straight from Heathrow to the office.

I was in Mr. Damiano's office, with the stale taste of aeroplanes still in my mouth. My feet ached. Mr. Damiano looked tired, too. His eyes were pouchy and black underneath, and his skin was sallow. For the first time, I wondered exactly how old he was.

"You remember how you made the garden, Rebecca?" asked Mr. Damiano. "When you first came?"

I nodded again. It was about two months after I began to work for Mr. Damiano that I discovered there was a backyard at the base of the office building. Mr. Damiano rented the yard, even though our offices were not on the ground floor.

"For storage," he shrugged, when I first asked him about it. But there was nothing stored there.

The door to the yard was kept locked and bolted. The lock was stiff when I turned the key, as if no one ever bothered to open it. I went down the three steep steps and I was in the yard. It was full of rubbish, and a lean-to shed sagged against the far wall. The yard was paved with greasy flagstones, grained with filth. The walls were high and dirty and they needed pointing here and there, but they were sound. Generations of London soot had gone into the brick. The Clean Air Acts had been passed, but the old dirt had stayed there.

Sunlight was leaking over the walls and onto the heaps of cardboard and black rubbish bags. I checked my watch and looked at the position of the sun. The yard faced southwest.

There was a rustle in the corner and I turned sharply. But I saw nothing, even when I went around the yard stirring the piles of rubbish with a stick. Nothing came out. In London you are never more than a few steps from a rat. I knew that.

I looked at the open door that led into the building. The door, piles of rubbish, boxes, shed, bins. Sound of traffic and footsteps beyond the high walls. I had been here before. I had been born into a place like this. Not my first birth, out of my mother's body, which I knew nothing about. Nobody remembered it. But my second birth, when Lucia lifted me out of my cardboard shoebox and brought me into the heat of the kitchen. My resurrection had happened in a yard like this.

I went back up the steps with the key in my pocket, to speak to Mr. Damiano.

I worked on that yard every weekend. I hired ladders and a high-pressure hose. I cleared the rubbish, and dismantled the lean-to. The wood was rotten and the shed fell apart as soon as I pulled at the planks. I filled heavy-duty plastic bags with the rubbish and arranged for a council collection.

For three weekends I worked on painting the walls. Painting the walls, leaning free from my ladder, thinking of nothing but the sweep of my brush and the tide of Dulux Weathershield in Brilliant White advancing over the bricks. As I painted I was letting light down into the yard. The sun came round and settled strongly. I saw how it would be: white walls, leaf shadows, light.

Mr. Damiano never came to see what I was doing. He knew about the project but seemed to take no interest in it. I would finish work late on Friday night, then I would be back again on Saturday morning, walking through the early streets in my oldest jeans.

I didn't want to plant flowers. I wanted things that belonged to the yard, ferns and ivies that would drip down the walls. There should be a seat and there should be a tall pot at either side of it, but I couldn't afford to buy them. In time, though, I would do so.

Next time I came to the garden there was a fig tree in the sunniest corner. It was in a terra-cotta pot and when I bent down I smelled its musky, fertile scent, and saw tiny figs on the branches.

The Turkey fig Adam had planted died in the frost. I would buy horticultural fleece this time and mummify this fig tree when frost threatened.

⟬⟭

"You remember how you made that garden, Rebecca?" asked Mr. Damiano again.

"Yes."

"It was nothing before. Rubbish."

In three years I had bought a seat and table for the garden and the two pots. I had allowed some flowers in. There was a sundial on the wall now, though I didn't know how to tell the time by it. I liked to sweep the flagstones, trim the ivies, and feed and water the pots. Mr. Damiano sat there in the evenings, often, with a bottle of wine on the iron table. The blue smell of his cigarettes filled up the yard. He asked me if I would plant some scented things and so I put a wooden tub of nicotiana and night-scented stock close to the seat.

"That's right, put them near," said Mr. Damiano. "My sense of smell is poor."

"Because you smoke."

He smoked too much and couldn't climb a flight of stairs without stopping to wheeze. He liked the garden. He would walk around it in his urban way, peering at the plants as if he didn't know what they would do next.

"You have the touch for this," he would say approvingly, like a man in a restaurant who is a connoisseur of food without knowing how to make the simplest dish. Right from the beginning he spoke to me as if we'd known each other for a long time. Once or twice I wondered if this was because I reminded him of someone. But I put the thought out of my mind. When people say you remind them of someone it means that you remind them of themselves, of their own life, of their own concerns. You are a mirror, that's all.

"You reproach yourself," said Mr. Damiano again. "Of course."

"I don't think about it."

"No, no," he said, but not as if agreeing with me. "Let's go downstairs, Rebecca. Let's go in your garden."

It was an August night and still warm. There was a light on the garden wall and when Mr. Damiano switched it on everything sprang into focus. The tide of London receded. The orange street-light murk vanished and the sound of traffic dimmed.

Mr. Damiano walked up and down, and I sat on the seat and watched the red point of his cigarette grow bright as he drew on it. The perfume of the nicotiana was strong. I thought of Mr. Damiano's hotels—the Sidney, Lampedusa, Villon, Langland, Sorescu, Cavafy, Sexton and Bishop—and all the people sleeping in them at this moment. Where the time was different, children would be playing with their baskets of toys. The hotels would be brightly lit at their hundreds of windows and they would have the privileged look that such places have at night, seen from a distance. Then, you can believe that the building holds everything you've ever wanted.

Mr. Damiano's gift was to keep that dream just as bright when you came close. As I thought of the hotels he had created and the fact that I was leaving them, they were like great ships in my mind, pulling away from the quay where I stood, lights blazing and music drifting over the gap between us. In London, in New York, in California, Mr. Damiano's ships blew their sirens on the water.

"We should change our olive supplier for Sidney," I said.

"Who are we using?"

"I Promessi Sposi. And those napkins won't work in New York. They'll think we're cheap."

Mr. Damiano sighed. It was hard for him to let go of his best ideas. He'd loved the thought of that patient, tiny darning. As I've said before, he had no time for the comfortless clichés of the luxury hotel. The bed heaped with overstuffed pillows and bolsters, the petty sewing kit and shoe wipes, the routine health spa toiletries, the gyms and massage services and pretentious bistros, the minibar which electronically registers everything that is taken out of it, the turning-down of the bed by tired middle-aged women who are working without papers, the offering of porn channels and crested writing paper. Mr. Damiano had sent me to visit many such hotels, to learn.

He wanted to give finesse to the thought of having everything you wanted. He wanted you to believe that your old nurse had known that you were coming and had got out the family napkins and held them up to the light and begun to darn. As you entered the hotel you entered a story where you had your own part, where you were considered, where you knew and were known. If you were afraid to sleep at night (and God knows how many people who have reached the peak of their careers are afraid to sleep at night) you would find a fire lit, and a book laid by your bed with the page marked.

"You are sure about the napkins?" asked Mr. Damiano.

"Yes, I'm sure."

"It was a nice idea," said Mr. Damiano.

"Yes, it was a nice idea."

Mr. Damiano had stopped walking. He stood beside the seat and rubbed the petals of the night-scented stock between his fingers.

"And so you're leaving me."

"Yes."

Mr. Damiano rubbed the back of his head. His hair was dark again. It had been graying, just a little, before I left for New York. I wondered if he colored it himself, or if someone did it for him. And if so, who would it be—what kind of hands—

"I am older than you think," said Mr. Damiano abruptly.

"How old do you think I am, Rebecca?"

"Sixty-two? Sixty-three?"

"No," he said. "I am much older than that. In my family we age very slowly. My father's hair was black at fifty. My mother did not give birth to me until she was almost forty, and then she gave birth again at forty-eight. We age very slowly, if we get the chance to age. You've worked well with me, Rebecca. You remember when you came here first? You told me that you knew nothing about hotels, as if that was a disqualification. But it was exactly what I needed. And you reproach yourself, and so do I. Let me sit down and tell you."

Flyer and Catcher

Out of the wood of thoughts that grows by night
To be cut down by the sharp axe of light—

Mr. Damiano had switched off the garden light. His bulk settled on the seat beside me. The dark was soft and comforting. Out of it his voice came heavily.

"I am seventy-one," said Mr. Damiano. "If my sister had lived she would have been sixty-three."

"What was she called?"

"Bella. It wasn't her real name, but we always called her Bella. Not that she was so very beautiful, but she was full of life and it looked like beauty."

A bird flew suddenly out of the ivy and across the garden. I couldn't see where it went.

"Our light disturbed it," said Mr. Damiano.

Suddenly the bird gave out a few notes, liquid and hopeful, testing for the dawn. The notes broke off. The leaves rustled again, and then were still.

"I think I told you, Rebecca, that my family were trapeze artists," said Mr. Damiano. But we both knew that this was the first time I'd ever heard it. The thought of Mr. Damiano's bulk flying through the air made me smile.

"I know. But I was not then as I am now. Trapeze artists, you know, are not fine willowy people. We have muscle. We are stocky, like this." He slapped his thigh. "I remember my mother in her costume. She worked until Bella was born. I told you, we age slowly in my family.

"My mother was strong. Strong arms, strong hands. I remember how she would warm up before every practice and every performance. She never hurried or cut corners. I can see her now, in a patch of sunlight at the back of the tent, stretching and bending, bringing her arms up and rotating them from her shoulders, bringing one foot up above her head, and then the other. She would skip with a skipping rope to build up her endurance. I used to count for her. That was before Bella was born, and my mother seemed young to me, although she was already in her mid-forties. She had dark hair which she rinsed with henna and the sunlight would strike on it. She was about as dark as you are—yes, the color of your hair is very similar. Bella inherited my mother's looks.

"After a performance my mother would towel herself down with a rough towel which was always clean and folded ready for her. She would towel every part of her body then she would rub oil into her muscles. It was a special type of oil, very expensive, in a dark blue bottle without a label on it.

"I remember once when we were touring in Austria, she took me to bathe in a lake which was called the Black Lake because of its water. It was black, peaty water and it was full of carp. They would brush against your legs when you swam. I didn't like the shadows of the carp. My mother swam under the water and she would rise up close to me and laugh. Water would stream off her shoulders. I would see the power in her and then she would let me swim on her back, out into the deep water."

"Did you like being a trapeze artist?"

"At first, I liked it. I was training from the time I could walk. Tumbling and exercising, three hours each day. Bending and stretching and doing flips in the dust. Every night I watched my parents perform. I watched the first performance, then there was an interval, then sometimes I saw the second performance if I hadn't fallen asleep.

"My mother was a flyer. Her costumes were made to catch the light as she flew. They were very expensive and she was always repairing them. The fabric would rub and split under the strain. Her sweat would rot it. My mother spent hours with the needle in her hand. She had to repair, repair, because we couldn't buy new.

"She was still a flyer but she knew she had only a few years left. Soon she would slow down and her coordination would deteriorate, no matter how much she practiced and how flexible she kept herself. And then one day she would fall.

"She thought ahead, and at that time she believed that I had the build to become a flyer, too. My father would continue to be catcher for me, as he was for my mother.

"Yes, my mother possessed foresight. In fact I believe it was more than that. There was a touch of second sight in her, but it wasn't steady. It came and went and so it was of no use to her. She would see pictures of the future but she wouldn't be able to interpret them. I remember once, when Bella was a tiny child, not more than two, my mother announced that she had seen Bella in a convent. She was sure it was a convent because it was full of nuns in their habits and there were bells, and there was Bella. My father laughed, and bounced Bella on his knee and asked her if she was going to cut her hair off and be a little saint. Bella didn't understand a word, but she said, 'Sì, Papà,' and we all laughed. 'Sì, Papà.' I can hear it now, and the sound of Bella laughing, not because she understood the joke but because she was glad to have made the big people laugh.

"Bella's birth was very difficult and after that my mother was never as strong. The act was limited.

"When I was four years old I was measured for a costume which sparkled all over and I went into the ring with my parents. Everyone clapped because I was so small. But they clapped more when they saw that I knew how to work. My mother sat me on her shoulders and walked the low wire with me. I knew how to balance, what I had to do. When she squatted I jumped down lightly on the balls of my feet as I'd been taught and I did a somersault and stood up with my arms outstretched. That was my first time in the ring. I didn't go up in the rigging, and the wire was only a few feet above the ground, but it was the beginning of real work for me. Everyone was glad and my parents were proud of me. But as I grew older, other things began to interest me. I would rather read than practice. Several times my father had to beat me.

"So, I was twelve and my sister Bella was four years old. I was a flyer. Don't get the idea that I was good: I was not. But I learned fast, I was supple and strong and I worked hard because I knew I had to. My father didn't miss anything.

"Bella was small for her age, with black curls around her face. She looked so young when she came into the ring that it made them gasp. You could hear the hiss of breath from beyond the ring kerb. She did not have to do anything to get applause. Just to be herself.

"Technically she was at the earliest stages. But already she had something. Her coordination was really astonishing. I don't think I ever saw Bella drop a thing from the day she was born. I remember that when she was two years old she could crack a fresh egg clean to separate the white from the yolk.

"Bella loved the ring, and she had something that my father hadn't got and I hadn't got. My mother had this quality when she was younger, but not as strongly as Bella. You would want to watch my mother, even while she was practicing the same thing over and over. And Bella was the same, but more. She had a spark in her."

"Were you jealous of her?" I asked.

"No. I did not want that applause anymore. I wanted to study, which was impossible. Families like ours do not study. I wanted to get away, which was also impossible. I wanted to be a student and sit in a big library with columns and high windows and read and read, and in the evenings to stroll with my friends along the riverbank and into cafés, and sit and talk about our thoughts. I never wanted to be measured for another costume. I wanted to smell water and coffee and fresh new books, instead of animal dung and human sweat.

"By this time we were in Spain. It was 1942 and there was no other place in Europe where we could be. My parents had joined a small circus which went from town to town in southern Spain. It didn't tour the cities, it wasn't good enough. It was a step down for us all. It was what my mother had feared. My parents didn't like it, but what could they do? We were the only artistes in that circus. It was a ragbag— badly trained performing bears, an African elephant which had skin trouble, a dwarf and a hermaphrodite, a couple of clowns, an equestrian act. We were out of place there. But it was the war. Spain was a bad country for us, but not as bad as everywhere else.

"How they used to beat those bears! I was used to animals being beaten, but those guys did not even get any results from it. The bears would shamble on their hind legs for a while and that was that. Even for country towns, it was not impressive. They had some plan of bringing in a snake charmer, but it never happened. I would go into the countryside to look for snakes myself. Anything to make life more interesting."

Mr. Damiano lit another cigarette, got up, walked up and down the flagstones without speaking. After a few minutes, he came back to me. His profile was deeply cut and harsh.

"A year passed. Bella was five. Every town we came to, Bella sparkled. It didn't matter who came, they fell in love with her. They threw coins into the ring for her, and my mother made her a sequined bag and she put the coins in it, curtseying to the audience. Bella did some tumbling, a few little tricks, and she developed her own balancing act on the low wire. Nothing difficult, but she seemed to flow from one position to the next like water. She was beautiful to watch.

"My mother would lead her out into the ring and then Bella would cartwheel her way round it, over and over, and then she would work on the low wire. Easy stuff, but she was so bright and happy that everyone loved it. And she remained small. She was five, but she looked less than four.

"My father was a good catcher. He should have worked with a girl, it would have gone down better. There was a girl called La Palomina who wanted to work with him. She liked my father and he liked her. There was sympathy between their bodies—you have to have that for the act to work. La Palomina could hang from a rope by her teeth. She was very good, but it would have meant a share going outside the family, and we couldn't afford that. She became famous after the war.

"So we carried on, me and my father. But it's not so interesting, a middle-aged man and a boy who's too old to be cute anymore. There's no magic.

"We did what we could. But Bella, down on the ground turning a cartwheel, had more magic than us, and we knew it.

"It was in those months that my father had the idea that Bella would work with us."

"You mean high up? On the trapeze?"

"No. She was far too young for an aerial act, even my father could see that. But she could be worked into the act. My father designed a special rigging. I would stand in the ring with Bella on my shoulders. My father would hang from the aerial ladder, catch her, and I would move away. Then he would swing with her. It was nothing at all but it would look pretty. In time it could be developed.

"We tried it. Bella was perfect. She kept her feet together, pointed the way we had taught her. She smiled. She learned to let go with one of her hands when he gave her the signal, and wave to the crowd as she swung. She blew kisses. Very pretty. They loved it."

"What happened?"

"Nothing. Nothing. It was a nice little act. Then we developed it so I lifted Bella upside down with her hands on my shoulders. I held her by the waist. My father caught her by the feet and she swung upside down. That was even better. Bella was perfectly self-possessed. She held her arms like a dancer. My father saw how good she was going to be. The next Lillian Leitzel, he said.

"My father knew that Bella was at the point where I would not need to hold her in the handstand. She would be able to balance on my shoulders. So we practiced over and over.

" 'I can do it,' Bella kept saying. 'Why don't you let me do it?'

"It was even more boring to practice with Bella than to practice with my father. I used to have a terrible fear that time had stopped and I was caught in it like a fly on glass who thinks he is treading his way into the air but will die still trapped. I think all adolescents know that feeling."

"Yes," I said.

"I would prickle all over with it. It was like a frenzy. I would see my mother sitting on the steps, mending my father's tights. I would see the bears dragging at their chains and a yellow village dog yapping round them, just out of reach of a blow from their paws. I could smell excrement and straw and dust. The heat was so great that the mountains vanished in a white haze.

"One morning Bella and I were in the ring together. My father had marked the exact place where we should stand. Again and again I squatted, Bella put her hands on my shoulders, I held her as she went up in a handstand, then I let go. She remained steady.

" 'Good girl,' I said. 'And now we're going to have a break. You can play.'

"I was teaching myself English, can you imagine? I had bought a teaching book from a secondhand shop, and I was on the fourth chapter. I took the book out from under the ringside bench, and sat down on the ring kerb. I didn't look at Bella. She would be practicing flips, or walking around the ring on her hands. Bella was always practicing, even when nobody made her.

"*This horse is lame. Please bring me a fresh mount.*

"I put my finger under the words and said them aloud. I wondered if 'horse' and 'mount' were the same thing, and if so, why there were two words for the same thing.

"*My horse is lame. Please bring me a fresh mount.*

"I pronounced those words with exhilaration. I was speaking English. I was educating myself. If I stared as far as I could, out through the tent flap, across the field and the clump of the town, into the yellowish dusty distance, nobody I saw would know what those words meant. But I knew.

"Then I glanced up. The ring was empty. For a moment I thought Bella had run out to my mother, then I saw her. She was climbing up to the pedestal board, where the fly bar had been left looped over. I had left it like that. She was already more than fifteen feet in the air, climbing into the dark. When we performed, it was all lit up, so you could see exactly where to put your feet. But Bella was climbing up steadily into the darkness. The rungs of the ladder were too widely spaced for her. At each step she stretched and grasped and pulled herself up. And she was making for the pedestal board, and the fly bar. She thought she was ready to fly.

"My book dropped. I thought of calling but I didn't want to scare her. And it was dark up there. If she looked away, if she misjudged, she might fall. Even Bella might fall.

"I thought what to do. It sounds long when I'm telling you, but it was no time at all. Like the space between one breath and the next. I was over at the foot of the ladder. I grasped it and began to climb. I knew I would be faster than her. I would be behind her and I could hold her and bring her down, safe. I could get to her before she reached the pedestal board."

"But you didn't get there," I said. In my mind the little girl cartwheeled through the air to smash on the floor of the ring.

"No," he said. "It's not what you think. I reached her. She felt me coming up behind her and she looked round and laughed. I could see the shine of laughter on her face, but she was still just out of reach.

She swarmed up the next rung of the ladder. I could see she thought she was going to make it and reach the pedestal board before me. God knows what she thought she was going to do once she got up there.

"I got her. I held her fast between the ladder and my chest. She didn't struggle, but her body went rigid. With one arm around Bella and my other hand gripping the ladder, I brought her down backwards. When I had got her feet on the ground I shook her hard and she began to cry. I made her look up at where she had been. She knew that she was forbidden to climb into the rigging. She knew, because my mother was always telling her. My mother knew that Bella's fearlessness was a danger as well as an asset. I was so angry with her that I was shaking myself.

" 'You see? You see? You could have fallen all that way down. You might have killed yourself.'

"But she hadn't fallen. She roared and screeched until my mother came, and then Bella snatched herself away from me and ran to my mother and buried her face in her skirt.

"I was afraid Bella would tell her what had happened. My mother would blame me for not watching my sister more closely. My father would hear of it and he would beat me. But Bella didn't say anything. She roared and stamped and screamed until her anger was dissolved. My mother scolded me for teasing Bella, but she didn't notice my book lying in the dust."

"So it was all right?"

"No."

How My Mother's Vision
Came True

To know the change and feel it,
When there is none to heal it
Nor numbed sense to steal it—

"No," said Mr. Damiano. He ground his cigarette into the flagstones with his heel. "Are you all right, Rebecca? You're not cold?"

"No, it's warm."

"It's very warm." He took a handkerchief out of his pocket and carefully wiped his face and the back of his neck. "Do you want a drink?"

"Yes, all right."

Instead of the lean-to, there was a brick-built shed in the garden now. Mr. Damiano kept a few bottles of wine there. It had electricity, and a fridge. Mr. Damiano disappeared inside, and light curled out of the shed and lay on the stones like a tongue. Bottles clinked, then there was the pull of a cork. Mr. Damiano came out of the shed with a round tray on the flat of his hand. He swiveled, switched off the light and closed the door behind him. All the while the tray in his hand remained perfectly steady.

Mr. Damiano put the tray on the iron table, poured the wine and gave me a glass. It was nice wine. It had a French stoniness in it, instead of ready fruit. I drank it slowly. My head felt as light as zero. Aeroplanes and fear and seeing Ruby in the fire-truck were canceling each other out. I could remember everything very clearly, but I couldn't feel it.

Ruby had not worn her bike helmet. She had taken it off when they left the park, because Adam was pushing her bike. If she had been wearing her helmet, would it really have protected her? Adam had taken time over buying the best type of helmet for Ruby, and making sure that it fitted. But it had been fastened around the handles of her bike.

Ruby was wearing a child-sized fireman's helmet, as the fire-truck raced alongside our plane. Where had that come from? My brain was still flying. I wasn't even tired. Maybe sleep had been a con all these years. You only needed it if you thought you needed it. I would not let myself go there. Today, I'd seen Ruby. It was still today. I wasn't going to let myself sleep, and turn it into yesterday. I wasn't going to let sleep separate me from Ruby's presence.

Mr. Damiano drank his glass rapidly, in silence, and then he poured another.

"Bella stopped crying," he went on. "My mother smoothed Bella's hair and wiped her face. She said she was going to finish the chicken stew, and she left us to practice again. Bella was still angry. She was burning with fury because I'd come up behind her and lifted her down just when she was near her goal. I could feel the stiffness of anger in her.

"I was almost fourteen and I had learned how to work safely when I was angry or tired or upset. I had learned how to get tension out of my body before I performed. But Bella was too young for that. She felt something and it was there in her body, instantly. I had plucked her off the ladder like a doll. I had humiliated her, and made her feel as if she and her plans were nothing. And maybe I had meant to do it. I have often asked myself if that is what I meant to do. I told myself I was trying to save her, but was that the truth of what happened? You know, Rebecca, you can ask yourself these questions many times, and you don't find answers. 'I wouldn't have fallen! I never fall!' Bella said. Yes, she was stiff with anger. I can see it now. But did I see it then?

"I should have told her to go and play. She spent too much time practicing anyway. She didn't need to practice. I had a little square of *turrón* in my pocket. I had been thinking of it all the morning, with part of my mind. Thinking of when I would give myself the pleasure of it. The taste of the *turrón* in my mouth.

"I could have given that *turrón* to Bella. She would have curled up on my lap to suck the sweetness out of it. She would have known that I was sorry. She'd have been ready to begin again.

"But I did not. Instead I said to Bella, 'If you want to work so much, then we'll work.'

"I squatted down. She stood facing me, between my legs. I took hold of her waist and as she sprang I lifted her so she rose up onto my shoulders in a handstand. We had done it many times before. I must have felt the stiffness in her body but I don't remember it. I'll tell you what I was thinking of. I was thinking: *How can I find out when I must say horse, and when I must say mount?*

"Slowly, I stood up, still supporting her by the waist. I walked to where the chalk mark was that my father made for us. I thought she was in position. I took my hands from her waist.

"'Point your feet, Bella,' I said. Maybe I said it too quickly. She needed more time to feel her balance, to get herself perfectly into position. Then she could make a line of her body, her feet together and pointing upwards so my father could catch her by the ankles as he swung forward.

"Her feet tipped and her balance changed. She was going over. I felt it and my hands flew up to grab her. But she came right over my head, backwards, and I couldn't catch her.

"She fell on her back in the ring.

"It wasn't far. She didn't cry. But I froze all over at once because she didn't cry. I was down by her side and her eyes were open, looking at me. Begging me to help her. She was trying to breathe but the fall had knocked the breath out of her.

"She was winded. That's all it was. I raised her in my arms to help her. I moved her and she made a noise I shall always remember. The noise of a child trying to scream who has no breath to scream.

"My mother came running. I must have called out for her without knowing it. She took Bella from me and laid her flat on the ground. She knelt beside Bella.

" 'Move your feet, Bella. Show me how you move your feet.'

"But Bella didn't move anything. She just stared at us, pleading for us to help her as she struggled for breath.

"She had fractured the top of her thigh bone, near the hip socket. There was a doctor in the town but he was attending a difficult labor at a farm in the hills. It was evening before he came back. My mother and father put a board under Bella and carried her into the house of the apothecary.

"My parents had no money to send her to the city hospital. There was a little charitable hospital run by the Sisters of Mercy, in a convent ten miles away. They cared for Bella there. She lay in a high, narrow, white bed with a crucifix over it, in a row of beds with crucifixes over them. There were twenty tortured Christs in that room.

"The sisters were good women but they knew little about Bella's injuries. They did what the doctor told them to do. She lay perfectly still, with a board under the mattress, with her leg in a heavy cast. They fed her from a cup with a spout. They knew nothing of what we know now. Now Bella would have had an operation. The bone should have been pinned, but even so it would have been difficult. It was a bad break, too close to the hip joint. Nowadays they would be able to do a hip-joint replacement if the pinning didn't work.

"Bella lay still. Her muscles wasted. She had sores on her elbows, her heels, her buttocks. She developed a chest infection. If she had not been Bella she would have given up.

"She recovered from her chest infection. My mother treated the sores with marigold cream, which she brought in each day and rubbed into Bella's skin secretly. The sisters didn't approve, because the doctor hadn't prescribed it. If my mother had left the cream by the bedside, they would have thrown it away.

"When the cast came off, Bella taught herself to walk again. She limped badly. No, it was more than a limp. She lurched as she transferred her weight. Already we could see that her injured leg was shorter than her healthy leg. My mother rubbed oil into Bella's muscles and massaged them to try to build them up again. Day by day, Bella was in pain. Her hair was matted from lying so long, and the sisters had cut it short. Her face was yellow with pain and lack of sun. She looked terrible.

" 'I'll carry you, Bella,' I said when I saw her struggling across the stone floor.

" 'No,' she said. 'I can walk.'

"For my father, life was over. That sounds like an exaggeration, but it was the truth. Bella came back from the convent and he had to watch her limping, lurching across the rough ground. My mother tried to go back into the ring, but it was no good. She was too old. What remained of our act was me and my father, a flyer and a catcher. But we never got the applause Bella had got, and nobody threw coins into the ring.

"We were touring new towns where no one had seen Bella waving and blowing kisses. She was just a crippled child, and Spain was not a good country for crippled children. So you see, Rebecca, my mother really did have second sight. She saw Bella in the convent and we all laughed. She saw the pictures but she couldn't interpret them. Maybe she was lucky.

"This is how my mother's vision of Bella in the convent came true."

"And then what?" I asked.

Living Statues and the Dwarf Shakespeare Act

"It was because of Bella that Damiano's Dreamworld came to be," said Mr. Damiano. "My future would not lie in libraries. I wasn't going to be a student. I had to earn money for Bella. I had to create a place in the world for Bella. I was never going to be a great flyer, but the circus had taught me the most important trick it possesses: to discover what people want, before they know it themselves, and before anyone else knows it. To discover it first, and act on it. It sounds very simple, doesn't it? You wonder why everyone doesn't find it out.

"I discovered it through our failures. By the time I was sixteen my father was finished in the air. He had rheumatism in both knees and it was affecting his spine. My parents knew they couldn't stay in the circus. When my father warmed up I could almost hear the grind of pain in his joints. He never complained, but as he swung his arms and flexed his knees he would make a strange sound, deep in his chest, like a steam engine. *Heu, heu, heu.* He made that sound to deal with the pain.

"I told you that my mother had foresight. She'd become skilled in mending costumes, and making new ones. She reckoned that she could set up as a dressmaker, with the bit of money they had saved. But for that, they needed to be in a city where there would be plenty of clients. Every small town already had its own dressmaker and the clients were taken.

"They rented a room in Valencia. It was cheap, as it deserved to be. It was small and dark and my mother had to go down three flights of stairs to the cold tap. But it would do for the time being. *Until I make money, and then I'll send you some every week.* I kept telling them that and I think they believed me. They wanted to believe me. My father was heavy and weary. It was as much as he could do to get himself through the days. Now I know that he was depressed, clinically depressed, but this wasn't how things were thought about then. He would go to the same café every afternoon and sit over his wine. My mother encouraged him. It was good for him to be out, she thought, in a man's world.

"He sat in the café and drank his wine. You won't know those leather bottles they used in Valencia then, to serve wine in the ordinary cafés. He would order a bottle, or half a bottle, never more. He would read the newspaper headlines, because he couldn't get through close print. I think he liked to sit there. He was not part of the circus anymore, not forcing himself out night after night with his joints burning, not needing to please anyone. He was away from the ring and from memories of Bella as she had been. He would go to the café about four o'clock, after his siesta, and settle there with his paper and his wine, and watch the people passing in the streets.

" 'He deserves his retirement,' my mother said. She was happy to work. She soon got clients, just as she believed she would. The hours were long but she had company. Clients were always coming in and out for fittings, or to talk over a new dress for a christening. They were ordinary people, small shopkeepers, the wives of policemen and minor officials. Nobody grand, nobody my mother wasn't easy with. They were quite happy to climb the three flights of stairs. Her prices were good and everything was finished as it should be.

"She never talked about the past. People assumed that she'd always been a dressmaker, but in another town.

" 'Your father doesn't need to worry anymore,' said my mother.

"I had changed a great deal. No more English language books, no dreaming, no imagining myself elsewhere. Even my body had changed. I was becoming solid, as I am now.

"Bella would come with me. That was agreed without question. There was no life for her in that room.

"We went north, to Madrid. The war in Europe was over. Everyone was moving, the whole of Europe washing from one side to the other. Like a stream after a flash flood, when the water runs thick and dangerous and you can't see the bottom of it. But in the middle of it all, people still wanted what they'd always wanted.

"We started with a street-corner act. Tumbling, juggling, a low wire lashed between street lamps. We had to watch out for the police all the time. Bella juggled with eggs, with oranges, with knives. She told fortunes. She was eight years old and when you looked into her eyes you believed that she had the right to tell fortunes. She knew more than some of the grown women who laid their hand in hers.

"We lived on bread and olive oil and oranges. Sometimes, when we were in the money, we bought rabbit stew from a street vendor. At first we slept in church doorways and then we rented a room half the size of my parents' room in Valencia. I buried a coin for every coin we spent, under the tiled floor of our room. We worked like demons, every day and twice as much on Sundays, when Bella would sit outside the richest churches with her crutches at her side and her beautiful eyes fixed on the fine ladies and she'd call out, 'For the love of God, for the sake of holy charity, bless me with bread.'

"Not that she wanted bread. She wanted money, and she certainly got it. Little girls in stiff dresses would mince across in their tight

Sunday shoes to drop coins into Bella's lap. Each time, Bella would make the sign of the cross.

"I watched from a distance in case anyone hurt her or stole her money. When they had all gone, Bella would signal to me and I'd come over. She would show me the money, and she would spit on the ground. Each Sunday I bought her two soft white rolls from the baker, and the rest of the money went under the tile.

"We saw through the people on the street as if they were glass. We knew who would give, who would linger to watch and who would rush onwards with barely a glance. We knew who would try to thieve our coins, and who would call the police. We knew from their eyes what they wanted. Late at night I would set two torches in the ground and the light would catch the passersby and draw them into our show. Sometimes we would buy a box of oranges and cut them into quarters.

" 'Refresh yourselves, ladies and gentlemen! With our compliments!'

"They would suck and spit out the peel and they would give more generously when the time came.

"They did not simply want pleasure. They wanted *to be given pleasure*. Once we had learned that, we used the knowledge in everything.

"The first Dreamworld was very small. My mother made the tent for us by hand. It took her weeks, working when she had finished her work for the day. It was striped in blue and gold. My mother made it in stripes so that she could use odd pieces of material, which were cheaper to buy. You could barely see the seams.

"Only a dozen people could be admitted at a time. We hired a boy called Jaime to keep the doorway while the show was on. He had to be fierce. The more they waited, the more they heard the pleasure inside the tent, the bigger the crowd grew.

"Inside there were cushions which my mother had also made. As well as juggling and fortune-telling, there was a Moroccan storyteller, a Fado singer, a snake charmer. There were sweet pastries, and wine. The light shone through the tent walls, blue and gold. We had spent all the money we had saved under the tile.

"Every day, what happened inside the tent changed, sometimes a little, sometimes a lot. One day there would be fruit, the next honeyed nuts. We hired a man who could do portraits in ten minutes. There was a gypsy girl who could make a fountain of silver coins spring from her ears.

"What happened inside our tent was a dream, a story. You entered and while you were there, your pleasure was everything. And then you had to leave, while your pleasure was still rising toward its peak. We worked until late, late at night. One in the morning, or two in the morning. The hours we worked, you would scarcely believe. I didn't think of Bella as a child anymore, and nor did she. We were partners. We shared the same dream. It was those who came to us who became like children. Not childish, but like children."

"What happened to Bella?" I asked.

"She died in Vienna, when she was thirty," said Mr. Damiano. "We were famous by then. The Viennese love shows, but they are very sophisticated. Not at all credulous. We had restored an exquisite merry-go-round. We had a medium who could speak to whole regiments of the dead. That was very popular. You would think you saw the rows of the dead standing there. We had a living statue team from Prague.

"Bella had flu. She didn't stop work. She wouldn't stop. She was booking a dwarf Shakespeare act from England and they were appearing at a fair in Innsbruck. Bella had to see them. She took the train west, saw the act, negotiated, stood on the platform for a long time waiting for the train back. I was away in Graz, visiting a scrap merchant who had a horse which he said came from the Imperial Fair at Kreuzburg. It was cold.

"Bella was half-poisoned with flu. When she got back, she found there was a quarrel between the living statues and the fire-eaters. Both acts were troublesome. I had already changed their accommodation, made sure their rehearsal times did not overlap and negotiated new performance times. They should never have troubled Bella. Instead of going to bed she stood in the evening cold while one side argued at her and then the other. If she had been well she would not have let them behave like that. But she was too tired, for once, to assert her authority.

"She developed pneumonia, she developed pleurisy, her lungs filled with fluid. Antibiotics didn't touch it. Her chest was weak, we knew that. The only part of her that was."

Our Business Is Pleasure

I thought of Bella, flat on her back, fighting for breath as she had fought all those years before, after her fall from Mr. Damiano's shoulders.

"We hoisted her up on pillows," said Mr. Damiano. "She was given oxygen. But we could see the darkness creeping up her face, from the lips. She died in the late evening. They all came to pay their respects, the fire-eaters and the living statues, all of them. When Sasha—our clairvoyant—came in, she covered her face with a white handkerchief and wept, so that she would not have to meet my eyes. Her professional status was compromised, she thought, because she hadn't predicted Bella's death. It's strange, what people consider important at such times."

"Yes."

"So you're going away, Rebecca. You're leaving us."

"Yes."

"Where are you going?"

"I don't know."

"You don't know." Mr. Damiano was silent for a while and then he said, "Not back to your husband."

"No."

"It's not yet time?"

"No, I mean never, it will never be time. We've separated. It's permanent."

"I doubt that," said Mr. Damiano, "unless he's found another woman."

"Of course he hasn't," I rapped out without thinking.

"Of course he hasn't . . ." Mr. Damiano repeated. "Why not?"

"Because he's—"

"Because he's a man in the prime of life? Because he's easy to love? Because he has an excellent profession? All those reasons?"

Mr. Damiano had turned to face me. His creased dark eyes were trying to make me laugh.

"He hasn't stayed in a box since you left him."

He has, I wanted to say. He's in our house now, fast asleep. The bedroom door's open. Down in the hall there's his case with his work for tomorrow in it. He works all the time. Sometimes he has colleagues round, sometimes he goes to see a film. He hasn't abandoned the life we had together. He's just . . .

Waiting.

Waiting. The word shocked me. I put it away in my mind to think of later.

"But you don't write to him? You don't telephone him?"

"No."

"Then I think the chances are high that he's found another woman," observed Mr. Damiano. He spoke so surely that for a second I could see this woman, too, as if Mr. Damiano had conjured her up. "If you went back to your house, Rebecca, I think the front door would be a different color. Yes. The first thing she will want to do is to change the appearance of the house. She won't want it to resemble the home where you and Adam lived together."

Our front door was blue. A beautiful duck-egg blue. It had taken me weeks to find the exact shade. Of course no one would want to alter its color. Adam wouldn't want it changed.

"She will tell Adam that it's time for something new. She will repaint your daughter's bedroom and take the furniture out of it, because it's not needed anymore. She will want to free him from the past."

"You can't do that. The past is what you are. Anyway, Adam doesn't want to be free of us."

"You think so ... Did you have a carpet in Ruby's room?"

"Yes."

"She will have removed the carpet and stripped the floor, you can be sure of that. She will have hired the stripper and done the work herself, wearing a mask so that the wood dust wouldn't choke her. I know what these women do."

"Why are you saying these things?"

His face seemed to glint and glitter. "Because they are true. And your husband's clothes will have changed, too."

"You seem to know a lot about it."

"I do."

"You've been there."

"No. How would I know where your house was, or where you lived when you were married? You never told me."

"Things like that are easy to find out, if you want to."

"Believe me, Rebecca, I haven't visited your house. But do as I say. Go there. See if the front door is still the same color. Then come back and tell me if I'm right or wrong."

⁘

It was more than three years and a hundred and thirty miles that separated me from Adam. Mr. Damiano did not see the film in my head that started each time I thought of Adam. Although it was my own film, I couldn't edit it. It started to roll and I was helpless to do anything but watch. The empty, sunlit house, the minute I spent by the mirror doing my hair, the open front door, the steps going down. The blue car driving innocently four streets away. It would happen and there was nothing to stop it.

I was afraid of what Adam saw. We couldn't comfort each other. He was locked into it, as I was.

People had rushed to tell us that we weren't guilty of anything. There was a bereavement counselor at the hospital, with the blondest hair I've ever seen. I couldn't listen to a word she said.

We couldn't have done anything. It was an accident.

But if it was an accident then everything is an accident. Ruby was born to us by accident. The joy of her was an accident. No matter how solid and safe it looked, all the time our household had been an accident, a frenzy of atoms butting against each other. And now it had all flown apart.

"You mustn't blame yourselves. It was an accident."

We couldn't have another child together. I knew it as soon as Ruby was buried. I could not keep a child safe. One stupid second, one mouthful of food going the wrong way, one reaction to a vaccine, one phone call from the teacher in charge of the school trip. I understood what it meant now. *All the ills that flesh is heir to.* Those ills were real, they were here and now. They were what we got, for being human. We inherited our lives by accident and we were haunted by what could happen at any minute.

The day I knew I had to leave home, I'd passed the primary school two streets away. Ruby had been in the reception class there.

A car was parked on the yellow zigzag lines outside, beside the notice in red lettering stuck to the iron gates, which read: *Stopping or parking here will endanger your child's life.*

Leisurely, the woman who'd parked her car there undid the seat belts that protected her two children and helped them out on the pavement side. They were only a step from the entrance gate. She wouldn't have to take them in. She could watch them safely into school from her car, which blocked the sight line of every other child cross-ing the road.

"Don't forget, VIOLINS," she hooted after her children.

I took hold of her open car door. I shook as if an electric current had got hold of me.

"Children could be killed, trying to cross the road here with your car in the way," I said.

She looked at me, her face blank and smooth and unsurprised. This wasn't the first time. Other parents must have got hold of her car door and shouted. She was bland, and smooth and sure of herself. Shut off from me and I couldn't reach her.

"They could be killed," I repeated. I thought I would kill her. I would drag her out of the car by the roots of her hair. But she didn't see it. Her right hand tapped the steering wheel.

"I'm just dropping them off. It only takes a minute."

"It only takes a minute to die," I said. She heard me then. Her eyes stretched, but she tightened her lips self-righteously.

"Please take your hands off my car."

"If I ever see you parked here again, I'll slash your fucking tires."

"Don't you dare threaten me."

"It's not a threat," I said. "It's a promise." I tightened my grip on her car door. I was pumping full of murder and she knew it. She rammed the car into gear and its acceleration shook me off and left me stand-ing in the road.

I would have hurt her. She'd known it and I knew it. I was going crazy with Ruby. This was what Adam would be left with, if I stayed. A crazy woman keeping guard outside the school our daughter no longer attended, until the school secretary had to call the police.

❧

"I'm tired, Rebecca," said Mr. Damiano. "I must sleep."

I saw that it was true. The fire and glitter had gone out of him. I was used to his gift for being any age when he wanted, but he was old now.

He sagged forward, then he clambered to his feet. He smiled at me, as he always did, with his formidable courtesy. With the warmth that made you feel he had a world to offer each time.

"I'm too tired to go home tonight," he said. His voice was thick and blurred. "I'll sleep on the sofa upstairs."

He planted the palms of his hands on the iron table, bracing himself for the walk across the courtyard. He'd told the truth when he said that he was older than I thought. He was old. It was easy to believe that he was seventy-one, or even older.

"Turn the lights off," he said. His head was bowed and I couldn't see his face. "Make sure the tent is cleared."

"What?"

He gestured impatiently. "You know. And we must watch Gottfried. He's been drinking. They all drink, if you give them a chance."

"Who do you mean, Mr. Damiano?"

"All of them, Bella, all of them. They drink too much and then they no longer give pleasure. But our business is pleasure."

"I'm not Bella, Mr. Damiano."

He was silent, supporting himself.

"I know that," he said after a while, very quietly. "You're Rebecca. I know you." But he stared up at me as if he was finding the lineaments of another face in mine. "Yes, I know you. How did you come to find me?" He stared at me and his face was tired and naked.

"Shall I take your arm?" I asked. "You don't look well."

He shook his head, ridding it of something.

"You've never been inside one of our Dreamworlds, have you, Rebecca? You're too young. It was all over before I knew you. But I'll make one for you. The last of Damiano's Dreamworlds, it'll be for you, Rebecca. I'll send an aeroplane overhead when it's ready."

"But I'm leaving—"

"I know. You told me. I heard."

Adam

If ever I forget your name, let me forget home and Heaven!

Six-thirty on an August morning. There is the promise of heat in the sky already, but for now everything is cool and still. In the distance the city is beginning to grumble.

Adam opens the back door and sits to lace his gardening boots. A blackbird stops tugging at its worm and looks at him, then seizes its prey again before the worm has time to slide back into the earth. Adam stands, walks to the garden shed, pokes about in the dusty dark for his garden fork and his spade.

The end of the garden, where Ruby's swing and climbing frame were planted, is overgrown with weeds and rough grass. This is where Adam is digging his vegetable beds. He's planning to make four beds, with grass paths between them, and their edges shored with wood. He has never done this before, and he eats few vegetables, but it's a project. The scuff marks where Ruby's feet used to strike the earth under the swing have gone. The careful holes where the climbing frame was securely fastened have been filled in.

Adam has staked out four oblongs where his vegetable beds will be. He sets in his spade, drives it deep at the side of the bed and lifts his first spadeful of earth and matted grass.

In an hour he has double-dug the first bed. He has worked methodically, shaking loose soil off the roots of the grass and laying the tough yellowish clods in a pile. The soil is clay. Adam has bought bags of rotted horse manure and they lean against one another, sagging. He's digging in the manure and a little sharp sand to improve the drainage of the soil. This, he's been told, is the right thing to do.

At the house-backs the curtains are still drawn. It is Saturday morning. Adam always wakes early, and never lies in bed after waking. It's the best way. He comes out of the silent house as fast as he can. He works in the garden, or runs circuits through the quiet streets. More often than either of these, he drives up to the hospital, whether he's on duty or not. These babies are not like other patients. They can ask for nothing and tell nothing. They need a minute, almost infatuated watchfulness that the NHS doesn't pay for. And because they can't vote or write letters or frighten politicians by speaking eloquently of their plight on television, they need to be spoken for, too, in the grim, sweaty tug-of-war that is hospital funding.

There are footprints in the dew, and a stink of fox. The spiderwebs are unbroken. Under the black, pointed leaves of the pear tree there are dozens of immature fruit. Adam lifts the leaves to check the size of the pears. This year he has encased several pears inside glass bottles. They grow inside the glass until they are much too big to slide back through the neck of the bottle. When they are ripe, he'll cut the stem, clean the outside of the bottle, rinse the inside, let it drain until fruit and bottle are completely dry and fill the bottle with Calvados. Adam will give the bottles to friends. His own drinking is strict. He checks himself, drinks beer and red wine but never spirits. He's seen too many doctors on the bottle, washing away the crowds of patients who clamor in their heads.

Adam settles the leaves over the fruit. A slug has got inside one bottle and eaten at the pear. But the slug has gone, and the hole in the flesh is small. As the pear grows, the damage may heal.

Carefully, Adam cleans his spade and fork with an oily rag, and places them back in the shed. But then he stands still, as if he has forgotten what comes next. He's seen something no one else would notice, under the shed. A small, dirty piece of Lego. He's certain it wasn't there yesterday. Maybe a cat has slunk under the shed, and pushed the piece of Lego out. Adam bends down, puts the Lego brick on his palm and turns it over with his finger. It is packed solid with dirt. He catches himself thinking that he could clean the dirt out with the point of a knife. He bends down again and scoots the Lego piece back under the shed.

Adam looks at his watch. Seven forty-five. Pascal will be here in fifteen minutes. And he's sweating. He'll get his gardening clothes off, have a shower, put on his running stuff before Pascal gets here. Crazy to have a shower before running, but that's what he feels like doing. There's time to make coffee and take it up to the bathroom. But he'll have to hurry.

The hot, fine prickling of the shower is good. He turns the water up until it's so hot it's only just bearable. Steam oozes around the shower cubicle. He lathers his body in a businesslike way, not really looking at it, not really feeling it. The touch of water is good. The touch of his own hands is disturbing.

A clean, worn towel, his running stuff clean on the bottom shelf of the airing cupboard. He rubs his hair dry. It's gray now, but it has stayed on his head, for which he's grateful. His body is much as it always was. He looks after it, without letting himself get too close to it.

He slaps the towel against his thighs, then tosses it into a corner of the bathroom. There, Pascal will be here in a moment.

The bell sounds one sharp but short ring. Pascal knows the neighbors are in bed and that these skinny terraced houses have thin walls. Adam runs downstairs. His keys, his water, that's everything.

Pascal, stronger and shorter than Adam, seems to bounce lightly on the balls of his feet even as he stands still on the doorstep. He's wearing a tracksuit. He dumps his sports bag inside the front door.

They jog away slowly down the street. The postman glances then rests his eyes on the intense blackness of Pascal's skin, the whiteness of Adam's.

"Morning," they call.

"Beautiful morning," he replies.

They are going to run along the river, loop through the playing fields, across the park and back through the allotments. This is their regular Saturday run.

Afterward they'll shower at Adam's, change and go out for breakfast.

Adam had never thought of running, before Pascal. It was Pascal who came with him to buy his first pair of running shoes.

"You will take the first pair they try to sell to you."

He showed Adam how to run his finger inside the shoe to check the fit at his ankles. He debated fiercely over grip and cushioning. He took hold of Adam's foot and squeezed it here and there and Adam was thrown back to childhood and the assistant pressing hard on the toes of his new shoes to judge where his flesh-and-blood toes fitted. The loose-limbed teenager who served them dropped his cool and wanted to please Pascal, find what he wanted, make the day good for him. That was the way Pascal worked on people. His serious, carved, intellectual face that you strove to please, his sudden smile that licked you like a flame and caught you alight.

They emerged with the running shoes pristine in their big square box and Pascal said, "Tell me the truth. You would have taken the first pair he offered you."

"Yes."

"Your heels would have been bruised in a week. You would have given up running because your back ached, Adam, and you would have thought it was because you were too old."

"You're right. You're completely right about that."

"But you are young."

"I am forty-eight, Pascal. I'm not immortal."

"Forty-eight is nothing for a man who keeps himself in shape."

⁓

Pascal was right. Adam was not too old. Adam runs. Sweat breaks over his skin, the firm, cushiony cuffs of the trainers grip his ankles and his feet thud on the grass. He accelerates, and for a moment believes he could accelerate forever.

They slow. They fall back from their rush of speed and hit the rhythm they'll keep to the end of the run. They're side by side and Pascal glances across and grins to acknowledge that this is it, now they've hit their pace, now all they've got to do is keep on. Even the brown, suspicious river is bright as they run alongside it.

The noise of breathing is what Adam notices since he began running. The snort and rush of it, like horses in a field, startled. How much effort breath takes. Not the slipshod breathing of city life as you ease from car to home. Real breathing.

He knows about breathing. All its mechanics and how it fails. The crushed butterfly lungs of newborns whose wings for breathing won't open. Collapse and scarring. Everything hard air does to soft stuff that isn't ready for it. The anguish of parents watching the monitors that they don't understand.

But he and Pascal run on. That boy there, fishing with his father. Adam wishes they would catch a fish now, before he's passed them. That it would be on the boy's line, the tug and thrum of it. That the boy would haul it into the air and go home proud.

⁓

After their shower, Adam and Pascal amble down the road to the café that for some reason has become their regular. It's not the best café around, but they like it. A thin little dark-haired girl is inside, cleaning the window, rubbing hard. She's new. In a few weeks' time she won't rub so vigorously and willingly.

After their run they deserve the fug of inside and sausages, bacon, eggs for Pascal, mushrooms for Adam. They drink tea. Pascal will not touch the coffee here, and he eats his full English breakfast with a mixture of relish and suspicion which is the same each week and has once or twice led Adam to suggest a different café, a more expensive one where they sell bagels and proper coffee. But Pascal refuses to change.

Pascal wipes egg yolk from his plate with the soft white bread. He looks up.

"Marie-Louise is pregnant," he says abruptly.

Adam feels his face spring into a shield of pleasure. "That's fantastic," he says. "Congratulations. I didn't know—"

"That we were trying? No. But it's taken us a long time. My sperm were not so active," says Pascal, astonishingly. Adam stares at him, unable to picture any other man of his acquaintance saying that with the satisfied candor of Pascal.

"But they got there in the end," says Pascal. He grins and lifts his mug as if to toast the success of his sperm. "Fourteen weeks."

"That's great," says Adam. He lifts his own mug of tea, to hide his mouth. His lips are not doing the right smiling thing. But his hand shakes and quickly he puts down the mug. "That's great, Pascal," he says again, baring his teeth.

But Pascal is watching him with narrow attention, the way he watches patients on the operating table. All the details of them, color and pulse and pressure. Pascal is a consultant anesthetist, and his reactions are knife sharp.

"Adam—"

"It's OK," says Adam. Then he does something he has never done before, because he can't bear the sensation of his own face, naked in the café. He bows his head, lifts his hands, covers his face with them.

"Adam, do you want to leave?"

Adam shakes his head. He can't leave. He can't stand up or walk through the café or go out into the bright street. It's coming over him, a rush, an acceleration he can't stop.

Pascal rises from his chair and comes round to stand behind Adam, his hands on Adam's shoulders, pressing, holding him down safe. Adam's breath tears in his chest as if they're still running, at another pace that no one can stand for long. His breath forces its way out of him and the noise of it is loud in his head.

It's early. There are not many customers in the café. An old woman in a woolly hat who notices nothing, a pair of working men who glance at Adam and Pascal and then down at their newspapers again. The dark-haired thin little girl stops rubbing her windows. She stands there, not sure what to do, with her cloth in her hand. She comes over to Adam and Pascal.

"Is he all right?" she asks timidly. Pascal shakes his head.

"His little girl has died," says Pascal.

Adam hears those words. *His little girl has died.* That's what Pascal said. Pascal didn't say when Ruby died, or that it was three years ago now and Adam's getting over it although, of course, a thing like that, you never really—*His little girl has died.*

Always, over and over, in her everlasting present, Ruby dies. She curls her hand into his, she tucks her thumb into her palm and her skin is sweaty but she's not embarrassed at all because she's only five and what she wants is to hold her father's hand. Her hand melts into him, her sweat is like balm.

"My hands are sweaty, aren't they, Dad?" she says, looking up at him.

The mug shakes on the tabletop and the tea spills because Adam's body is shaking the chair and the chair is touching the table. Pascal lifts the mug and gives it to the girl, who is still standing there, cloth in one hand. She dabs at the table with her cloth.

"I'll get you some more tea," she says.

"I'm sorry," says Adam. "I'm sorry, Pascal, I'm so sorry, I'm so sorry—"

He hears the echo in his head. Rebecca said that. She wept and he listened but he couldn't weep. She sat in Ruby's bedroom and he told her she must stop sitting there. In the dark and smell of Ruby she was happy, she said. He was afraid it was becoming an obsession. He asked her if she would see the counselor who worked with parents after a baby in the unit died. Not the blond counselor, a different one. This one was good, he said, but Rebecca stared at him as if he was trying to steal something from her. As if Ruby was still in her arms and he was trying to take her. But it hadn't been like that. They buried Ruby together. He carried her in the light woodland box made of compressed cardboard and she weighed enough to bow his back.

He can feel her weight. His shoulders hurt. It's not finished, he's not at the end of something or even beginning to get there. It is all still to come, only now beginning and he hasn't felt it yet. He's like a man who has put his hand into a fire and stares at it for the first second and feels nothing.

"We'll go home now," says Pascal.

Adam walks around his house. It's full of soft afternoon light now. He's far away from himself after so many hours of grief. Grunts and salt and mucus and tearing sounds he would never have believed would come from his throat. His pillow is wet. He pulls off the pillowcase and the pillow itself is wet with mucus and tears. He wonders if it can be washed, or only the pillowcase. Rebecca would know.

Pascal brought him to the house and then went away, back to Marie-Louise, as Adam wanted. He would have stayed, but Adam didn't want him to do that. Pascal's life was separate. He had his own things to deal with. And besides, Marie-Louise was pregnant.

Rebecca never saw him cry. He touches the head of the bed that he and Rebecca shared. Rebecca chose it. She polished the wood with beeswax and it still has that deep, complicated shine. There is a pattern of fig leaves cut into the wood. Adam traces the pattern with his finger and it seems to burn, so clear it is, so intentional in its design.

Adam walks into Ruby's bedroom. There are no curtains at the window now, so the room is full of sun. The curtains with the dolphins on them have gone to the charity shop in a black binbag. There's a white, quilted mattress protector on her narrow bed. He sits in the shabby little blue armchair where Rebecca used to sit when Ruby was a baby, feeding her. He can't picture them anymore but he can remember the smell of the baby's room at night. Rebecca's milk had a sweet, thick taste. He tasted it, too. They'd intended to re-cover that little chair for Ruby, but they never got round to it.

The room is quite empty. He walks around it and because there is so little furniture and the boards are bare, it makes the echoing sound of a room in a house for sale. An expectant sound. Rebecca sat here in the dark waiting for Ruby and he told her she must stop. She must give up her obsession. She was damaging herself. But here he is himself, far behind her, only now beginning to mourn.

His little girl has died.

Not a year before or three years before. Not a second ago. But now. Now. He goes to the window. There is the pear tree. There at the top of the garden are his earnest, laughable vegetable plots. There's the shed with Ruby's Lego hidden beneath it.

"Wait for me, Rebecca," he says, without realizing he was going to say it. "I won't be long."

He throws up the sash window so that the air can flood in and at that moment the doorbell rings. His heart leaps in his throat, with terror, or with hope maybe, that it's her, she's heard him and already she's here as if there's no distance or time between them. The bell rings again.

Down the stairs, and then he steps lightly across the hall floor, as if what might be there might also be scared. As if it might run at the sound of his footsteps.

But there they are. Pascal and Marie-Louise, side by side, their faces breaking into relief as he opens the door. And he sees at once that of course Marie-Louise is pregnant. How could he have missed it?

"We've come to fetch you," says Pascal.

"You are having dinner with us," says Marie-Louise, "and after that we're all going to the cinema. And then you are sleeping at our house." She waits for a beat, smiling at him, and then says, "Please," and takes his hand in her own dry, warm hand, and continues to hold it.

The Moscow Veteran

And to get to him—to his very heart without
papers I entered the Kremlin...

The man sat or perhaps was propped—he had no legs—on a flat
wooden trolley. One arm was whole and perfect, the other ended below
the elbow. He wore a military uniform and his eyes were a startling
pale blue. Linen blue. In his good hand he held a cup for money.

Automatically, Joe shelled a few coins into the cup. The man's eyes
caught him and he stopped. Suddenly it seemed wrong, brutal almost,
to drop the coins in the cup and walk on as he had done dozens and
dozens of times before. He knew what the man's story would be. There
was nothing to say, no advice to offer. He would be a veteran of the war
in Afghanistan with a veteran's pension which was now worth close to
nothing. There was no money for a wheelchair. He had his wooden
trolley. He had nothing to gain from talking to Joe. And yet...

An old woman hobbled past and dropped a few kopeks into the
cup. Her pension, too, would be worth almost nothing. But these old

women never passed the veterans without giving a coin. And they would always speak to them. "There you are, son, God will bless you. God will reward you."

There was no stopping these old women from talking about God now. They packed the churches, and young men and women packed them too, carefully following rituals relearned after decades of disuse. The young women covered their hair, the young men bared their heads.

The old woman made the sign of the cross and fumbled in her worn-out purse for the last coin. She had everything God needed in order to exist, Joe thought. Poverty and innocence and goodness and lack of hope for anything on earth. What she and all the other old women had always believed had turned out to be true. Earth was a vale of suffering, fitfully illuminated by acts of kindness such as a stall-holder tipping an extra chicken foot into the scale. But this almost never happened and could not be counted on. Only God, suffering, united himself with your sufferings. . . .

"Take this, son, God will reward you."

"Have a drink," said Joe, and dropped in more money, rouble notes this time, enough for a bottle of vodka. The man raised his eyes and scanned the face that Joe knew would always bear an expression that marked him as not from these parts.

"You're not from round here, are you?"

"No. English. But I live here in Moscow."

The man's blue eyes held Joe's.

"Why?"

"I'm a writer. I do my research here. I'm writing a book about Stalin."

"About Iosif Vissarionovich?"

"That's it."

"There's a real man for you. If we'd had him in charge I wouldn't be sitting here."

"No."

"We didn't lose wars in Iosif Vissarionovich's time. Plus, you never saw a soldier begging in the streets. Write that in your book."

The blue eyes went wan. He was tired, in pain.

Everything had moved on, but not him. The war he'd fought was history, a failure, not a victory. Everyone was glad to forget it, and glad too that now the West was getting a good taste of it and understanding what the war had been about and why it had had to be fought.

He was tired and maybe the phantom legs hurt, and the phantom hand. The wooden trolley looked homemade. It must be hell to sit on. How many hours would he sit here?

"You done your military service?"

"We don't have it in my country."

The man shook his head slightly, incredulously. "You were a student, right?"

"No, it wasn't because of that. No one does military service in Britain. It's been abolished."

But he could see that the veteran didn't believe him. Joe was just another example of the smart ones, the ones with money and education and pull, getting out of what poor kids got stuck with.

Joe felt the fat of his wallet knocking inside his breast pocket. The urge burned in him to give and go on giving until it was all gone. And then walk home with his head bowed, without enough money for the metro.

The notes he'd given were plenty. Any more and the man would think he was crazy. And people would notice. There were always pickpockets hanging around.

Joe felt inside his breast pocket. Without removing the wallet, he opened it. The wad of notes was between his fingers. It wasn't a fortune. Enough for a meal out with Olya at the good pasta place on the Arbat. Folding his hand over the notes he bent down.

"Here. Take this."

The man glanced at the edge of the notes as he swallowed them into his one remaining hand, and then disappeared them inside his clothes. It was so quick that for a second Joe stopped believing he'd given the money at all.

The man looked up. The pallor of his eyes. His skin. He looked terrible.

"Someone comes and takes you home?" asked Joe.

"Yeah. Someone comes. You're crazy."

"I'm sorry," said Joe. But he said it formally. *Forgive me. I have a bank account and a credit card and an apartment and a passport. If I want I can be on a plane to England tomorrow. I can slip out of everything that holds you.*

Joe walked on. That old woman scouring her purse had done more than him. The flowing crowds of passersby opened and absorbed him. Everyone in the world seemed to be walking. Joe felt flimsy and he knew it showed from the way he was jostled aside. He was in Moscow but not of Moscow, passing his life as an observer. Olya had gone to see her sister in Yaroslavl. She would be back—when? Five or six days. Olya wasn't happy. Her sister would be saying to her that she should leave Joe. That it would be a big step but that in the end Olya would be happier. Joe would never give her what she wanted. And Olya would smile at her sister with her dark, soft, unhappy eyes and say, "You don't understand our relationship." Olya would come back tender and remorseful toward Joe, as if she had somehow betrayed him by talking of him.

She should leave me, thought Joe, walking. It would be better for her. She wants—

She wants what? We call it wanting children but it's not really that at all. We could have a child but that wouldn't make things better, in fact it would make them worse. What she wants doesn't exist, at least it doesn't exist in me anymore. To tell you brutally, Olya, it's been given away already, to someone else. And I can't get it back, not because I don't want to, but because there are some things you can't do twice.

You're not from round here, are you?

No. I'm not from these parts.

He would walk on. He would get a ticket and go into the Kremlin with the holiday crowds. He'd thought he was walking aimlessly but of course he wasn't, his body knew where it was taking him.

He'd only been back to England once since Ruby's funeral. He'd seen Rebecca then. He knew where she was now, because she'd kept in touch. She always did that, he always knew where she was. Once, out of the blue, she sent a long email about the flat they'd shared and about the meals they cooked and how far away it seemed, like another world. Now she worked for a guy who owned hotels and she was traveling the world and it was good for her, the best thing for her now. Or so she wrote. But as far as Joe could see both she and Adam were still in shock, blundering about, saying things they didn't mean and doing things they didn't understand. Or they were like people who have been shot and will fall any second but don't know it yet.

It must have been a shell that blew off that blue-eyed veteran's legs. Or maybe a land mine. He wouldn't have known what was happening, at the moment of it. To see and feel your body explode—that's impossible. *I am losing my legs, my hand.* Nobody thinks that. They will say it afterward, in the past tense, but it takes a long time.

What a color his eyes were.

The things that Olya wanted from him no longer existed. He had given them to Rebecca and they were gone. This wasn't how it was supposed to be. Most of the things he read in newspapers and magazines and novels supported the idea that relationships had a life like fruit or flowers. They germinated, they bloomed and ripened, they died and left space for the next one to grow. Sometimes the process was ugly and painful but this was more or less how it worked.

But for him it hadn't been true. There wasn't anything left to grow. He had loved Rebecca with—

(He had never even slept with her. Not really. It was years since they'd dismantled the flat. Men don't behave like this, they move on.)

With his whole heart, that's what he'd loved her with. That's why Olya couldn't find it, that's why she was unhappy and had these long conversations with her sister that he wasn't supposed to know about.

"He's not cold, no, I know he's not cold but there's something I just can't get past..."

"He's English, Olyenka."

⁓

"... and to get to him—to his very heart—"

Joe repeated the lines to himself. Mandelstam wrote them in Voronezh, the city of ravens, in exile, in February 1937. He would die at the end of the following year, after his second arrest. He would be last seen picking over a rubbish heap in a transit camp at Vladivostock. He was writing in those lines about Stalin, the man who would murder him. Maybe he was trying to save his own life, maybe he was trying to understand the murder inside Stalin's heart. His heart of hearts.

Joe walked faster, head bowed, trying to imagine what it was like to be inside the writer of the poem, who tried to imagine inside Stalin's heart as Joe has tried to imagine inside Stalin's heart. But there was no comparison between Mandelstam and Joe. No contest. Mandelstam had to understand Stalin with his own life. And I get paid for my understanding, thought Joe. People buy it. His book about the death of Nadezhda Alliluyeva has sold well.

But it wasn't easy to get away from Nadya, even after the book was published. She still possessed him, even though he was supposed to have moved on from her. He was writing of Stalin at war, Stalin in fugue. He had intended to go on. He'd wanted to write of Stalin at the end of his life. Stalin, toxic with rage, suspicion and the terror of death. When he died his face bore an expression which no one who saw it was able to forget or to describe as it deserved. At last, Stalin got the face he earned, perhaps. And Stalin's arm, the arm crippled in childhood by a blow from his father, was raised to ward off death.

But in his heart Joe kept going back to the earlier days. He could not get away from the image of Nadya as a young woman in the heart of the Kremlin, mother of two children and stepmother of a son, on the night of 8 November. She and Stalin have just celebrated the fifteenth anniversary of the October Revolution. There's been a party at the apartment of their friends the Voroshilovs.

Power was all so recent for them, thought Joe. It must have seemed so fragile still. Like found money. The Revolution only fifteen years behind them. These comrades, these people who envisaged a different world, have got what they wanted. They are the masters now. Sometimes, at these parties, they must have looked at each other, incredulous. Here they were, against all the odds, in the heart of the Kremlin and with their hands on its ropes of power. What they don't yet fully realize is that those ropes will drag them, too. They will be taken to places where they don't want to go, and they'll do things of which they would never have believed themselves capable.

At the party that night, there's a row. Something between man and wife made ugly and magnified a hundred times by the fact that nothing is simply between man and wife anymore. A man shouts insults, a woman runs from the room. But the man's Stalin and the woman is Nadya, who is now thirty-one and who loved her husband so passionately at seventeen that all her family were afraid for her. They knew it wasn't healthy to love like that, crazily, with no barriers, nothing held back, nowhere to retreat to if it all went wrong. There was nowhere in Nadya's body or her heart or her mind that he hadn't penetrated and made his own. Her family knew her nature and her seriousness and idealism. The way she made him perfect in her own mind so that he was the ideal revolutionary who would lead her, along with the whole of his people.

When all that began to crumble it was ugly stuff. Terrifying. She could not get back those parts of herself he had possessed. She could not destroy Stalin-within-her, without destroying herself.

The next morning Nadya is found dead, shot through the heart with a pistol that her brother has given her. Her daughter is six, her son eleven. After her death, everything changes. Family life ends. Stalin reads the terrible letter his wife has left for him. He sees her lying in her blood. And there's something deep in him that feels more than shock and anger and grief for the end of a woman whom he has loved. There's a humiliation in the core of him. She has had the choice between life with him in the heart of the Kremlin, and death. She has chosen death. When she was a girl of seventeen she loved him with all her heart. She took on the child of his first, dead wife and she gave him two more children. But now she prefers death to him, and in her coffin she is smiling and at peace. Her face shines with unearthly radiance. She has got away, she has insulted him and then escaped. But such an insult must be avenged.

He wants revenge. When his first wife died, he thought he had lost the one person capable of melting his heart. Now he knows it wasn't true. Let them wait. They'll find out. They don't know anything yet.

Joe spent a long time looking at photographs of Nadya, searching their grains. In her open coffin, surrounded by flowers, her face is calm. Her eyelids lie peacefully over her smooth, closed eyes, her mouth is slightly parted, the pure lines of her face are clear-cut. There's no sign of a death struggle, or of the inner torment which must have thrashed through her before she wrote that final letter and picked up the pistol. She really does look like someone sleeping. She's got away, she's escaped. The story given out was that she'd died of appendicitis.

He'd showed Rebecca that photograph once. He told her the story of Nadya and Stalin. Joe's work often bored Rebecca, but that photograph didn't bore her. She stared at Nadya's dead face and then she said, "But it's all wrong, isn't it? She looks so peaceful. But she's left her children behind to suffer."

Joe thought of the children when they saw their mother lying deep in a bed of flowers and radiant with light. Somehow the children hadn't really occurred to him before.

"She couldn't help herself," he defended Nadya. "She wasn't in a normal frame of mind. She was suffering too much."

"Never," Rebecca said. "Never, never, never. Not if I had children. I would never do that to them."

"You can't be sure of that."

"Yes, I can. Some things you can be sure of, even about yourself. I would never kill myself if I had children. I would never leave them."

"She was tormented."

"Tormented! How do you think they felt for the rest of their lives? They must have hated her," said Rebecca.

"Her children?"

"Of course. She'd failed in the most important thing parents have to do."

"What's that?"

"To make their children believe that life is good. Or if they can't manage that, at least make them believe that life is bearable. That there are ways to bear it and that they will help the children to find them."

"Yes," said Joe slowly. "Probably you're right." He'd been seduced by the dead woman, and Rebecca understood it. Because Nadya was beautiful and he responded to her story and the final glamour of the flowers and shadows which surrounded her, and the drama in the men and women stepping past her coffin while Stalin watched and watched to see who came and who did not. But Rebecca had seen into the heart of it. Anger, abandonment. The hardness of Nadya's dead flesh. The sordid day-to-day of a household where there's no family love anymore. When the book was published he sent a copy to Rebecca and Adam, and they wrote back to thank him, but he is sure that Rebecca will not have read it.

After that conversation with Rebecca, Joe had wondered if her adoptive parents believed that life was good. But he hadn't asked her. Her adoptive father had died of bowel cancer, and her adoptive mother had osteoarthritis and lived in a home in Whitstable. Rebecca went to see her four or five times a year. She was particularly fond of small, ripe Caribbean bananas, and Rebecca always took a large bag of them. In the days when they shared a flat Joe had offered to go with her, but Rebecca had said no.

"She'd start thinking I was going to marry you. She's like that. She's always trying to find a purpose for me. You know, Joe, to her I am like some kitchen implement that's strange to her and she knows it must have a use but she hasn't discovered it yet."

"Probably it's essential in the cuisine of another country," Joe had answered, and they'd laughed.

"... and to get to him—to his very heart—"

By now Joe knew it wasn't possible. Years of research and writing wouldn't do it. He was not a poet. He was not going to pay for knowledge with his life.

He was in the Kremlin now, inside its brilliance of gold and white. He had no permit or papers, any more than Mandelstam had had. But things had changed and he did not need them. Only money, for the entrance ticket. Ordinary people swirled about, a bit in awe and a bit cautious, keeping close to the walls. The architecture was intended to dwarf them, and they knew it.

He was no closer to solving the mystery of Stalin. His readers believed he'd illuminated it for them. They loved the way he wrote Nadya's story. They wrote letters to say so. They said that he had made Stalin come alive for them. They were waiting eagerly for his next book.

He had made Stalin come alive for them? My God. What a monstrous thing to do, if it were possible. Joe looked around at the gold, the white domes, the dazzle of it all and the squat brutality under all that beauty. He turned slowly through 360 degrees, staring. Crowds of Russian tourists walked purposefully past him, with an air of holiday devotion. They made Joe feel like a Methodist at Lourdes.

He was in the heart of it now, all right, but the heart was empty. Or at least it was empty for him. No broad-cheeked Georgian, no Minotaur with glistening black hair and mustache and high, supple boots, waited in the inmost heart of the inmost heart, to tell Joe the truth about himself. Stalin's fingers were exceptionally sweaty. They made greasy marks on the papers he handled. He could not bear people to notice things like that about him, human things. Mandelstam made that mistake in his poems. He put what he had noticed into the poems.

There was music in the Kremlin now. A choir of priests in training sang their hearts out to raise money for restoration funds. Young, strong men who once again believed that the church was a route to stability and advancement. He thought of Stalin training for the priesthood in his youth, and believed that he could hear the wheel spinning, spinning, coming full circle.

He thought: *I can't write about these people anymore.*

He thought of Rebecca. For three years he'd left her alone, knowing that she'd left Adam. They'd written and telephoned and once he'd seen her in London, where she'd come to his hotel late and wearing an unfamiliar, sharp little black suit and a pink linen shirt. Her hair was brushed off her face. She had looked awful in some indefinable way that seemed to lodge in her eyes and mouth. She'd talked endlessly about her employer, in a flood of trivia that stopped all conversation. And he'd just let her carry on.

"Come and visit me in Moscow," he'd said, and her mouth had trembled for the first time.

"I don't think so," she'd said. "I'm afraid of aeroplanes."

"But you travel all the time for your work. You've just been telling me about it."

"That's for work. That's different. I know that I have to do it."

"Either you're afraid of flying, or you're not afraid."

And she'd looked at him as if he'd revealed such innocence that it was a gulf she couldn't even call across.

"It's to do with ways of being afraid," she'd said at last.

⁘

I'll leave, he thought, as the trainee priests raised their voices again and the sound rose in a pure jet toward the roof. For an instant the oppression of the past lifted. It wasn't possible to believe that it had never existed, but it was possible to believe that the present was equal to it, and could bear its weight without being crushed.

"Forgive us, Lord, forgive us," sang the choir over and over.

I'll leave, thought Joe. I don't have to stay here. I can go anywhere I want to go. I've been locked into this story for long enough.

He thought of the way Rebecca's mouth had trembled when she said she was afraid. He thought of how he would go to her, but not yet.

Golden Fleece

Golden fleece, where are you, golden fleece?

This is one of the poems Joe was always telling me, in the days when we'd sit after our supper and pour one glass after another down our throats. Not drunk, no. Just hazy, with the city and all its lights slung out below our windows.

"Well, where is it, then?" I asked when Joe had declaimed this poem once too often, first in English and then in Russian. I never liked the sound of that language in his mouth until I heard him use it in Russia, to speak of everyday things. "Where is this golden fleece that's so wonderful?"

"Don't you know the story?"

"Of course I do," I said a bit too quickly. If I didn't know then Joe would immediately tell me. I preferred to look it up by myself, later.

"It's a symbol. The golden fleece is a symbol."

"Of what?"

"Of happiness. No, that's not right. Of desire."

"Well, for God's sake. Why can't they just search for the thing for itself? A golden fleece is nice enough to have, without mixing it up with happiness and desire."

He didn't argue. He laughed and stretched and yawned and agreed with me. It was one of the nights I woke and had a nightmare and yelled out and he woke up straightaway in spite of the wine we'd drunk. He did what he always did. He got into my big bed beside me and wrapped his arms around me tight and lulled me with things we never said or remembered in daylight. I fell asleep easily.

Looking back, how many times did that happen? I've forgotten. So much of it went out of my head when Adam came. I've been remembering a lot of things since I've been on my own.

Can it be true that Adam's changed the color of the front door?

I left Mr. Damiano sleeping. He'd worried me, the way he looked so old all at once. I gave him a while to settle, then I went upstairs after him, to the inner office where he would sleep on his couch sometimes.

He was fast asleep. He was lying on his side and he was snoring, quite heavily. He was still wearing his suit, he hadn't even taken off his tie. I wondered if I could loosen the tie without him feeling it. I bent over him and very gently I managed to loosen the knot, just a little. I didn't like the thought of him sleeping with something tight around his throat. That would lead to bad dreams.

He lay on his side with his knees drawn up. He hadn't put anything over himself even though there were blankets in the cupboard which he kept for such occasions. Beautiful soft fleecy blankets. Everything he kept about him was good. I opened the cupboard and found a blanket and laid it over him, then I tucked it in around his feet.

He looked better so. He looked more cherished. I stood and watched over him and thought of everything he'd told me in the garden. He'd given his life to me, maybe because there was no one else to receive it. All those stories, all that history. I would never have been able to imagine such a past for him, but I believed it, every word of it. A man like him could only come out of a past no one in his present could guess at. Maybe he'd been only an average flyer but then barely anybody is a flyer at all. I could see Bella's accident just as he had made me see it.

I wished I'd known Bella. I liked the sound of her. The two of them had stuck together. They'd done well, I thought, thinking of the first Dreamworld they'd created when Bella was only a child. She'd have liked his hotels. She'd have seen the point of everything he did.

He snored, and his breath rattled in his throat. It was an old-man sound. Something troubled his dream as a fly troubles a horse and he twitched and then was still. Before tonight I would have thought he wouldn't like me watching him when he was like this. He wanted to be seen in his prime, with all his power alive in him. That was how all his employees saw him. The woman called Elena who was his personal assistant before me spent a month inducting me into his service, as if it was the performance of a mystery.

I sat down at the little desk in the inner office, took a sheet of paper and began to write.

Dear Mr. Damiano,

It is three in the morning and you are having a sleep. I wish I had not told you so suddenly that I was leaving. But I had to. Otherwise I would still be with you in twenty years' time. Maybe it wasn't Ruby on the runway. Maybe it was all my imagination. You didn't say that, although I expect you thought it. Anyone would. But I think she was there for a purpose.

I'm going to see if Adam has changed the color of his front door. I have to do some other things first. But I'll be back.

I've dealt with the outstanding emails.

With love from
Rebecca

He would know what that signified. We'd talked one day about people who cram the word "love" on the end of emails to acquaintances whom they don't love in the least. Mr. Damiano said it was just normal, acceptable hypocrisy. I said I wouldn't write it.

"So if you write love, then it always means love?"

"Always."

He smiled and raised his eyebrows.

"At the time, it means love," I corrected myself.

It wasn't true that I'd dealt with the emails, but I made it true over the next few hours, while Mr. Damiano continued to sleep. It was light by the time I left. The streets were pale and quiet and cleaners were unlocking the outer doors of offices. I went to the studio apartment I rented, not far from the office. Going there was only the first step.

I showered for a long time. I packed clothes. I thought of setting out without sleep and I was sure I could do it, but while I was waiting for the kettle to boil, the long day and the night and everything that had happened came up and hit me and I was on the bed, flat, falling, with no time to pull the covers over me or take off my shoes.

The sound of the phone pulled me out of a sweet sleep. It was Mr. Damiano. He sounded twenty years younger than he'd been the night before.

"Rebecca. I want you to come to my house. Can you come now?"

I sat up and blinked. Sun was flooding onto the bed. I hadn't closed the blinds, or undressed.

"What time is it?"

"Did I wake you?"

"Give me a minute."

"I'm sorry."

"No, it's OK. I needed to wake up. What time is it?"

"Nine-twenty."

I'd only been asleep for a couple of hours, but I felt as if I'd been deep in dreams for a hundred years.

"What day is it?" I said suddenly.

"It's Friday."

It had been Wednesday when I got back from New York, I was sure of that. Wednesday night. The time was different, but not that different.

"Mr. Damiano, last night when we were talking in the garden—"

"Not last night, Rebecca. The night before last." I heard the smile in his voice. "You're not awake yet."

"No—"

"I shouldn't have let you go like that."

"But I told you. I can't keep on working for you. I thought you understood that."

Mr. Damiano made an impatient sound, as if asking himself when I would ever get the point.

"I don't mean that. That is all under way. Elena short-listed for me yesterday, from a pool of contacts she maintains. I saw two candidates for your job yesterday evening. Marina will start work for me on Monday. I am flying to New York tomorrow morning, to the Sidney. Things are not going well there."

He had his power back. I had seen him as an old man, bowed over and heavy. I was wrong. Or maybe not wrong, but seeing only one way in which the kaleidoscope of Mr. Damiano could settle.

"Come to my house now," came his full, strong voice. "I am not happy with the way we left each other."

He gave me the address, and we said goodbye. I already knew where he lived, though I'd never been there. No one in the office had been there. There was a myth in the company that he had no home. He was later and earlier in the office than anyone, and then there were the blankets in the cupboard and the couch where he often slept.

I knew so many separate things about Mr. Damiano, but I still wasn't sure how they joined together. He loved horses, and once told me that he used to bet heavily and that he'd bought a share in a small Italian restaurant with his winnings. He still ate at that small, dull restaurant almost every day. There was no better food in London, he said.

He no longer placed bets. He liked to go over to Ireland, to the races at Leopardstown and Punchestown. He loved the business of it, the thousands of lives, human and animal, knit up on the chance of a horse's hooves beating on the turf. It was play and he loved play.

"Play is the best thing human beings do," he said to me, smiling.

⁓

I had been asleep for twenty-six hours, it seemed. How was that possible? But it felt good as I showered again and put on my jeans and a white T-shirt, to show myself and him that my job was over and the little black suits were tucked away in a cupboard. The sun fell everywhere. I'd never seen a day like it for glisten and dazzle, and this was the dirty heart of London. What would it be like elsewhere? There was dust all over the apartment. I would clean it before I left, I thought. I had enough money to keep paying the rent for a few months, so I could leave my possessions there, but there were not many of them. My working clothes already had the look of garments which could gladly go to a charity shop and be picked up more or less as a bargain by people who more or less wanted them. I would be rid of all of it. Everything I needed for now would go into one bag.

I was ready. My heart beat hard, as if something frightening or wonderful was about to happen. It was a long time since it had beat like that. I had been calm for so long now. Nothing had brought tears to my eyes since I'd sat in Ruby's bedroom and found the scent of her still there, like treasure. Nothing, until I saw her again, on the runway. My heart beat and I felt afraid. I didn't know where this would lead me. I walked to the window and the light dazzled me and prickled my eyes. There was the bright sky and the trees shaking their electric green leaves in the morning wind and the rush of London and I was not separate from it anymore. I could not hide in the stiff, chill pocket where I had hidden since I left my home.

It was a narrow, white house in a narrow, white, quiet street. It had an old iron bellpull and when I pulled it down I heard the sound in the heart of the house, and then Mr. Damiano's tread. He opened the door to me. He was dressed in one of those pale linen summer suits that English men can't wear. It looked fine on him. He was upright and smiling.

The house was everything I hadn't expected. Beautiful rugs criss-crossed each other, trees stood about in the corners of rooms, the walls were covered with fine, silky Turkish carpets, there were piles of cushions and low divans. It looked like the tent of a traveling merchant.

"Sit down. We'll have coffee."

A woman I had never seen before brought in the coffee. She was dressed in black, with a broad strong face, and she looked about fifty. It surprised me when she spoke in English.

"Angela is my housekeeper," Mr. Damiano explained.

It struck me that he had layer upon layer of lives. Maybe there were other houses, quite different, in Rome or Alicante or Berlin. More housekeepers. *More Rebeccas,* I thought. It was a thought that chilled me. But his smile was real. Even if it was only an illusion, his skill was wonderful.

Angela served the coffee and went out. All the doors of the house were left open and soon we heard her begin to sing. The volume rose and fell. She must have been moving around, working. Her voice was strong, not sweet, but true. She was singing "Blue Moon."

"She has a good voice," I said.

"We go to Covent Garden together. Angela has to explain the stories to me. They are so far-fetched that they must be true, I think."

I drank my coffee. It was very peaceful here and I noticed that my hand holding the cup was perfectly steady.

"You slept well," said Mr. Damiano.

"Yes."

"Because you had come to a decision."

"Yes."

"I haven't asked you here to make you change your mind, Rebecca. I asked you because I wasn't satisfied with the way we parted. I was too tired to think of you properly, as I should have done. You are leaving my employment, and I have been very happy with the work you've done. I intend to give you something."

"But I've left with no notice—I've made things difficult for you."

"No. You have made me see that I should go to New York. That's good. This business was not built by sitting in an office in London. I have been behaving like an old man. You're laughing at me, Rebecca. You think, 'Of course he is an old man. He should behave like one.'"

"I don't think that today. Maybe I did think it last night, just for a while—"

"You mean the night before last—"

"Yes. But you have renewed yourself."

"Aha! You found the right word, Rebecca! That's because you are a native speaker. That is the word I wanted to find for you, after what you told me about your aeroplane, and that you saw Ruby in the fire-truck. But I am not a native speaker and so I have to say it like this, with words that aren't quite right. Because I don't know when a horse should be a horse and when it is a mount. So, I will say it in my way and you will understand me.

"I look at your face, Rebecca, and I see that the worst thing that can happen to you has happened to you. It's there, look. Anyone can see it. It has made its mark on you and the mark will never come off.

"You take it with you wherever you go. But maybe you renew it.

"No, I am not explaining this right. My horse has turned into a mount. What I want to say is, you take it with you, Rebecca. What you are now is the woman that Ruby's death has made. And with that— well, that's enough."

He paused. There was a film of sweat on his forehead. For a moment he looked drained and old, as he'd done in the garden. But then he gathered himself and shook off his age.

"Eat one of Angela's almond biscuits. They are excellent. And then I'll show you what I have for you."

After we'd drunk our coffee and eaten the biscuits, he rose and went out. I heard his voice and Angela's from the kitchen. I couldn't hear the words. Suddenly her voice rose in protest but I still couldn't understand. They were not speaking English.

They sleep together, I thought. They got out of the same bed this morning. There was that feeling about them, and Angela was one of those women with a face that could lighten with her mood and a fine body under that dull dress.

Well. He was not mine after all, my Mr. Damiano. He had another name, in Angela's language.

Her voice was quieter now. They'd resolved whatever it was.

It's not possible to listen to a couple talking privately in another room without a pang of some kind. But I didn't need to say to myself what the pang was. He was coming back.

He held out a small, flat, brown-paper parcel.

"Open it, and see if you can tell me what it is."

The parcel was tied with string. It had been tied up a long time ago and the knots were difficult, but I picked them loose. The paper was old and fragile. I unwrapped it carefully and there was a folded piece of cloth.

"Take it out," said Mr. Damiano.

I unfolded the cloth. It was made of strong, silky stuff. A panel of blue and a panel of gold were stitched together. The piece of cloth was about a yard square. Mr. Damiano looked at me expectantly.

I stroked the cloth. Blue and gold, different pieces of fabric sewn together into one . . . I had it.

"Your mother sewed it," I said. "It's the tent of your first Dream-world."

He slapped his hands together. "I knew you would remember! It's for you, Rebecca, to mark the time we've spent together. And your excellent work for me."

"I can't take it from you. You've kept it all this time."

"Of course you can take it, if I give it to you. Take it with you. Put it in your bag. It doesn't take up much space, and feel how light it weighs. My mother chose material which was tough and would survive use. It has barely faded. Take it."

I folded the cloth carefully, corner to corner. He was right. It folded almost to nothing. I thought of the queues outside the first Dream-world, waiting to come in, and how Bella had told fortunes.

"I'll keep it forever," I said.

Mr. Damiano shrugged expansively. "Of course you will. And if you lose it, never mind."

It was time to go. Angela remained in the kitchen, singing and clat-tering plates. Mr. Damiano came into the hall. As he reached to open the door for me, I reached for him. I felt the weight and bulk of him for the first time, the shock of his body after so much of his mind and voice. His warmth and smell enveloped me. This close, the color of his hair had a certain deadness which made me know for sure that Mr. Damiano tinted his hair. We held each other, not moving, locked together, while Angela sang in the kitchen. And then the door opened and I was gone.

The Deep Blue Sea

We dip our heads in the deep blue sea
The deep blue sea the deep blue sea
We dip our heads in the deep blue sea
On the last day of September

Dearest Rebecca,

It was an email from Joe. I sat in the Internet café and read it through once, and then again. St. Ives had an Internet café now. The town was so much changed from the days when Adam and I first came. Everywhere, the differences between places were being smoothed out.

He had always begun with those words when he wrote to me. *Dearest Rebecca.* I'd taken it for granted, but now I wondered. Right from the beginning, Joe's endearments had made me feel that I had a place in the world.

Dearest Rebecca,
I am on Vancouver Island now. I've begun a new book, but this time it's not going to be history—or, if it is history, it's of a different kind. I don't

know if I'll ever publish it. It's just a story. I've never written anything like it before. I think it's for you. It's been strangely easy to write, as if the story was there all the time, waiting for me to notice it.

No more Stalin, Rebecca. I'm finished with that. I'll never get to the end of that book about Stalin's fugue.

I couldn't stop thinking about Nadezhda Alliluyeva and her death. You were right, Rebecca, when you saw the horror of how she left her children. I couldn't let go of her, even after I'd finished the book about her. But now I have, and it's killed the book I was trying to write. It was always Nadya who interested me, not him. Strange, isn't it? The mark Stalin makes on the world is so great. A stain, a mark that spreads like a greasy fingerprint on papers in an archive. We'll never get rid of it. And yet as a subject he is barren. I can rehearse everything he did and everything he was, and it comes out dead on the page. It's the effect he has on other people that matters. I try to see him alone in a room, eating or sleeping or whistling a tune he likes, and every time I fail.

I can think of the things that may have run through his mind when he was in the dacha. An argument, a cry, a blow. A woman running out of a room. A wound smelling of blood that has already congealed, and a letter lying on the floor which he knows he should not read, but which of course he will read. A face that was alive with love for him, but now it's shut like a stone. Children who feared him and men who danced for him like bears. But I cannot imagine myself into that room where he is alone. I've come to the end of trying.

You told me a long time ago that story was all you had. You were angry with me for trying to reinterpret your story, maybe even trying to change the way you looked at it.

All you know about your mother is that she gave birth to you. All I know about my father is what my mother has told me. I can't remember him at all. He was a flyer. My father flew and my grandfather flew and I know almost nothing about what they did and what drove them. They went to war, both of them, one in each generation, but I don't know anything about it.

He would never talk about it, my mother says. When there was a program about the war he wouldn't watch it. He never went to reunions. "He'd had enough of all that," my mother said.

There's a small museum of aviation here at Victoria, close to the airport. That's how my story started. I walked around those aeroplanes and imagined men inside, starting up the engines. I could see it, feel it. One of the characters might be my grandfather. And there's a woman, too. I see her alone in a room which she has painted herself. I watch the way she moves and hear the song she hums under her breath.

Do you remember telling me about how the midwife sat down with a long form to fill in, on your first ante-natal visit? You couldn't give her any of the details she needed, about your family medical history. She was very tactful about it. She must have come up against the situation before, you said, people who don't know who they are or where they come from. I recall your exact words: "It's not only that I don't know my mother or my father. They've cut me off from the whole chain of my ancestors."

I felt for you then, though I may not have shown it. You don't want my pity, any more than I want yours. But in thinking it over, I've come to see that it isn't true. No one can cut you off from the chain of your ancestry. They can't do it by mistake, or even deliberately. It would be the hardest thing in the world to do.

You've got all the information inside you that everyone else has got: the genetic map, the mitochondrial DNA. Your features rise up from the swamp of the past, just like everyone's.

Nobody really knows their ancestors, even if they're living beside the graveyard where their great-great-grandparents are buried, or in the house which their family built and lived in for generations. They may possess papers, objects, maybe money and property. But they don't possess the lives of the past, any more than you do.

But they may possess stories. I was thinking about what you said, Rebecca, and that the most important thing you haven't got about your family are their stories. That's why you got so angry when I suggested that there was another way to interpret your shoebox. It was your story and it was all you had and you were going to cling on to it. No one was going to wrestle that shoebox out of your arms.

So I thought I would give you another story. It's presumptuous of me, isn't it? Lucky I'm not with you so I can't see you slap me down with a look.

If you don't want it, you don't even have to read it. It's not finished yet, but when it is I'll email you to find out where you are, and then I'll come and give it to you.

I'm not being completely honest. In fact, my dearest Rebecca, I'm not being honest at all. I'm not writing this story entirely for you. How could I? I'm also writing it for myself. I want to look at the features of it. I want to see my grandfather's lips move. I want to hear the words that will come out of Florence's lips. She's called Florence, the woman I told you about, the one who's in the room alone. At least, she's alone now, but soon she won't be—

So I am not going to write any more about Stalin. Olya was right, I should have written Volodya's story, but I can't do that, either.

I'm writing about the people who have been there all the time, waiting. I'm writing about you, and me. And you wouldn't believe how fast I'm writing. All those years of struggle and research and drafts, and no book; and now I'm going to write this one in a matter of months. I can feel it.

Don't take fright. Don't sheer off, Rebecca, the way you do sometimes. All I'm asking you to do is to be my reader.

Yesterday, I saw a grizzly bear. We were on one side of a gorge, with our guide. There was a slippery path, and a steep drop to the river below. The river roared through the gully. They have close to six feet of rain a year there. Enough rain to bury you standing, Mikey said. He's our guide. We'd camped the night before. Did you know that you can't leave a trace of food in a tent in bear country? You have to seal it in boxes and hang it in trees well away from the camp.

Mikey touched my arm. He spoke quietly. I knew that he wanted to draw my attention to something without alerting the others.

"Look down by the water. On the other side of the river. There's a grizzly."

I looked down. The bear was easy to see, though I wouldn't have known it was a grizzly. It seemed to be playing with the water, right by the edge, where it churned through the rocks.

"He's hunting salmon," said Mikey. "Didn't expect to see him here."

I could tell that although Mikey took a certain detached satisfaction in the presence of the grizzly, he wasn't in the usual sense of the words pleased to see him. And I could see why. The bear had climbed down his side of the gorge. He could most certainly climb up again, on ours.

But he was at a distance. None of his senses registered us through the roar of the water.

Mikey didn't mention the presence of the grizzly to anyone else in our group. We walked on through the wet, in single file.

But as we went on it occurred to me that we weren't walking into safety. Phew, no more bears, that's a relief. It wasn't like that. We were simply walking into the territory of being less close to a grizzly bear. There were pretty much bound to be bears within calling distance all the way we walked.

You know how they say that you are never more than three yards from a rat, in the city? And yet you rarely see one, unless it's your job to do so.

So here I am, Rebecca. To be exact, here I am sitting in a pool of electric light, with my iBook burning blue. I'm drinking whiskey and I'm about to start writing again. I'm in the territory of bears. They are all around me, even if I can't yet see them. I can sense them, smell them. You know me, Rebecca, I'm an indoor man by nature, and words are the kind of bears I hunt.

With love,
Joe

I must have been smiling as I read it, because a young guy who was wiping the tables smiled back at me.

"How're you doing?" he asked.

"Fine." I glanced round. The place was full and there were more backpackers barging in the doorway. Too much trade for one pair of hands.

"Do you need any help here?" I asked.

And now it's September. The thirtieth of September, to be exact. The families and children left weeks ago, and even the students have to go now. Tomorrow, people will be permitted to let their dogs run on the beaches again. Porthmeor has a washed, innocent look to it. The light's changed too. It's golden now, rather than white.

I can walk freely, where there would have been a hundred camps set up on the sand in August. Family camps: children, parents, grandparents, young girls with their boyfriends, maybe a son-in-law who keeps staring at gaps in the canvas walls that surround him, as if he plans a breakout.

But in some of the camps everybody looks content. Even happy. I want to get close, to find out how their happiness works. I want to watch from the very first moment, when the first member of the family dumps an armload of chairs, cushions and mats on the sand and then another comes up with rolls of windbreak under each arm, and a big smooth stone for hammering in the poles. They don't want to lie in the naked air of the beach, with people like me watching. They're very genial but they know what they want, which is themselves.

They want to turn outside into inside, but with fresh air. They build their canvas walls well, debating wind direction and maximum exposure to sun. The baby's tent is set in the shade with a bouncy cradle outside it.

Wetsuits, surfboards, barbecues, newspapers, cool boxes, baby gym, an inflatable dinosaur, spades, buckets, blankets, fishing nets, footrests, ice cream, sun cream.

The sun cream takes up hours. Running after the two-year-old with a sun-cream spray. Applying and reapplying the sun cream to every inch of the flesh. Behind the shoulders, on nipples and foot soles. Everyone has the same expression during the anointing process. Serious and dreamy, as if they're slowly falling in love with themselves.

There's a young girl, the daughter of the camp, with the boyfriend who's come on holiday with them. He's skinny and gawky and she's beautiful. She fills her palm with cream and approaches him from behind where he's lying facedown. But as soon as he feels her hands on his flesh he twitches, rolls over and shoves her backward into the sand. The grandma screams with laughter. The girl's left with her hands full of sun cream and sand. But she doesn't seem to care. Next moment, she's kneeling beside her boyfriend, helping him fill in a wordsearch.

(I have to imagine this. I didn't see it. They were safe from my eyes inside their camp.)

She's so perfect and he's so imperfect and yet she's the one who's trying to please him. She jumps up and starts pegging wet swimming costumes onto a line that runs across the top of a windbreak. She uses little red plastic pegs, like dolls' pegs.

⁘

The camps are gone. It's the thirtieth of September now. The last day of September. We used to play a game to that song, at primary school. One girl (it was only the girls who played) would make an arch with her arm, her outstretched hand braced against the rough stone play-ground wall. All of us would hold hands and make a long chain which wound through the arch as we sang.

The captain said it would never never do
Never never do never never do
The captain said it would never never do
On the last day of SeptemBER

As we sang the last word we would jerk our arms down hard and if you were the girl who was making the arch you would brace yourself against the wall in case you were pulled off your feet.

The games we played were full of mystery. They were like adult conversations we'd overheard. But it was us playing them, not our mothers and fathers.

We dip our heads in the deep blue sea
The deep blue sea the deep blue sea

We dip our heads in the deep blue sea
On the last day of SeptemBER

I have a job, for a few more weeks. The café has had a wonderful season and I've done well with tips. I have a room with what are called sea glimpses, and a sour-smelling en-suite. There's a pretty oak chest on which I've spread the piece of silk that Mr. Damiano gave me. The fragment of his first Dreamworld. The silk is fragile and I've spread it out of the sun, in case it fades.

I sleep lightly. Every time I wake there's the noise of wind and sea. Gulls walk on the roof at night and their big claws scrape the tiles.

I am beginning to think of what Ruby lost. The life Ruby didn't have. Her life, that didn't spread out and grow. She used to talk about what she would do when she grew up. She'd realized that people left their parents to find homes of their own, and she didn't like it.

"If I was living in another house, you wouldn't be able to make my dinner."

I told her she could stay living at home for as long as she wanted. "But you won't want to, Ruby. You think you will now, but you won't. Not when you're grown up."

She looked at me, frowning. She thought I could look into her future as if it were rolling out on a TV screen. Much later, when she was in her bath, she asked me with false casualness, "Can kidnappers make children live away from their houses?" I told her that they could not. My adoptive mother had told me the story of the Moors murders when I was eight years old. She did it to make me careful.

"You can't trust anyone, man nor woman," she said. "They come up to you all smiles and sweeties. It's inside that they're bad, where you can't see."

My head was loaded with terror each time she sent me to the shop for bread. My adoptive mother chastened me with the thought of what could happen if I stepped out of line. The bad people who would seize me. The teachers who would tell me off. The cars that would run me over. She filled me with terror.

I did not terrorize Ruby. I was determined she would live in the sunlight. And now I am alive, and Ruby is not.

I think for a long time each day of the life that Ruby lost. I think less of my grief, my longing for the feel of her and the smell and touch of her. I try to think less of this. I think of the space of years Ruby missed. The houses she would have inhabited, away from us.

I sit on my mat with a towel spread on it, staring out at the sea. I might swim. I've got my swimsuit on under my dress. The sun is warm, and there's no wind.

I haven't visited Ruby's grave yet. It is behind me, within sight. It's the north of my compass. I walk along the top of the graveyard every morning, on my way to work. My view is Ruby's.

⁓

There's one family group left, twenty yards from me. A big burly woman, about fifty. A matriarch. Two daughters with her, or maybe it's a daughter and a daughter-in-law. A son who has hammered in the windbreak with skill and precision.

The woman keeps standing up, shielding her eyes to watch the four little children playing at the water's edge. Her grandchildren, presumably. Well she might watch them. I've been uneasy ever since they were let go on their own. People don't know what this sea is like.

I am clenching my arms around my knees. Before I know that I'm going to do it, I get up and walk over to the big woman.

"The sea can be dangerous here—you'll get a big wave suddenly. And they're very young..."

"I'm keeping an eye on them," she says, not taking offense, just stating the fact. She has the face of a Viking. Big jaw, stern blue eyes.

"But by the time you got down to them—"

She sees what I see: the vastness of sand between us and the children, playing where the waves break. The children are knee-deep, maybe thigh-deep—the water's swirling around them—

"If they were mine I'd be down there," I say, not caring now what she thinks. But she doesn't get angry.

"Maybe you're right," she says, and strides toward the sea. The space between her and the children narrows. They have heard her voice. They turn and leap and splash their way toward their Viking grandmother.

My heart steadies itself. I go back to my towel, and there's Joe, standing where I was lying, shielding his eyes, watching me.

"I've been to the Tate," he says, as I come up to him.

"Oh—have you?"

"Yes. I've been watching the expression on people's faces as they come out. They look as if they've had a bit of good done to them, don't they, Rebecca? Like people coming out of a church service. Only it's a church where they're not members, so they're extra respectful."

"It's good for the town."

"I daresay."

We are in the deep blue sea now. We've waded out into the loudness of the waves. From here, the shore is a foreign land. Joe swims ahead of me with the strong breaststroke I'd forgotten. He used to swim like that when we went to the Baths on Thursday nights, adults-only night. They would turn the lighting down to try to create an atmosphere, but they couldn't change the smell of chlorine or the after-echo of a hundred school galas trapped under the glass-and-iron roof.

Joe has grown broader. I noticed it as he walked into the sea. His chest is more muscled, his thighs thicker. And his swimming is surely better than I remember it.

I swim slowly, keeping his wet black head in sight. He's swimming properly, dipping his head down in the water and lifting it to breathe. But the water's cold, even at the end of the season, and it tires me. I won't swim far. I turn on my back and float, resting before I swim back to shore.

I hang, suspended. My arms are colder than the rest of me. I could yield now, neither on earth nor in heaven.

There's a small plane overhead. It's not very high. It'll be going to the Scillies, maybe. It's hard to judge distances when you're floating. I could reach up and touch it with a wet finger.

"I saw a seal," says Joe beside me. He's smiling as he treads water. "It was this close. It looked at me, like a dog. More intelligent than a dog. And then it dived."

"Did you touch it?"

"Of course not. You're tired, let's go back."

But Joe's not tired. He dives and comes up shaking drops of water from his hair. He dives again, deeper, and rises in a stream of bubbles.

"It's wonderful here. Why didn't you tell me?"

We swim back side by side. Joe looks happy today, and hopeful. Maybe his life will be as he wants it to be. He's so clever, I think, as if Joe's a new person whom I'm seeing for the first time. So talented. He has succeeded in what he set out to do. Everyone reads his book, or pretends to do so. There's talk of him presenting a TV history series. I look at him and realize that he would be good on TV.

We climb out of the water and now it's the air that seems cold, and the breeze chill on my skin. We rub our bodies down and put on clothes. Joe glances at me, but I keep on combing my hair, not meeting the glance. He has so much to offer. He's been going hiking every weekend out on Vancouver Island, he says, and swimming three times a week. It's true, his body is firmer, more fully muscled.

But what hangs between us is that I have never wanted it.

"You look well," I say.

"I am well," says Joe.

"Are you staying?"

"No," says Joe. "I don't think so. I'm going back to that cabin. I need to get on with my writing."

"The cabin with the bears?"

"That's the one. I'll live there for a while. Six months, maybe a year. You and Adam must come out and visit." He looks me full in the face.

"What makes you so sure?"

"You'd be a fool not to, Rebecca."

"He may have changed the color of his front door. He may not want me there."

"The trouble is that you think nothing of yourself. I know why that is, but you do damage, Rebecca, because you don't know the power you've got."

"I'm sorry."

"You've got no call to be sorry. You're not getting any declaration from me, Rebecca, don't think it. All I'll say is that I love what you are in my life."

It's like the slow release of a vise on my heart. I hold his words in my mind, to think of later in the hope that they're true, and that I no longer need to feel the guilt I have always felt toward him. He said the words as if they were true.

We are clothed, side by side and eating chocolate. Joe gets a wad of paper out of his backpack.

"I've printed the story off for you," he says. "Here you are. It's not finished. I thought it was going to be a short story but it'll make a novel."

"Can I read the rest when it's done?"

"If you like. But this is the part I wrote with you in mind. The rest won't be like that. It goes on to the next generation, my father's generation. The story's taken on a life of its own. That's why I need to get back and work on it."

"Have you seen a bear at the cabin yet?"

"Yes. A black bear comes most evenings now. My neighbor says she's got cubs off in the woods. But she's all right as long as you don't scare her."

"You like it there."

"I do. I like it more than I would ever have believed possible. I'm content in my cabin, Rebecca, along with the bears."

The Birthday Party

Adam touches the doorbell and it rings smartly. A pink balloon bounces from the door-knocker. From inside there comes a crush of happy, excited voices. It's Lisa who comes to the door, dressed in a yellow shirt and cream trousers. Her hair is brushed back into a ponytail, and she looks years younger than the woman who sat night after night beside the incubator that contained her daughter. Then, her brown eyes were set in stains of shadow. Now, they glow with pleasure.

"I'm so glad you could come," she says. "We weren't sure—I mean, I wanted to ask you, and then Ramzi said maybe we shouldn't, you're so busy and—"

"I was glad to be asked," says Adam. It's true. There's something about Lisa and Ramzi and little Amina that has stayed in his mind. Lisa talked to him one night about Ramzi's family. They hadn't been able to accept her. That was the way Lisa put it, in words that didn't seem to contain a judgment. They lived in Huddersfield, where she and Ramzi had both been brought up, but in different parts of the town. They'd gone to the same comprehensive. She'd seen Ramzi's parents at school parents' evenings, but she'd never spoken to them.

Lisa and Ramzi didn't remember when they'd first met, but when they were sixteen they started going out together. Well, not going out exactly. They had to be careful, because all Ramzi's cousins were at the school as well.

In the end they had to leave. "It got too difficult." They came down south and both got jobs. Her family had visited, but not his. None of them had come to the wedding. It was too difficult. She'd written letters to Ramzi's mother, and sent photographs. Ramzi had phoned to tell them of Amina's birth, and he'd sent them a copy of the Polaroid photograph which was taken a few minutes after her birth. But they hadn't sent a card back or anything.

"I know I shouldn't be angry with them, they can't help it. It's for Amina I'm angry. They don't know she's alive, not properly. If she doesn't come on all right—well, they won't know about that, either. Not the way they should. Maybe they'll even be—"

"What?"

"I shouldn't say it." But she whispers it. "Relieved. Because then they'll be able to pretend that she never existed. And that makes me so . . . well, angry."

"I'm sure they don't feel that," says Adam. "She is their granddaughter."

Lisa shrugged her thin shoulders.

"Amina's responding well to the antibiotics," went on Adam. "Once we get this infection under control—"

"Yes. Ramzi's coming in at ten, when he finishes his shift. She looks better than she did this morning. He'll see the difference."

Ramzi worked in a call center, as Lisa had done before Amina was born. Ramzi was doing well, he was a supervisor and they thought highly of him. There was a chance of management training. But what Ramzi wanted was to do a degree in engineering. It would happen,

Lisa said. They were only twenty-two. She would go back to work, get herself promoted. They would share the care of Amina whilst Ramzi studied.

"Only now I feel I couldn't ever bear to leave her, not for an hour," said Lisa.

It was over many weeks that he learned all this. The closeness of the unit was a strange thing. It seemed so personal and yet in an odd way it wasn't. Some parents found it very hard to cope, when they finally took their babies home. They'd longed for it and counted down to it and yet it frightened them once it came. They didn't feel safe without a nurse within call. They weren't forgotten, no, it wasn't as crude as that, but some stayed in your mind more than others. Amina, for example. A still baby, a baby who knew how to conserve her energy. She'd had a lot of problems but he'd always had a hunch that Amina would make it. He'd felt that they were in it together. She knew that he was trying to help her. He talked her through it, as he did with all his patients.

"Now, Amina, what this drug's going to do is fight the infection in your lungs. You're off the CPAP, we're not going to go backwards now."

Nobody outside neonatology understood the amount of character there was in his patients.

<hr/>

"Come on inside, Ramzi's borrowed a camcorder and he's filming them having their tea."

He follows Lisa down the flat's narrow corridor into the living room.

And there's Amina, in a pink ruffled dress with her scant hair tied up in a matching ribbon. She sits in her highchair at the head of the table which has been placed in the center of the room. There are five other babies, on their mothers' laps or crawling round the floor. Bunches of pink balloons hang from the walls and the table is heaped with sandwiches, cakes, biscuits, crisps, feeding bottles, dummies, wipes, tissues. How young they all are. The fathers look even younger than the mothers. One dad is showing Ramzi a function on the camcorder. By the window a boy in jeans and T-shirt jogs a grizzling newborn infant.

They all seem to know who Adam is. Lisa must have told her friends that he was coming. She settles him into an empty chair next to Amina, and brings him a glass of lemonade. His eyes note the child. There are the hollows at her temples, the typical translucency of a child born at twenty-seven weeks. Her wrists are so narrow that he wonders where they found the gold bracelets that clasp them. As he watches, Amina leans forward, fastidiously opens a sandwich, removes the cheese slice inside it and eats the bread.

"She likes cheese really," says Lisa. "But she's got a thing about opening up things if they're closed." The baby stares intently at her mother, then at the door she has bitten into the bread.

"She's sitting up well," says Adam.

"I have to keep remembering she's not really one at all. She's only nine months."

"She's doing fine." She looks fragile but he knows how tough she really is.

Here's Ramzi with the camcorder.

"Is it all right if I take some film of you with Amina? For her, when she's older. We can tell her, that's the doctor who took care of you when you were born."

"Of course."

Amina is still regarding her bread. Suddenly, with immaculate timing, she holds it out to Adam.

"Thank you, Amina," he says, taking it.

Scrupulously, Ramzi takes the lens off his daughter and films around the whole table, lingering on each child.

"We'll have the cake soon," says Lisa. "They're getting tired."

"She's done so well," said Adam. "She's beautiful."

Ramzi puffs out his cheeks, lets his breath escape slowly.

"Now we can say that," he says.

The other babies are much bigger than Amina. They crawl, or

stand holding a table leg. One of them makes a staggering run from the hands of his mother to the hands of his father.

"They're all my friends from the baby group," says Lisa. "We started off meeting once a week, but it's more now, isn't it, Mel?"

"Most days, really. It keeps us sane," says Mel.

"More or less," says the girl who seems to be the mother of the newborn baby as well as another who can't be more than fourteen months. She hoists her big square boy onto her hip and touches Amina's cheek gently with a finger.

"She's a little princess," she says. "Anytime you get tired of her, Lisa, you send her down to me."

There are no grandparents here. Nobody over twenty-five, he guesses, except him. On the table there's a bunch of pink and cream roses. Lisa sees him look at them.

"Ramzi bought them for me. They've got a scent as well."

"Everybody gets presents for the baby, but I think the mum deserves something," says Ramzi.

"You hear that, Ross?" calls Mel.

"Ramzi, get the camcorder ready, I'm going to get the you-know-what."

They draw the curtains and switch off all the lights. The babies stare uncomprehendingly. One starts to cry but is quickly silenced with a dummy. And here's Lisa coming through the kitchen door with the cake held high, its one candle alight. Carefully, she sets it on the table before Amina.

"Ooh, Lisa, did you make it yourself?"

"It's lovely."

"Where'd you get the teddy bears?"

"Tesco's," says Lisa. "They sell them in packets."

And then, hush. Lisa bends by her daughter. "It's your cake, Amina. You're the birthday girl."

The baby's eyes shine dark in the glow of the flame.

"Happy birthday..." begins one voice, and then they are all singing. For the first time, maybe, Adam thinks as he sings, since they were children themselves with their own birthday cakes and candles. And now they are the grown-ups, the parents learning how to give birthdays to their children.

"...dear AmINa..."

"Now, we're going to blow out your candle, Amina. Big breath. One, two, three..."

The candle falters, rises again.

"Go for it, Lisa."

"Show your mum how it's done, Amina."

The candle blows out. The curtains are drawn back.

"You cut the cake with her, Ramzi. Ross'll film it, won't you, Ross?"

And there they are. Father and daughter look the same way, into the lens. The father holds the knife and guides Amina's hand.

"Make a wish, Amina."

The knife goes down clean into the pink and white icing.

They come to the door to see Adam off.

"Are you going back to the hospital?" asks Ramzi. He has Amina in his arms, curled up and drowsing.

"No. I'm taking some leave. I'm getting a train down to Cornwall tonight."

"I hope this weather stays for you," says Lisa.

"They say it will."

"You need your holidays."

"Thanks for coming, we appreciate it, don't we, Lisa?" says Ramzi. Suddenly he has authority, standing there with his baby girl in his arms. He is twenty-two but he is a man.

"It was a pleasure," says Adam, with truth. And before he knows he's going to do it, he adds some truth of his own.

"It's not really a holiday. I'm going down to Cornwall to see my wife."

It's just a shade of expression in Lisa's face but he knows she has been told. Someone in the unit has talked about Rebecca, and Ruby.

"She's been away for a while. Things were bad after our little girl died."

They say nothing. Lisa makes a little sound of sympathy.

"So we're going to spend some time together, down there. It's where my family comes from."

"Nice place to come from," says Ramzi. "I went there once when I was a kid."

"I've never been," says Lisa.

"When we got back from our holiday, I asked my mum, 'Why do we live in Huddersfield when there's places like Cornwall?' She wasn't best pleased."

"We'll take Amina one day."

They glance at each other.

"I hope it goes well," says Lisa to Adam. "You know, if it could be the same for you, as it is for us. I mean, look at where we were a year ago."

"I'll come and tell you, on Amina's next birthday," says Adam.

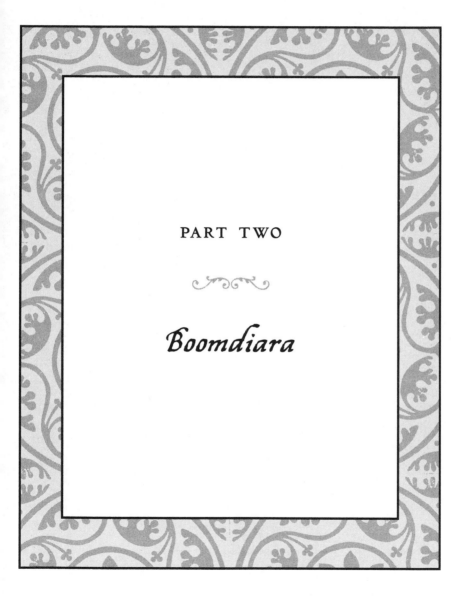

PART TWO

Boomdiara

Have you left the ground in murkiness, all clammy, grey and soaking,
    And struggled through the dirty, dripping white?
Have you seen the blank sides closing in and felt that you were choking,
    And then leapt into a land of blazing light...

Dearest Rebecca,

I enclose the story so far. Most of the action takes place in 1917—
the prologue a little later.

Olya and I are finished. It's really over this time. I've had enough of
messing her about. All right, I'm ready to acknowledge now that messing Olya about is exactly what I was doing. You told me once that I
ought to leave Olya if I wasn't going to give her what she wanted. I was
very angry with you then, wasn't I?

But it wasn't Olya who stopped me writing about Stalin. I've told
you some of the reasons already, but there's one more that I haven't
told you.

He was a young man whose name I don't know. He was sitting on a
wooden trolley, begging. He was a veteran of one of Russia's many

wars. A killer, and an innocent as well. He'd been conscripted because he couldn't get out of it. No pull, no clout, no college place, no connections. Just a boy with blue eyes and no education.

He lost his legs, Rebecca, both of them. Imagine it. He can't get artificial legs, because there isn't the money. So he sits on his wooden trolley, and the pensioners who have no money themselves give him what they can.

He told me that if Stalin was still alive, it wouldn't have come to this. They would have won the war. Iosif Vissarionovich wouldn't have left veterans to rot in the street.

What could I say? I said nothing. It wasn't my war. I could write about Nadya, and what I've written I've written. I'm not ashamed of it, but I can't go any further. I cannot get to the heart of what that man was.

All I can do is stand here with my head bowed, and ask Olya to forgive me. I've used up too many of her years. I've taken up love that ought to have led to the life she wanted. She wanted children, she wanted us to have a real life together.

I can't argue for how you came to be in that shoebox, even though it's a key event. That bloody shoebox. You're not still carrying it around with you, are you, Rebecca? I hate the sight of it. It's not you. It's not what you are worth. Don't just leave it behind: bin it, burn it.

I've found a woman who might have been your ancestor, and a man who might have been mine. Because that's what we are, aren't we, Rebecca? Brother and sister.

And I wanted to write about flight. Do you remember what I told you once, about Mandelstam's baby aeroplanes? I expect you've forgotten. Why does the thought of those aeroplanes move me so deeply? Why do I stare up into the sky when a certain type of aeroplane passes—an old-fashioned plane, flying low? It looks fragile, but at the same time it looks as if it's really flying, really riding those waves of air.

When I was a child I slept under my father's coat. It was an RAF greatcoat. It was heavy. It pressed me down and it had a smell which was peculiar to that cloth and which I've never smelled anywhere else. I used to think it was the smell of my father, but I think the smell of aeroplanes was mixed up in it, too. And if war has a smell there would have been the smell of war deep in the fibers of the coat. He never talked about the war to my mother, and maybe he wouldn't have talked about it to me, even if he'd lived.

His own father, my grandfather, flew those baby aeroplanes of the First World War. The men in my family father their children late, and so they don't stay around to father them for long. For most of my life it's felt improbable to me that I had a father at all.

I don't remember him any more than you remember your mother. I'd love to have known him. Sometimes I get a sensation in my head, in my mouth almost, like a taste or a smell. I nearly remember him, but then I don't. I try not to reach after it too much. The thread that links us is so slender that I'm afraid it'll snap if I strain it too far. It drives me crazy. Maybe there's a sensation like that in your head.

All those months inside your mother's body, those hours when she was yours and no one else's, and you were hers. The fact that the relationship between you didn't continue doesn't invalidate it—that would be like saying that love isn't real unless it lasts forever.

Yes, I wanted to write about flight. Flight was such a pure thing when it began. They made machines that followed any crackpot shape they had in their imaginations. Those baby aeroplanes looked like bundles of sticks. But how beautiful it must have been, when the only purpose of flying was flight.

But of course it changed, almost at once. There began to be other purposes for flight, because as soon as a man picks up a stone, he thinks of throwing it, and then of what his target will be.

When the First World War started, there were a hundred planes in France. Most of the generals couldn't see the point of them. When it ended there were twenty-two thousand. This is what we do with our inventions. This is what we have to do. You and I grew up in a time of peace, but that was by accident. What shapes our lives is war. I tell you, we haven't absorbed those blows yet. We are still reeling from them.

Only we don't see ourselves reeling. We don't have young men on the streets without legs, on wooden trolleys.

I wanted to write about these people who might be our forebears. Maybe I started off by trying to manipulate them. But my characters weren't having any of that. They are like children—they seize their own life in both hands and race off with it.

And characters see through the tricks in the writer's mind. Will might be my grandfather: the dates are more or less right. Florence's daughter might be your grandmother. But however much I try to write without knowing what I'm writing, I can't help seeing that Florence is closer to you than that. And if Will's my ancestor, then he's also the man I see in the mirror.

You'll see how rough the story is. This is work in progress—or so I tell myself. In December I'm going over to France to do some research. But maybe I won't ever really finish this story. It's going to take me a long time to write about the next generation, my father's generation.

Writing it is the point of it. Being with Will and Florence is the point of it. It's like those baby aeroplanes. They've got nothing to do with anything except flight.

You're my reader, Rebecca. You can read me as no one else can. Here we are, brother and sister, writer and reader.

But don't, for God's sake, feel you've got to like it. Or comment on it.

And so my story opens. My characters are in a graveyard. Maybe I'm wrong about this, but I think that sometimes we recognize history as a sensation—a smell, or a touch—before we can name it or know what it really is. If it's our own history, that is. Even if we've never seen those graveyards, we know about them. They are our key events.

With love,
Joe

Prologue

A field is enough to spend a life in.

It's a raw seam of earth with wooden crosses set into it. Committees are working hard on it. No one has ever had so many graves to deal with. Everything must be considered. How are all these dead to be looked after, and introduced to history?

A gray, wet sky. It has rained all morning and will rain again. Here comes a woman with a child stepping at her side. They're nothing remarkable. There are many such figures here, erring between the rows of graves. But this woman, unlike the others, is not dressed in black. Neither is the child in mourning.

The woman has a piece of paper in her hand which she consults from time to time. It's a map, maybe, or a plan. Everything here is new and raw and temporary. Even the graves look as if they might shift from one week to the next.

The task is enormous. The earth around here heaves up bodies wherever it's touched. They must be identified, catalogued, put to rest, memorialized. And yet there must also be something for those who remember the scent of skin or the timbre of a laugh. At the very least there must be a place to visit.

She's found it, or she thinks she has. The numbers match. Woman and child stop. They stand side by side for a minute, looking at what they've come to find as if it's trying to conceal something from them, until the child, overcome perhaps by the atmosphere, turns and burrows her head into her mother's waist. Mother and child bend together in the shape of giving comfort.

What to do? What to say? These fields have been ploughed up for the sake of the dead. Nothing else will ever grow here, that's a promise.

It begins to rain. The field looks even more provisional. A small aeroplane makes its way westward and both woman and child look up, arrested by the sight of it. The plane's noise comes and goes as it falters across their field of vision.

"Look, an aeroplane," says the little girl.

"Yes."

They don't kneel at the graveside. They don't drop flowers or plant a rose—besides, that is contrary to the plans of the committee. After a while of standing, the woman wipes some touches of rain off her face, takes the child's hand and begins to retrace her steps.

Florence, 1917

Will was naked the first time I saw him. He was in the bathroom and the door was open. Not wide open, but wide enough for me to see inside.

He should not have been there at all. We don't have visitors so early. Who had let him in? I wondered. And then I wondered if Madame Blanche would blame me for it, when she returned.

I stayed safe in the shadow of the door. I leaned forward, just a little. The room was full of sun and steam, and against the far wall there was the big claw-footed bath that Madame Blanche had installed. No one in town had a bath as fine as ours, with its wide gushing taps and the powerful pipes running down to it and away from it. Built to last a lifetime, and plumbed in only a few miles from the front.

It was Madame Blanche's one act of faith. Petit Paul would continue to stoke the furnace, hot water would pour from the taps, the bath would fill and men would clean themselves. The house would stand and we would do well.

At the end of each week Madame Blanche comes out of her private office after doing the books. She always seeks me out then.

"We are doing well, Florence," she says gravely, as if letting me know the fate of some invalid who is precious to us both. We never speak of the fact that the house is hers, the bath is hers and the profit is hers. I have never seen inside those account books.

God help Marguerite if she doesn't buff the porcelain to shining whiteness each morning, and again between clients. The bath must appear pristine, as if no one else has ever lain in it.

I like the bathroom in the early mornings, when our bath lies in its lair like a lion couchant, waiting for the officers. Nothing has happened yet. The towels are folded. Danielle and Marie-Claude run about in their kimonos with their hair scraped back off their foreheads, like little girls. And so do I. We drink our coffee in the garden before we dress. It's cool and the dew is on the grass in the orchard. Claire holds my hand and we go to visit the hens.

But this man was in our house at ten o'clock in the morning. He bent forward and sluiced his face. He took the long-handled bristle brush and began to scrub his back. I watched. He groped for an enamel can of clean water that stood on the edge of the bath. He lifted the can high, and poured fresh hot water over his head in a long stream.

I knew that the water would be fresh and hot. These things were my responsibility that day. Madame Blanche was away on a visit, but she might come back at any time, perhaps in two hours, perhaps in two days. She never tells me, or anyone. She opens the well-oiled front door with her silent key and she's suddenly there among us. Her eyes go straight to the rumpled bed, the smear on a glass, the girl with her face red and sweaty after romping on the orchard swing. And especially she sees everything I've done. I am in charge now until she returns. I'm her deputy, her aide-de-camp, her lieutenant.

Will was naked. The fresh hot water parted his short hair and flattened it, and the sun shone on it. Water flowed over his face, his shoulders, his chest. The clean water disappeared into the milky, dirty water that lapped his waist. He sat in his dirt. He wasn't young, I saw that at once. He was more than thirty, thirty-five maybe. Heavyset.

The men who come to us are dirty. They don't know it themselves, because they are so used to it. (Madame Blanche would correct me if I said that they were men. They are officers. We don't take men.)

But they are all dirty. They smell of raw earth and sweat and metal. They smell of smoke and explosives. They aren't aware of it. They wash before they come to us and they comb their hair and put on fresh clothes if they have them. Sometimes they wear lemon cologne. It makes no difference. All of them smell of war and it's the dirtiest smell there is.

This is why Madame Blanche installed the bathroom. No other establishment has one to match it. I was doubtful because of the expense, but she was right, as always.

"It will pay for itself ten times over," was what she didn't say.

Madame Blanche never talks about money, but when you come to know her you soon realize that everything she thinks about and speaks of has the tang of cash in it somewhere.

Have you ever held a handful of coins up to your nose and sniffed it? That's another dirty smell, not like the smell of war but somehow akin to it. I am not saying that money is dirty, however. I am not such a fool as that. Money is why I am here. Those round dirty coins which stand for pigs or orchards or good square meals or your child sleeping in a safe warm bed with a full belly.

The men arrive. They drink wine in the garden if it's fine, in the salon if it's rainy or cold. Marie-Claude plays the piano. I pass around slices of sweet cake. Nobody eats it, but it looks nice: cake with wine. It has a feeling of home. Marie-Claude wears a white dress with lavender ribbons, or apricot ribbons. She plays the piano ardently. I make sure she only has one glass of wine, because otherwise she becomes tearful and tells everyone that she would have had a place at the Conservatoire if it hadn't been for the war. This strikes the wrong note. The men become uneasy, because it reminds them of their sisters, who also take music lessons and dream of concert platforms. They don't want to link girls like us with their sisters.

Marie-Claude plays on. The sun sparkles on Madame Blanche's carp pond. From time to time she takes a young man aside in her motherly, discreet manner.

"Would you like to bathe yourself?"

Madame Blanche's bathroom is the talk of the town. These young men know what to expect. And they long for it. Deep, hot water, a cake of lemon soap and a towel that is big enough to wrap around you . . . it's oblivion.

I can never make Madame Blanche understand that "to bathe" is not a reflexive verb in English. One of the reasons I am her aide-de-camp and her lieutenant is my command of the English language, but that doesn't mean she's prepared to learn from me.

"Do take a bath, if you like," I murmur. "The bathroom's awfully nice."

Madame Blanche's eyes slide toward me and I catch a gleam of satisfaction in them.

The men emerge from the bathroom as happy as babies. There's still a tang of war on their clothes, but we can't do anything about that. Even Madame Blanche hasn't gone so far as to suggest that we open up a laundry. It would probably be illegal, anyway. I think that their uniforms are the property of the Crown.

⁘

Will's uniform lay on the bathroom chair. I watched his back, with the runnels of silky water going down it. His arms were tanned, and his face, and there was a line where the white flesh met the tanned flesh.

The sun was falling directly onto the bath and he was in his own sun-lit world. He knelt up in the bath and began to soap his private parts with a care and thoroughness which I approved. He splashed more water over himself and as he did so he began to sing.

I love the flowers, I love the daffodils
I love the butterflies, I love the rolling hills
Boomdiara boomdiara
Boomdiara boomdiara
Boomdiara boomdiara
Boomdiara boomdiara
BOOM

I love the motor cars, I love the aeroplanes
I love the—

But he felt me at the door. He swung round and I saw his face full-on, frowning and wary. An adult face, not a boy's face. The door was only a little way open and I stepped back quickly but I think he saw me.

I hurried back along the passage. I would not have put it past him to leap out of the bath on a wave of dirty water and come after me. I've seen how quick the reflexes of these men can be. At the turn in the passage I waited and listened. After a while the singing began again, loud and deliberate now, like a challenge.

Boomdiara boomdiara
Boomdiara boomdiara
BOOM

Petit Paul, who stokes the furnace for the baths, glided past me press-ing himself sideways against the wall so as not to touch my skirts. Madame Blanche has drilled him. He is not to look at the young women here. He is not to burst into rooms. He is to knock, and wait.

He's timid, anyway. He doesn't want to touch us or look at us. He's an undersized boy of fourteen who will be tall if he gets enough to eat. He is desperate to stay here because this is where food is, and war is not. If it means walking around with his gaze fixed on the floorboards all day, so be it.

I knew I mustn't stand there. There were a hundred things to be done without fuss or haste, in the way Madame Blanche likes her household to run. I should go and listen to Marie-Claude talking about the piano lessons she used to have, and the day that her teacher told her that she had real talent, my child, real talent. If she could empty her heart to me, maybe she wouldn't feel the need to burst out with it in company. I had to order the meals for tomorrow, and make sure that Danielle kept the dentist's appointment I had made for her. She's afraid of the dentist. She thinks he'll pull her tooth out, and she's right. It must be pulled. Her breath is rotten. I had to visit Gabi in her room and inquire about the terrible period pains from which she's suffering. Next, there were roses to pick, and my blue linen walking skirt to mend. I had to make sure that lunch was on the table at twelve sharp so that the girls could lie down for an hour before the bell rang for the first time.

I wondered again who had let the man in the bath into our house at ten o'clock in the morning. No one ever comes as early as that.

And if I listen carefully enough to Marie-Claude, I thought, and ask the right questions, she will be in a good mood and will play for a while to Claire before she goes for her nap after lunch. Claire will sit on my lap and one of her small round fists will beat gently against my breast in time to the music. She is not aware that she is doing this. Her early days flood back to me, when she beat her fist on my breast like that as she fed. And I told her: *You are mine, mine. I will never abandon you.*

Perhaps Claire is musical.

Perhaps Claire should have piano lessons.

Perhaps, if I listen to Marie-Claude and make life sweet for her, she'll be willing to teach Claire. And then, when Claire's older—

❦

I went up the stairs to the attic floor, rapidly but without the appearance of haste. I have learned this from Madame Blanche. It's also from her that I've learned to appear cheerful and agreeable to the girls and to our visitors, while remaining utterly faithful to the program set out for me. I have learned these things from Madame Blanche and when she's away I practice them still more carefully. She may return at any moment. Once or twice she's doubted me. I knew it instantly. She looked at Claire with that long, considering gaze I've seen turned on a girl who wasn't pulling her weight. As if wondering how and why my child was in Madame Blanche's house, eating Madame Blanche's food, living under Madame Blanche's protection. And I was flooded with fear, and she knew it.

I opened the door to Claire's room. She was standing in front of the washstand while Marguerite washed her face. Standing still like a good girl, her eyes squeezed shut in mute protest. Why does Marguerite have to wash Claire's face as if it's a plate?

"Thank you," I said, "I'll do her hair today."

Marguerite went out, banging the door not from annoyance but because to Marguerite doors exist for slamming, food for cramming into your mouth, men for "you know what" as she calls it. But she's willing and above all she's cheerful, which is a cardinal virtue in this house. No long faces, please!

Claire leaned against my knee as I brushed out her soft, bloomy curls and wound them around my fingers.

"I've got you a new ribbon," I said. It's red, Claire's favorite color. I tied the ribbon into her hair and she stroked it proudly.

"Sing me the new song, Claire," I asked her.

I have been teaching her:

Buttercups and daisies,
Oh the pretty flowers,

Coming 'ere the springtime
To tell of sunny hours.

She knows all the words. She's very quick.

"Go on, try to remember," I urged her. She screwed up her smooth face.

"Boomdiara!" she announced. "Boomdiara, boomdiara, boomdiara, boomdiara—"

"No, Claire. Not that song."

Where can she have heard it? Has he been up here? They are not allowed up here, in the attics. I don't have Claire downstairs in the salon when the visitors are here. In some establishments they have the children dressed up with their hair curled, like little monkeys on sticks. None of our visitors knows of Claire's existence. Only the more experienced of them can tell that I have given birth to a child, and children so often die or are given away that there are no questions asked.

"Boomdiara," sang Claire, looking straight at me.

She might have heard the song rising from the open bathroom window. To divert her, I picked her up and swung her high above my head so that she shrieked with laughter. I lowered her until her stomach was resting on my head, rubbing against my hair. I rocked her there and she laughed and laughed in the bubbling, unwilling way that Claire laughs, until she had laughed the song out of herself. And out of her memory, I hoped.

Madame Blanche

Madame Blanche is back. We know it without seeing her or hearing her. The flowers in the garden stand erect, and the cat who has been sunning himself on the front doorstep uncurls and disappears. The girls sit up straight, unless they are working.

I'm in the kitchen when I hear her footsteps. She is wearing a pair of lilac glacé kid boots, buttoned at the side, with low heels. The sound of her footsteps is both delicate and solid. It's unmistakable. And inside me there's the usual shiver.

I might be afraid of her. I've seen things which ought to make me afraid. No one is more ruthless, when she thinks she has cause. She knows too much about me, just as she knows too much about everyone in this house. Each of us, at some weak point, has yielded up her secret.

I'm in the kitchen, because Solange gave notice this morning, on the grounds that the noise of the shells is getting on her nerves. But it's a bit late to be so sensitive. The shells can be heard in England, let alone here. One of the men told me that he walked on the cliffs in England, and heard the shelling.

Solange gave her notice this morning, and said she would go at once, never mind the wages owing to her. She chose this morning because she knew that Madame Blanche was out of the house.

"She makes me feel like dirt," Solange said, as she threw her belongings into her bags. Angry, stored-up words spurted from her. She was angry with herself, too, that she hadn't dared to say these words to Madame Blanche. "But what's *she*, I should like to know? Putting white gloves on her hands while her feet are wading in pigshit, that's her."

I stayed, because I saw how close to the edge she was. Solange might go crazy with a kitchen knife, slashing our velvet curtains, our plump salon upholstery, maybe even the dresses we wore.

"And what's *she*, I'd like to know? What's she that's so wonderful?"

"You know what she is, Solange," I said mildly.

"You're dead right there! I do know! And I'll make sure everyone knows what she is, before I'm finished."

She would say nothing. Everyone in town knew Madame Blanche's business. It was only the detail, the manner of it all, that they didn't care to know.

"You want to get that kiddie out of here, if you ask my advice. Your Claire. Find yourself a decent feller and get off out of here, m'm'zelle Florence. I'm saying it for your own good."

She moved close to me and looked into my face, part of her liking the drama of it, part of her, I still believe, really caring what happened to me. We had never quarreled. Solange was always good to Claire. She made apple purée for her, and chicken soup, and let Claire climb up on a stool to play with pastry.

Claire will miss Solange.

"It's not as easy as that," I said.

"Get away from here and nobody'll know what you've come from. What you've been."

I moved away from her and went to the window. "I know you mean well, Solange," I said. "But I have to think of Claire."

"It's true, a decent man won't take another feller's leavings," said Solange, without the least malice in her voice. "They like to think they're the first, even when they know they can't be." Her face changed from anger to plump pleasure. She was thinking of how she had caught the miller. She had tricked him into believing that he was the first.

Now she's packed her bags and off she's gone, trudging up to the crossroads to meet the miller. She knows that he's sixty, well past the age of military service, a prosperous and not completely ugly widower. Maybe she thinks he's a jolly feller because of his red shining face and the way he likes what he calls a good handful to get hold of on a winter night. She won't credit that he's said to have killed his first wife. Not that he ever used violence, he's not the type. That wasn't the way he took his pleasure.

He's a type that frightens me. They set their minds on one thing and they can't be diverted, no matter what. Where a normal man would yield or forget or just grow bored, a man like the miller goes on planning and working until he gets what he wants. He's got something wrong with his hands, too. I don't want to think of Solange in those hands.

He killed his wife day by day, with the drip of meanness and cruelty and lovelessness. He mocked her flat chest and the way she scurried to please him. He stared at her while she ate until she could not swallow a mouthful. I knew her, and I know she was glad to die. Anything to get away from the private torments he had devised for her.

I told Solange about her death, when I heard that the business between her and the miller was serious. She stared back at me, blank and mutinous. She told me that people had got it all wrong. She knew exactly what they were saying and it was all lies, the lot of it. In fact it was libel, she said, bringing out the word with triumph, trumping me.

She wanted her ignorance. She clung to it. Or maybe she was more of an optimist than I'd thought, and she believed she could change him. There's a third possibility, I suppose: that she hated it so much here, in this house, that any alternative was to be preferred. But I can't believe that.

So, here I am in the kitchen, taking Solange's place for the day. Carefully, I put a long metal spoon through the savory crust of sausage and white-bean casserole. A dish from home. I stir gently, so as not to pulp the beans, add a handful of parsley and replace the lid. The girls will be hungry. They are always hungry and they like big country dishes, cassoulets and casseroles and juicy hams. When our visitors are here we crumble sweet cake, but behind the scenes we draw up our chairs to the long oak table which is black with age, and tuck into a meal which lets you know you've put something in your stomach.

Madame Blanche makes sure that our establishment is not affected by food shortages.

"Florence?" says Madame Blanche. I don't startle and I don't immediately turn round. I bend to swing the heavy pot back into the oven. The oven's heat buffets my face and I'm aware of Madame Blanche's eyes on my back, on the nape of my neck, on the coils of my hair, on the muscles which flex in my arms as I push the metal rack firmly back into the oven.

She sees everything. She'll notice that my hair is not as smooth as it should be. She will think I have been with one of our visitors.

"So. Who was here, Florence? Anyone new? Anyone interesting?"

I turn to face her, wiping my hands on a kitchen cloth.

"Major Blackie and the two captains who came with him before. One went with Mariette, one with Lucie. The Major stayed in the salon, listening to Marie-Claude."

"And Gabrielle?"

"Still in bed. I've given her raspberry tea. She's really unwell."

"It's the fifth day? Or the sixth?"

"The fifth."

"Annoying," says Madame Blanche. "She should be able at least to help in the kitchen by now if she can do nothing else. It would free you. So, Solange has left us. Well, that's only what we expected, isn't it? In another day or two I would have given Solange her *congé*, but it's better that she left of her own accord. That business with the miller wasn't reflecting well on us."

And she smiles at me, broadly, as if we've cooked up Solange's departure between us, conspirators in this as in so many things.

"In fact, it was one of the reasons for my absence today," she goes on. "The new cook is engaged and she arrives tomorrow. We can give our dear Solange away to the miller without a care in our hearts."

A repulsive and unlikely image rises in my mind. Down the church aisle, out of the doorway and into the sunlight rolls Solange, locked onto the arm of her miller. She is a nightmare of orange-blossom and white lace. Behind comes Madame Blanche, smiling her broad, inscrutable smile, and following in a procession are the girls in their best dresses, chattering and laughing and throwing rice. Thank God, I don't see myself.

"Why are you smiling, my dear Florence?"

"No reason."

"When I was young I also used to smile for no reason. It's nice to see it," she adds, looking at me with those eyes which I thought were black the night I met her. But they are not black, they're a deep purplish-brown, the color of dates. She has beautifully cut eyelids, but her eyes have a sheen on them which defies you when you try to look into them. It is so hard to make out her expression. And yet sometimes, just often enough to keep you tantalized, there is something bewitchingly personal about the way she looks at you. As if she has seen all of you, down to the bone.

"So, nothing else new?"

"An officer from the aerodrome," I say casually. "His name is William Hazell. Not young."

"Who introduced him?"

As she asks, I realize I don't know.

"A pilot? A squadron leader, perhaps?"

A squadron leader! Well, I've never been able to fault Madame Blanche for lack of ambition. But in fact I've no idea what he was. Pilot . . . observer . . . maybe even a balloonatic . . .

A birdman, anyway.

"He went with Mariette," I tell her.

She nods. "Mariette has had a busy day. Remind me to give her the velvet rose in my top right-hand bureau drawer, to trim her black straw."

"Yes."

"And you, my dear Florence? What have we been able to do for you today, apart from stirring the pot, which I saw you do so competently."

"Captain Marwood came in later. Just for an hour."

"Very good. That's the fifth time—or the sixth?"

"The sixth."

"If he has friends, Florence, encourage him to bring them."

Lifelong friendships are forged quickly here. Lifelong doesn't mean the same as it does in normal life, although that's not to say it means any less. One fine afternoon four young brother-officers may sit in our salon, smoking each other's cigarettes, asking each other to hum the songs they have half-forgotten, so that Marie-Claude can play them. Even though she'd prefer to impress us all with Liszt, she likes the warm, rapt faces and the way they sing along when she plays.

They lean against each other and talk in their own language which I have to learn just as much as the other girls, even though my English is perfect. If they are from the aerodrome, they talk about good shows and bad shows and Archie and dropping eggs. They laugh at each other's jokes, clothes and singing voices. They talk about having the wind-up sometimes, though always with a laugh and always in the past tense. They bite their nails and their hands shake. But as long as all their nails are bitten, and all their glasses spill over if they're filled too full, and all of them get the wind-up sometimes, then the badness of it is divided, too.

They are like us, although it feels wrong to say it, even inside my own head. If each one of us had to live the days we live alone, how would this life be possible? But we have patterns and they weave us together. We are a group, just as the men are a group. Imagine if they heard me say that.

We look out for each other. Mariette will perch on Gabrielle's bed to show her how the velvet rose looks on the black straw, and let her know that Madame's really on the warpath this time, so Gabrielle had better slap on rouge and get herself down into the salon sharpish. *"And you're silly about drink, Gabi, you ought to try a couple of brandies. It gets you through with that nice warm feeling inside you."*

Sometimes I wonder how the men manage to peel away from their friendship for long enough to go to bed with us. But even when they're in bed with us, they don't separate from each other, not really. We're part of the group life they live. One goes with Mariette this time, his friend the next. It's as close as they can get to going to bed with one another, which they would never do. They compare experiences afterward. They talk about our breasts and our hips, but not about the things that really surprise them, such as the smell of us and the hair we have and where we have it, and the way our bodies look so much larger when we are naked than when we are dressed, and the way we are still in control when they have lost themselves and are panting and gasping as if their lives are in our hands. They don't talk about any of these things.

"Will you remember me, Florence?" one of them asked once. He had rolled off me clumsily, and was lying on his back smoking a cigarette. He was a nice boy, with red hair and fine, thin skin. And a smile that let me know he was no fool. I can't remember what he was called. He came a few times, then he stopped coming. I do remember that he was eighteen, six years younger than me. But there was something else. He was one of the few, the very few, who realized that I had a child.

While he was smoking his cigarette, Claire began to cry, out in the garden. A sudden, piercing yell and then a silence that quivered. She was trying to get her breath. She must have fallen hard.

No one came to her straightaway. The silence broke and she began to cry again, hard and rhythmic. I sat up in bed to listen. It was a strong, angry cry so I knew she hadn't hurt herself much. But why didn't anyone come? And then feet came running across the terrace.

"Oh, Clairey, I thought you'd half-killed yourself, and now look at you, only a beensy little scratch on your knee. I can't even hardly see it—"

It was Gabrielle. She'd be pressing Claire's red, wet face against her neck. Gabi loved to hold Claire.

"You come along with Auntie Gabrielle, she's got something to show you, if you're a good girl...." Her voice receded. She would be walking down into the orchard, carrying Claire, who wasn't crying anymore. The red-haired boy was watching me.

"My sister's got a boy and a girl," he said. "Twins. She harks just like you did, when one of 'em sings out. She can tell if it's anything wrong, just from the noise they make. She says there's all sorts of crying."

"Yes."

"It's your kid, isn't it?"

"Yes."

"Does she live here with you?"

"Where else would she live?"

He nodded, and got up from the bed.

I listen to Madame Blanche's lilac heels tapping away down the corridor. She will look into every room she passes, pausing, assessing, a word here and a word there, a smile for Mariette, a long, considering frown for Gabrielle. Then to her own apartments, as they're called. Her bedroom, and her little private salon where she receives her own visitors. She will be drawing the pins from her hat now. Another name will be lodged in the account book she keeps in her mind. William Hazell. She will remember that he is from the aerodrome. She will remember the colorless voice in which I gave her his name.

Here's Marguerite.

"'selle Florence, Claire's ready to say goodnight."

"I'll be up in a minute, Marguerite."

I want to pick up my skirts and race up the two flights of stairs to the attic room where Claire nestles in her cot-bed, rosy and big-eyed with sleepiness, right hand curled around her plush mouse, left thumb in her mouth. Half asleep already. But I wouldn't want anyone to hear the beat of my footsteps, the eagerness in them, the way my whole body longs to catch Claire up and press her, press her tight to my heart at the end of yet another day in this house, which is also our home. I don't want Madame Blanche to hear the hunger in my steps. I don't want her to note anything more in the account book she makes of my soul.

Dearest Rebecca,

(If you've got this far . . .)

What I realized after thinking about Florence and writing about her was how weary she is. She's a young woman but she's weary. She's being used up. She prostitutes herself so that Claire will survive and she will survive. The officers are clean, the house is elegant, there's a garden, there's music, the food is good and plentiful. But the fact is that Florence is there to be used until she's used up, like the other girls.

Madame Blanche has her eye on Florence, that's true. She makes an exception of her. She's grooming Florence. Maybe that offers a way out. But otherwise, if Florence is lucky and she doesn't start drinking or drugging herself, she might put by enough to start a little business of her own one day. A dressmaking business, maybe. That's about her best bet. Solange thinks she can start again elsewhere and maybe find a man who will take her on, but Solange is fooling herself, and Florence knows it. The miller has taken her on and he intends to punish her for it.

Florence hasn't got much choice—not in that part of the field of history in which she finds herself. No housing benefit for Florence, no help with childcare costs.

She's tough in her way, you'll have seen that. She's very controlled and very observant. She makes herself live from hour to hour. Has

Claire had her face washed, is the piano tuned, will it soon be time to pick the baby turnips? Her mind is full of those things. She finds comfort in them; at least, she thinks it is comfort.

She will never tell anyone everything. Even Claire won't guess how much her mother loves her. When she's older she'll believe that Florence is too tough on her.

The thing about wartime love stories is that usually there are no boundaries or barriers. War breaks them. But that isn't going to happen here. A woman so weary, so controlled, so wrapped up in her child, and a middle-aged man who is married and whose wife is expecting a child that he doesn't want. (I'm going ahead of the story, and telling you what Florence doesn't know yet.) Will isn't a boy, he's not one of those fresh-faced handsome public schoolboys we all know about, with a book of poems in his breast pocket. He's a middle-aged man. He's got a wife, and a child coming that means almost nothing to him. He's not a cold man, but he's tired, too, like Florence. He's worked for an insurance company for years. He wanted to be an architect, but he'd never tell anyone that now. It was too big a leap for a boy whose father was a tin-miner.

Will learned to fly before the war. They didn't have a child for years and he saved and paid for his pilot's training. He would go off to the aerodrome Sunday after Sunday. His wife hated it.

Florence doesn't know any of this yet. But I'm letting you into the story.

Speaking English Perfectly

The room where I sleep is long enough for a single bed, and wide enough for the door to swing open. It is in the attics, next to Claire. There's an iron bedstead with a striped ticking mattress, darned linen, a darned white counterpane. There's a rag rug on the boards, and the walls are white. I scrubbed the boards myself, and polished them with beeswax and turpentine, and I painted the walls white. The dormer window looks out and away, over roofs into treetops and sky. My window faces west, away from the war.

It looks toward England. At home our house faced east, into the morning. We had a courtyard where grapevines grew over pillars. My mother would point north, and east.

"England is that way, Florence. Over the sea. One day you'll go there."

But she said it as if it couldn't happen, and it never did. My mother told me how the wind always blew in England, even inside the houses, and how dark it was in the winters. She hadn't been back in more than twenty years. But sometimes in August, when it was so hot that she lay on her bed in her chemise and I lay close, she would say different things. She would say that they had Romans in England, just as we had them in Orange. But up there they built for war, not pleasure. No wonderful amphitheaters and circuses. They built a wall across the land, from sea to sea, and patrolled it with soldiers.

"Why did they build it, Maman?"

"To keep the wild people out, Florence."

I don't have blinds at the dormer window, or curtains. When I wake up the sky is there immediately, to let me know what the day will be like. At night the stars come so close you'd think they were elbowing their way through the glass.

My bed is narrow, but not too narrow for Claire to cuddle in beside me when she wakes in the night. I hear her as soon as she stirs and I'm out of bed before I know that I'm awake. I scoop her out of the tangled cot and press her face against my shoulder so she won't wake anyone. When she was a baby she smelled of mashed potatoes when she woke up red and sweaty. Now she smells of vanilla. In my bed she tucks close to me, at my back, with a bunch of my nightdress in her fist. I lie awake a little longer and watch the stars. Sometimes there's a moon and the clouds fly over it so fast it feels as if we're flying too. I wish that time would stop and we would always be here, safe, with Claire curled into sleep and the house still and silent beneath us.

Madame Blanche didn't want me to have this room. I have a perfectly good room downstairs with a thick red carpet, green silk curtains, a washstand and a wide bed. Madame Blanche is very proud of our rooms. Everything in them was chosen by her. They are elegant, restrained, tasteful, she thinks.

"Except for the mirror," said Gabrielle. She was in my room, leaning over the dressing table, fixing her back-hair. "Look where she's put it."

I looked. "Dressing-table mirrors are always like that."

"Not that mirror," said Gabrielle in her quick, cutting voice. "The one over there."

"Oh, yes," I said, smiling, as if I'd known and understood all along what the mirror over there was for. And the china figures in Mariette's room that I'd never looked at too closely. A book here, a picture there.

"She makes me laugh. Like they haven't got the point already. Like they don't know what kind of house they're in."

That was when I first came. Gabrielle remembers what I was like then, but the others don't. They all came after I did. There's a lot of coming and going here.

But Marie-Claude thinks her bedroom is lovely. She dusts it and polishes the furniture herself, and when she has a day off she washes all her ornaments in soapy water, rearranges them and replaces their labels if they're stained or faded. Marie-Claude collects china baskets of flowers. They all have different names and Marie-Claude makes labels for each basket, in her best handwriting, decorated with curlicues and sprigs of flowers. *Country Garden, Rose Bower, Maiden Dreaming, Sweet Violets.* Marie-Claude is saving up for *Bridal Posy.*

I told Madame Blanche I couldn't sleep downstairs. It gave me bad dreams. She didn't like it, but she gave in. She doesn't come up here. No one does, except Claire, and sometimes Marguerite.

"You'll have a room of your own," said Madame Blanche the first time we met. It was late December, the first winter of the war. I was five months pregnant with Claire. I was on my way north, to find work.

The question is, what was Madame Blanche doing in the third-class carriage? I didn't think of it until much later. She had plenty of money. What was she doing on those hard, dirty seats which smelled of coal?

Now I believe that she had spotted me as I changed trains, among the market women and closed-faced men and raw boys going to be soldiers. I must have given so much away, while I thought I was hiding it all.

⁓

The young woman is traveling alone, late in the evening, in a third-class compartment of the Paris train. She is wearing a dark blue woolen skirt and jacket, edged with black braid, well-cut and obviously handmade. Her hair is dark, thick, smooth, drawn into a knot. Her hands are gloved and her expression composed. (This is what I saw in the mirror as I stood in my bedroom at home for the last time. I looked perfectly calm, even serene. Perhaps a little pale, and it's true that there was a rash on my neck, hidden by my high-collared blouse, and a cluster of tiny spots on the left side of my chin. I never have spots. My lips were pressed firmly together. I took a good look at myself, like a burglar checking that no signs of his intentions will give him away as he strolls casually down the street, whistling and glancing up at shuttered windows.)

⁓

As she changes for the Paris train, the young woman signals a porter to transfer her luggage, which consists of a valise, a large basket and a hatbox. The porter heads up the train to the first-class compartment, and she has to pull at his arm and tell him that no, it is the third-class compartment she wants. He becomes surly after this, expecting a small tip or none. He slams the luggage into the third-class compartment in a way that conveys his disrespect. She flushes, scrabbles in her bag, overtips him. He walks away, flicking the coin she's given him.

Once in the compartment, the young woman reaches up to stow her hatbox safely in the rack. The movement shows that her waist is thickened by pregnancy. When she has reassured herself that the hatbox is not going to be crushed, she squeezes into a seat between two market women who smell of wine. She closes her eyes and appears to fall asleep as the train jogs north. But her gloved hands are not sleeping. They clutch the small black bag on her lap as if it contains her whole life.

∗

So, as you see, I left plenty of clues. Half of them would have been enough for Madame Blanche.

∗

It was a corridor train. There were people standing in the corridor and among them was Madame Blanche. At the next station, the two market women got out, barging the other passengers with their empty baskets. This was the stopping train, not the express. I leaned forward and watched the two women clamber down the steps, hoist their baskets and go off down the tracks together. They were home. It was a halt in the middle of nowhere, no lights. They would cross the cinders, find the muddy lane that meant home. It was a fine night, with a moon. There would be cottages where they were expected, maybe even welcomed. They would talk of prices and how the market had gone. Maybe they'd lie about how much they'd made, and keep back a few sous for a jug of wine the next time.

I wanted to be them. They looked as if they'd already barged their way through enough suffering and sorrow to get the measure of it. Now they'd be lifting the latch of the door, scolding the dog, checking that the fire had not been allowed to go out.

In the train window my face looked back at me. My hair was still smooth from the brushing I'd given it that morning.

If I went north I would find work. I could cook, or sew, or work in a laundry. I knew how to do all those things. I would look for a job where accommodation was provided.

I would become a widow. My husband had died in the first days of the war, before I knew I was pregnant. He had left me nothing to live on and his family had never liked the marriage.

- But if you are a widow, why are you wearing blue?
- I have not got enough money to buy mourning.
- Silly girl, doesn't she know that half the world hasn't got money to buy mourning? Stick your clothes in a vat of black dye, that's what you do. When they try to come up, bulging and roiling in the inky water, thump them down with a stick. That's the way to get the dye even.

It was a good, easy story, but it had holes in it already.

The north was where I was going, close to the war. People wouldn't ask so many questions there. There would be plenty of work. There were new factories opening, to make munitions. They wanted women workers there.

I shivered. It was getting cold already. This was the north. The smell of the engine smoke nauseated me, and the smell of sweat and onions. I must get out to the corridor.

The door was heavy and my vision was starting to break up into patches of blackness. There was sweat on my face. I tugged the door but it wouldn't open. I pulled again as hard as I could, hurting myself.

It gave way and I was in the corridor. The noise of the train was fierce out here. Every vent rattled but there was more air. Two men crouched on their haunches, playing cards, and they looked up at me as I pushed past them. I had to step high, between them, and I held my skirt close so that they could not see my legs.

There was a draft. I got as close to the window as I could and pressed my forehead to the glass. I breathed deeply and the clean air pushed down the nausea that was trying to swamp me. I was getting the better of it—

"Here," said a woman's voice. "Have some of this."

It was the silver cap of a flask. The smell of brandy made me gag and I pushed it away.

"No. Drink it. You'll feel better immediately."

Her voice made me follow the instruction. I lifted the silver cap and drank, and as the brandy went down my gullet, my nausea dissolved into fire.

"That's not enough. Drink more."

I drank more. I drank off the capful and she refilled it. I drank that, too.

"You haven't eaten," she said.

"No—" It was true. The ham and cheese sandwiches at the buffet had looked stale.

"I have some biscuits. They're very good. They're oat biscuits."

I thought her eyes were black. They were hard to read, but her face was concerned, and I thought it seemed kind. Rain had begun and it made runnels which joined and parted on the black windows. We seemed to be going faster now, banging and rattling into the night.

"Thank you," I said. "I feel much better."

"You should be careful, in your condition," she said. "Are you traveling alone?"

"Yes."

"And you're going all the way to Paris. You won't be there until morning."

"I know that."

"It's a very slow train. No matter. As long as you have someone to talk to, it's tolerable. And something to eat and drink."

"Are you going as far as Paris yourself?"

"Beyond Paris. Towards Béthune, do you know it?"

"No, not at all."

"You're a southerner, of course. But from where?"

"From Aix," I said. "Aix-en-Provence."

"Ah, yes. I know it well."

Better than I do, in that case, I thought, and nearly smiled. She caught it.

"What makes you smile?"

"Nothing."

"That's nice. It's only the young who smile for no reason," she added. "Once you grow older, once you have cares of your own—" and her glance slid down over my waist. "They don't last long, those care-free years."

"No." The brandy was working in me. I felt bold and indifferent. As long as the journey lasted, I had nothing to fear. I was a passenger like everyone else, with a ticket I'd paid for in my bag. No one knew who I was or where I came from, and they certainly didn't know where I was going. In the racket of the train we were all equal. Even the smell of drink and the quarrel of the card players didn't bother me anymore. I was equal to them, too. Until the train stopped it wouldn't matter who had a home to go to, and who had none.

"But there's something in your voice that isn't at all southern," she said.

"My mother is English. We always spoke English together," I said. Maybe her quickness had startled it out of me.

"English? Really?" The strength of her interest surprised me. "And so you speak English perfectly?"

"I suppose so. If my mother speaks English perfectly, then so do I."

"Say something to me," she demanded suddenly. I laughed. "Speak to me in English," she insisted.

"Do you understand it yourself?"

She shrugged. "A few words here and there."

"It is a truth universally acknowledged," I began rapidly in English, "that a single man in possession of a good fortune must be in want of a wife."

"Ah, that's very good!" she exclaimed, as if enchanted with me. "One would think it was your mother tongue."

She had not believed a word I had told her. I put this aside to think about later.

"And you can speak to anybody, just like that, in English? You can understand everything they say?"

"Yes."

"It's remarkable," she breathed. Then she gathered herself and spoke more blandly. "You are going to stay with relations," she stated.

"No."

Why not tell the truth? We were on a train. She would only remember a pale young woman from Aix-en-Provence, who spoke English. I could say what I liked.

"You are going to join your husband," she guessed again.

"No. I have no husband."

"Ah."

"I'm a widow," I said, a little too late, and a little too brazenly. But I didn't care. "My husband died in the war."

"Ah," she repeated. "Well, there are many like that. You are certainly not alone."

"On the contrary, I am completely alone," I said. The train swayed and I caught hold of the window strap to steady myself.

"It only seems so," said the woman, surprising me.

"What do you mean?"

"You are talking to me. You are not alone."

I shrugged. "Well, of course, if you want to be literal—"

"You're talking to me. I am interested in you. Who knows where that might lead?"

"It'll lead to Paris, and then you'll get off the train and go in your direction and I'll get off and go in mine."

"Not necessarily. Listen. The train's slowing down. When we come into the station, allow me to take you to my compartment. There will be no difficulty about the ticket. It's not reasonable for you to be traveling in third class, in your condition."

It was her look that captured me. Intent, grave, almost motherly. She put her gloved hand on my arm and said again, "It really isn't reasonable. You'll be much better off with me. Just as far as Paris, if you prefer."

No. It was like that, but not like that. I must tell the truth. It was my own weakness that captured me. I was hungry, and tired, and afraid. She offered shelter, and the chance that when the train stopped I would know where I was going. I had brandy boldness then, but no real courage. It wasn't until Claire was born that I began to have real courage.

"*On s'occupera de vous,*" she said.

At the next station a porter fetched my bags immediately, and transferred them to the first-class compartment. I felt as if a protective veil had fallen between me and the rest of the world, whereas before I had been naked.

The train began to move again, and I sat back and rested my head against the cushioned softness. I could scarcely hear the rattling of the vents and the thump of the wheels. The little lamps above each seat glowed softly.

"My name is Blanche Lepage, but I am always known as Madame Blanche," she said, as she reached up to unpin her hat. "Please call me that. There, that's better. Would you like to make yourself a little more comfortable? No one will come in. Take off your jacket, loosen your collar. It's a long journey at the best of times, and now, with the war—even the Paris taxis have been commandeered to take reinforcements to the front. Who cares how long it takes us to travel on our own little affairs?"

I stood to take off and carefully fold my jacket.

"Your skirt is tight," said Madame Blanche. "Do you want to loosen it?"

I had let out the waistband already and my skirt no longer hung well. I would have to alter it again. I really didn't know what women did about clothes when they were pregnant. It wasn't something I'd ever heard discussed. If my mother had had another child after me, probably I'd have known.

We sat down opposite each other. She wanted to talk, I could see that. She sat firm and upright, not allowing her back to touch the cushioned seat. I straightened myself.

"You have nowhere to go," she said.

"Not yet. I shall find work."

"What sort of work?"

"Any sort."

"What experience have you got?"

"I can nurse."

"Nurse—what, you're a trained nurse? But they won't have you in any hospital, my dear. You must know that."

"I'm not a trained nurse. But I assisted—a doctor I know. And I can cook, clean, sew, launder. I've heard there are jobs in munitions."

"There are, and there'll be more. But again, not in your condition."

"My condition won't last forever."

"What do you mean? My poor child, if you intended to do something about it, let me tell you that it's much too late. You would be risking your life."

"I didn't mean that." I flushed deeply, from shame at my own ignorance, from not knowing the depth of the waters under me. "I mean that babies are born after nine months, aren't they? And then I can work."

"And then you will have a child to care for. Unless you give it away."

"Give it away? To whom?"

She laughed. "That's exactly the question, isn't it? To someone who doesn't want it, I daresay. Who won't take care of it. Or into an orphanage, where it'll grow up to be a servant if it's lucky. You've never been inside an orphanage, I daresay. From the point of view of those in charge, it's a good system. The babies can't tell anyone what goes on.

All they can do is cry. And after a while they stop crying. No. Let me talk to you seriously, my dear. But good heavens, here are we talking like this, and I don't even know your name."

"It's Florence."

"Just Florence?"

"Florence Hirondelle," I said, and again she didn't believe a word of it.

"You'll allow me to call you Florence? After all, I'm old enough to be your mother."

She was, just. She would be somewhere in her late thirties, I thought, although it was difficult to tell. I could now see that her eyes were not black. They shone in the lamplight. They made me think of fruit: black grapes, which are not really black at all, or ripe dates. She had beautiful hands. They were small and strong and flexible, and she wore expensive rings. A sapphire in a nest of diamonds, a solid ruby set in claws of gold.

"Well, Florence," she continued, "I have a little proposal to make to you. Don't feel that you must answer me straightaway. We have plenty of time. We can chat, get to know one another. I have a basket here. We can have a little late supper. You like cold chicken? Good. So there's no hurry. You don't have to make your decision until we get to Paris."

Her voice was calm again. It had roughened when she talked about the orphanage. Her voice was like the muffled beat of the train wheels. It was carrying me onward, elsewhere. It was what I wanted to hear.

The Aerodrome

It's a fine, brisk day. The sky's packed with fast-moving white clouds, and there's no threat of rain. The atmospheric pressure is steadily high, and the barometer is set at fair.

Inside the tents, heat has collected. There are rows of camp beds, neat in the gloom. The smell is of holidays and childhood. The heavy khaki canvas filters out the sun's brilliance and turns it green. It's very still. When you come out of the tent, the world looks pink for a few minutes.

Will Hazell lies on his back on the camp bed third from the tent flap. His arms pillow his head. Will breathes in through his nose, out through his mouth. The sound of his breathing is soft, but definite. It's a good sound. He listens to the draw of his breath, watches the rise and fall of his chest. You could go into a dream like this for hours. He can switch off and watch an ant walk from one side of the blanket to another. It doesn't bore him, no matter how long it takes.

His mind is stretched, blank. It's something to do with the way they sleep, or don't sleep. The way hours of green calm are punctuated by a fury of sound and heat and smoke, the buffet of shell explosions, the brilliant edges of clouds, the zizz and stitch of machine-gun fire. The frenzy of not knowing what the hell is going on and yet being in charge of it. Only afterward it starts to make shapes. The shapes make it safe. The clipped clichés make it safe. Say them over and over and over and they'll come true.

It was a bloody good show over Oppy. How many hostiles? Did you see me side-slip? I had the bugger on my tail. Thought I'd stall but I pulled out of it all right.

All of them learn the clipped words, no matter where they come from. It's a new language and you wear it like a mask. No one has seen or described these things before.

Frizell told his story in the Mess, how he held his course at five hundred feet along the railway. There was Archie everywhere and he could see the men looking up and pointing their rifles at him. He knew where he had to lay his egg. There was a junction outside the station. The Huns were bringing up troop trains, packed with reinforcements. That was the language you had to use. You didn't speak of men.

Frizell leaned against the piano and shaped what had happened. But Will had seen him land, seen Frizell walk away unwounded from his shot-up plane. His face was wet and wild, and one hand went up as if to tell the sky what had happened. Frizell halted and stood directly in front of Will. He was a big man, the handsomest man in the Mess. His skin was brown, his eyes the blue of water with Robin starch in it. He stopped in front of Will and seized his hand. Frizell's grip was icy. He was a boy, Will thought. He stopped in front of Will because his father wasn't there.

"God has been good to me. . . . He has been good to me," he stammered. His eyes had a gloss on them like drunkenness, his face was out of shape. But in the Mess, Frizell was back to himself. He had gone down to five hundred feet but it wasn't enough. He had gone down to three hundred feet, two hundred feet, a hundred and fifty. He'd kept the track bouncing dead below him as the Nieuport took the rip of bullets along the port wing and Archie exploded all around him. There was a machine-gun emplacement on the station roof. Frizell had seen the face of the gunner through the smoke. But he held on and there was the train. He dived and laid his egg just where he ought and then he pulled the nose up sharp, so sharp he nearly stalled but the explosion pushed him on up. He had got the train. He was so low by then that he nearly hit a nest of telegraph wires. They were still firing on him. There was oil leaking everywhere and his engine had missed all the way back, with the wind against him.

The wind is always against them. The westerly prevailing wind pushes them deep over the German lines, and doesn't want to let them come home.

God has been good to me. . . . He has been good to me. Frizell won't want to remember that. They were all pressing close around Frizell in the Mess. The blaze in his face had gone out. He was himself again, the handsome bastard with the luck that everyone wanted.

⁊❦⁊

Green calm goes on collecting in the warm, quiet tent. Beyond the tents, beyond the fields and hangars, beyond the aerodrome—but not so very far beyond—there's the front. The sound of the guns is like that of an unfamiliar but vital industrial process. A few miles from Will, men in trenches are sweating, packed into the tiny homes they've created from boards and mud. They pick lice from the seams of their tunics. The lice crunch and bleed a little dark brown blood. The men boil up water and swallow the rum issue. They bind the sores on their feet and grease their guns. Will knows what they do, but he is not part of it. He is a birdman and his job lies above.

He has been six days in France. These first two to three weeks are the most dangerous for a new pilot. He was sent out from England in haste. He knew how to fly but not how to fly and fire and navigate and keep watch at the same time. They'd half-trained him.

Policy dictates that there are never any empty seats at the Mess table. From a distance it looks as if no one ever dies. One face replaces another, as if on a shift system. If Will learns quickly, if he makes a fast, strong climb toward the knowledge no one back in a training camp in England can give, he might get through. They've given him a Nieuport and he trained on a Pup. He's flown the Nieuport every hour he's had. He'll fly it until he knows it. He'll get the better of it.

He lies still in the tent. His eyes are not quite shut. He's aware of light and shade: more light as someone lifts the tent flap, shadow again as a body fills the entrance, light as the newcomer pads toward his camp bed, lies down carefully so that it won't creak too loudly. They are careful of each other's sleep.

When it gets warmer they'll put the camp beds under the trees in daytime. That's where they'll rest, between shows. Will's always had a dream about sleeping in a bed out in green fields. Safe and snug in the blankets, white sheets up to his chin while the clouds sail overhead and the world goes on with its work. Snug as a bug in a rug. There won't be white sheets, of course. One hour they will be lying on their backs, faces stroked by the warm summer wind, and the next they will be bucking in high cloud, riding the lumpiness of air that looks so pure from below.

You need sleep so much. He would never have thought he would need to sleep so much. Twelve hours isn't near enough. He sees that same desire in all the faces around him. They want to be in the black, as he does. Pinned down by heavy clothes, by coats.

For the next few hours he knows he won't die. Out of habit, he has begun a letter to his wife, and it lies beside his bed.

I hope you are . . .

What does he hope she is?

In the tent the light is green. Outside, the grass is thick and deep by the hedges. Will has walked through it, waded thigh-deep in it, watched its pollen brush off onto him. Where one of the tents has been moved recently, there's a long yellow oblong with new green shoots among the etiolated grass. There are scuff marks where the entry was.

Cow parsley, buttercup and wild garlic are flowering, wood pigeons roll the sound of summer over and over inside their throats. It's idyllic. There's a stream, a little bridge, a farmhouse. There's even a rumor that someone's got hold of a cow and there's going to be fresh milk in the Mess.

You can stroll about in the fresh air and the sunshine. You don't have to zigzag or keep your head down.

Each pilot and observer and mechanic has made a tour of the front line. You need to know what it's all about and what you're here for. There is the artillery. Aerial photography and Morse information will give those guns their fixes. There are the men, sunburned, troglodytic, who will look to you for protection against hostiles flying low during troop movements, machine-gunning the infantry just as you will machine-gun the enemy infantry. They watch you warily, as if you're another species, which you are. There is the close-up, intimate, permanent chaos of the line, from which those men can't escape, and into which you can't enter.

From above, Will knows the front line as the men will never know it. It is unsheeted for him on these pure blue mornings. No one has seen a war like this before. His plane swoops over it in a second. Our lines. Hunland.

Even if all you can see is smoke, the camera sees more. Keep on taking photographs. They will show more than you can see.

Will thinks about coming down in Hunland, and being taken prisoner.

"Might as well put your toothbrush in, sir," says Spit Quinn, his mechanic. "There's plenty to do. I heard of a man once, went up in a

BE2 with the *Complete Works of Shakespeare*. But don't let the squadron leader see you packing your pajamas. He reckons it's defeatist."

❦

Will carries chocolate in his breast pocket. He pictures himself offering it to French children who will, in return, hide him in the outhouse of their conveniently nearby cottages. Better to picture the unwrapping of chocolate than the long living fall from seven thousand feet, arms and legs whirling. Or a flamer.

Are you conscious all the way down?

Will hates his own ignorance. All his life Will has fought for knowledge. It's his brains that have got him where he is. Otherwise he would be where those others are, trench fodder, hunkered in mud that won't go away even when it's summer. He would be itching in a khaki uniform that fitted roughly and bore the sweetish smell of lice.

Who would have thought that a scholarship boy would even enter death on a different plane? He's at the top of the ladder here. He's so high up the ladder that he's not even on it anymore. He's in the clouds. And when he's not flying he comes down onto green fields beyond the range of guns and shells. He sleeps in a bed, he eats at a table, and lights a cigarette without cupping it in his hands to conceal its glow when he inhales.

"When you get a blockage, this is where it'll most likely be," says Spit, tapping the barrel of the Lewis gun. Will Hazell nods, but in a perfunctory way that makes Spit glance at him again. Is he taking all this in? Does he understand what Spit's trying to do: pack survival into his new pilot?

What Spit doesn't yet know is that Will's nod means that the knowledge is safely in, and Spit can go on.

"Get a blockage you can't deal with, you're unprotected," warns Spit.

❦

Spit and Will have more in common than the Nieuport. Spit would know his way blindfolded around the household Will Hazell comes from. He would recognize the food on the plates, and the knit of worry and satisfaction on Will's mother's face as she watches her children eat so fast their plates are empty in five minutes. He'd know those washday Mondays: cold bacon clapped between two hunks of bread, and don't come back till your sister fetches you. Backbreaking, short-tempered washday Mondays. At the end of them Will's mother sits at the front door, luxuriating in a cup of tea while her clean laundry cracks in the wind.

A granite tin-miner's cottage for Will, with five children, two adults and a skinny black dog sharing four rooms and a kitchen. A red-brick terrace in Manchester for Spit Quinn.

Will's father was quick, too, but no scholarships came his way. He worked far out under the sea. The sea boomed overhead, waiting its chance. One day it would get into the tunnelwork. That was always the sea's intention, as sure as it was blind. Joseph Hazell had the instincts of an engineer. He understood the materials that surrounded him, the balance of pressure and counterpressure, water and stone, the moley tunnels feeling their way out, braced and buttressed and infinitely vulnerable. He picked up the minute signs of stress that meant the balance was out of true. A creak, a crack, a pooling of water where no water was before, a candle that blew out and stubbornly wouldn't relight. Warning signs.

If Joe Hazell says it's time to get out, you drop your pick, get out and don't wait for nothing. It's the sea you've got on top of you.

The Atlantic of Will's childhood. He didn't know it was called the Atlantic, not till he grew older and learned what the world was and where he was in it. The schoolmaster had an old wreck map he brought in and unrolled to show. In those days the edge of the map was drawn so it looked as if you were falling off the edge of the world.

He knew the sea long before he knew what it was. Green and turquoise, a cold glove prickling all over his body as he went in naked with the other boys. They dived off rocks, skinned their knees and elbows scrambling out of the sea, watched the thin blood trail and coil in the clear rock pools. They clapped a hand over their privates to protect them from the razor-sharp mussels as they scrambled over the rocks.

The sea was alive with rips. Will got caught in the rip once, when he was ten. He knew what to do but it still shocked him. The rip took hold of him like the arm of a strong man hauling him off for mischief. It was colder than the rest of the sea, and it knew exactly what it wanted to do with him. It wanted to take him and drown him.

He looked at the land and it was moving in the wrong direction. Will knew he had to swim on the cross, until he was out of the rip. He knew not to fight it. Fighting made you weak, and then the sea did for you. He knew boys who had fought—well, he didn't know them, but they were part of the story he grew up with, their drowned selves bobbing in, swollen, on the tide, their fingertips and their soft eyes eaten out by crabs.

As the rip seized him he knew those boys were close. He twisted sideways and pushed down the panic that rose in his throat and wanted to stop him from swimming and breathing. The sea was running rough now. It hadn't been rough before. It was the rip getting hold of him.

He didn't fight. He turned on his stomach, kicked out, steadied himself into the strong breaststroke that could take him a mile or more. He swam on the cross. He was ten years old, skinny and strong. He was caught in the rip. He was not going to die yet.

It was very cold. He wondered where the others were. They'd come up on shore and he'd gone off across the rocks and hadn't said where he was going. He hadn't told them he was going to swim out.

He swam on, bubbling and gasping. He seemed to be low down in the water, or else the water was up on top of him. The rip pulled at his naked body, wanting it. He couldn't feel all of himself anymore.

Bright water slapped in his eyes. He saw pieces of sky. He was swimming into deeper water, out of the bay. It was the only way to get out of the rip. No one from shore would see the smallness of his head in the bouncing of the waves. No one would help him or look for him until it was too late.

Suddenly a thought rose in him which he had never thought before. His father was under the sea, beneath him. He was down there, in his tunnel, burrowing out under the sea. He had a lamp and he was dry, or only wet with sweat. If Will reached down, through the water, the sand, the rock, he would touch his father's hand.

He swam out of the rip. It came all at once. The fringes of it made a last pull for him, but they were weak. The rip slid off him and he was out into clean deep water. The swell pushed him and the waves pushed him, but there was no rip anymore.

He was very cold, and far out. Not as far as he'd ever been, but far enough. He trod water and raised his head as high as he could, to see where he should come in. If he got caught again he would drown, but he wouldn't get caught. There was the place he would aim, where there was an apron of sand between the rocks. He would come in there and he would be safe.

But for a moment he stayed out in the deep water, sculling with his hands and treading with his feet. He was intensely aware of the veiny passages beneath him, where his father was. His father might look up and think of the world above him as he worked. He would never think of Will being there too, almost within grasp.

❦

Will is alive. He'll do what the other pilots do. Sometimes, on the way back from a show, they play in and out of the clouds. When the pursuit is over and death has packed up his bags for the day.

They run their machines down the seams of a cloud. They hide in caves no one has ever seen before. Inside the shine of the sky there are these caves, the color of irises. They bare their teeth for joy at the beauty of it, these fighting men in their tattered aeroplanes. They reach out to touch it, like corporals in muddied, bloody khaki who can't see any reason not to pluck a dog rose from the hedges as they march.

I hope you are . . . I hope you will be . . .

Sweet Dreams

No, Rebecca, I'm not going to tell you about Will's wife. Not yet. I'm not even going to tell you her name. This is the story of Will and Florence.

Will dreams. His body twitches. He throws up his right arm to ward off a blow.

There's a fight going on. Two figures, knotted together. Both of them are naked, so close that he can't see if they are both men or not. But they must be. Only men would fight with that deadly poisonous intent. One of them is trying to force the other down onto a bed. There are grunts and groans, but neither cries out. The bed is a camp bed like his own. *It won't take your weight,* he wants to warn them. *It'll collapse, can't you see that?*

And then he sees something else they don't see. The beds are not beds at all. Really they are planes, frail with struts and wires. They will never take that pressure.

"*She's spinning,*" a voice says, very quietly.

"*Look out, old chaps,*" says someone else in a lazy drawl, as if the whole thing is a gigantic joke.

They are right. The pilot has lost control. The bed that was a plane spins faster and faster, into its own vortex. In the blind heart of it the two men are still fighting. They do not know what is going on.

Will's lungs ache with agony and terror. He tries to cry out, but his voice is crushed down into his lungs. There is no air where he is.

Watch out for the rip! Watch out for the rip!

He wakes struggling. There is Frizell standing by his camp bed, looking down. He's in flying kit, with his goggles pushed up above his brow.

"What time is it?" asks Will quickly.

"Five," says Frizell. "You all right, old man?"

He is carrying his gauntlets, tapping them against his thigh. The skin of his hands is golden brown. Will swings his legs off the bed, stands, pushes his way toward the flap of daylight.

It is still the same afternoon. Warmish, but more clouded now. At the far end of the field a man runs up to bowl against a single batsman and a single fielder, as if the stutter of an incoming Pup engine has nothing to do with them. Frizell looks up, shades his eyes, scans the sky.

"That'll be O'Hagan back again. Yes, it's him. Good-oh."

Will swallows the ugly metal taste in his mouth. His heart is still hammering. He watches, until the hedge hides it, another man enjoy the best moment of all: landing safe back at your own aerodrome, with your machine more or less intact, yourself and observer (if you have one) more or less unscathed.

"You didn't look as if you were having sweet dreams," says Frizell, offering Will a cigarette. Will takes one, they both light up, but Frizell forgets to smoke his. He stares at the cigarette in his hand as if wondering what it is.

"I'd be a fool if I was," says Will.

"What?"

"Having sweet dreams."

"Too true," says Frizell, his face clearing. For a moment he looks his real age, which Will knows is two months short of twenty.

"Where're you going?" he asks.

"Taking Dutton on his familiarization. They're sending us pilots who haven't even completed their gunnery course. What the hell kind of chance have they got? Then when we complain about the lack of training, they say it's impossible to train anyone for what they'll find out here, anyway. Which of course is true. And then Trenchard can't deny the Army anything. Well, he can't, you've done your conducted tour of the trenches, you can see that he can't. If the Army asks, we say yes."

Will nods. Frizell is pitched and tense, still thrumming somewhere with the dangerous elation that made him burst out about the saving hand of God.

"You play the piano, don't you?" asks Frizell.

"I do."

"That's awfully handy."

His piano-playing has been called many things, particularly by his wife, but "handy" is not one of them.

"I'd tell the padre if I were you. He always wants to know if any of the new chaps have musical talent."

Frizell smiles briskly, glad to have sorted out the piano-playing, glad to find a way of drawing Will into the life of the Mess. It can be tricky with the old men.

"If he likes music," says Will, "I heard a girl play very well yesterday, not five miles from here."

"What, was there a concert?"

"It was in a private house."

But Frizell doesn't seem interested. The gap in the hedge approaches. There is the little plank-and-rail bridge over the stream. On one side of the stream, cricket and sleep. On the other, the smell of oil, the sound of machine tools, the roar of engines being tested. Runways, hangars, mechanics, the Battery wireless, all the apparatus of war. Frizell steps onto the wooden bridge, waves and vanishes behind a screen of hawthorn and cow parsley.

There is nothing that can compare to it. First the climb. The Nieuport's got a good rate of climb. You can feel the power of it pushing you up through the clouds. They're wet and clammy and you can't see anything. They press in on you and you think that the thick white tunnel is never going to end.

And then you burst out into the light.

Story Development at
30 September

Dearest Rebecca,

You've got this far, at least. The more I write this story the more I see how much there is left to write. But I don't want to bore you. And it may not be the kind of story you like—you may not feel for Will and Florence as I do.

And then there's Will's wife. I haven't found a name for her yet. She's pregnant and she writes letters to him two or three times a week. They've already been married for ten years. But he's detached from her and maybe she is detached from him, too. They live together. They sleep in the same bed. She asks him about things that have happened at work, and she listens carefully, frowning. But then she'll drop a little remark which makes it clear that she thinks Will should be more careful at work. He's too outspoken, he makes it much too obvious that he's cleverer than Mr. Davidson.

Well, that may be true, but Mr. Davidson is the chief accountant, so it's not very clever. Will was passed over for promotion last time, and that doesn't surprise her. Can't he make the effort, for her sake if not for his own? He's got his pride, she understands that. She knows all about his pride by this time, she should hope.

She nips out remarks that cut him, and she knows what she's doing, and he knows it, too.

Rebecca, I've been thinking about Olya. Even Olya, as generous as she is—you can't imagine how generous she was—she's been changed by what happened between us. Everything got tarnished. She wanted to give me everything but I wouldn't take it, that was the worst thing, worse than what I couldn't give her.

I've disappointed her. I've played around with her hopes and dreams of the future. And they were hopes and dreams she had a right to have, the hope of being loved with the whole of someone's heart. She wouldn't even have minded if it hadn't lasted. She could have coped with that—even if I'd been unfaithful and gone off with someone else. But not with the way it slowly became clear to her that I'd never loved her in the way she wanted, and I was never going to.

I didn't mean to do it, but on one level I knew I was doing it. Disappointing her, I mean.

You know that smile she has, the way she gets joy from things that most people don't bother about—giving away a bottle of fruit she'd preserved herself, or taking the neighbor's children for an ice cream. I didn't kill all that but I changed it.

She went to her sister more and more often. She began to criticize me. She would say harsh things but with such a painful look, as if it hurt her more to know these things and say them than it could ever hurt me to hear them.

If we'd had children they would have been her children. I can see it. They'd have had Olya's eyes. Three pairs of Olya's eyes, all of them looking at me, all of them baffled and accusing because I hadn't turned out as they'd hoped. I can just see a son of mine with Olya's eyes and it makes me shiver.

Will's not a boy. He's a man in his mid-thirties. He's thickset and he's got gray in his hair. He hasn't rushed into this war straight out of childhood. He's got an adult life to lose.

Well, this is as far as I've got. I'll have more of the MS to send you soon, but here's my outline for the rest of the section. It's very rough.

STORY DEVELOPMENT

More on Will's past. Will's father, Joseph Hazell, injured in tunnel collapse soon after Will escapes the rip. He can't work underground again, though he recovers enough to work as gardener. Low wages & employers who make it clear they are doing him a favor by taking him on. They give him part of his wages in produce.

Will begins to steal from his father's employers. He's clever and doesn't get caught. His mother knows but says nothing—uses the extra stuff as it appears, to feed her family. Will brings her black grapes when she's ill. She brushes the bloom off them. His father both knows about the thieving and refuses to know. This goes on for years.

After five years Joe Hazell is unable to work because of his injuries. He dies at forty-three.

Will decides that when he is a man he will get himself into a job where no one can tell him what to do. (But he will not achieve this, because there's no money or influence to get him into a profession. Will is picked up as an exceptionally clever boy and goes to grammar school on scholarship. His father's employers pay for his school uniform. He steals from them all the time, gladly.

But he has to leave school to take a clerical job when his father dies, because his mother needs the money. He will work at a higher level than his father and enter a different class, but he will still be an employee and work in a hierarchy where he is not in control.)

My father's RAF greatcoat. Mum putting it over me on winter nights, on top of the bedclothes. The weight of it. Heavy wool which I thought had a smell of the war. The way the coat would slip when I turned over in bed, as if it had a life of its own. The weight of it years after Dad died. The way I would think about the stories Mum told me about Dad. *This is important.* This must be how Will feels about his father.

What happened to the coat? Must ask Mum if she remembers. If she has still got it.

Will hates the thought of being in anyone else's power. He hates what Madame Blanche does to Florence: her grooming of Florence.

Madame Blanche. She will die when a German plane (Albatros?) drops a bomb wide after raid on local railway station. She'll be wearing her lilac kid boots. She looks up and sees the Albatros but doesn't recognize it. She thinks it's an English plane. She thinks that Will may be the pilot. She looks up, thinks she recognizes his face through the goggles. The plane dives on her.

(But she's a tough practical woman, so this scene must not be loose or overemotional in any way.)

Madame Blanche really in love with Florence. Jealous of Florence's child, not maternal. Grooming Florence to take her place or more.

Madame Blanche walking in the attics at night, noiseless, spying on her household. Florence and Claire don't wake.

One night when she is doing this she'll find Will and Florence together, sleeping. They won't wake. Clasped, but not sexual. Florence has had a bad dream. Will clasps her. She feels his arms around her as she falls back into sleep. Moonlight falls on the bed but it's not romantic at all—in fact it is rather desolate.

? Cut the war graveyard scene opening? Have Will live? Florence and Will are together at the end, after the war? The pair of them together, back in Cornwall, at Chysauster. Claire playing hide-and-seek in and out of the ruined houses, above the bones of Will's ancestors. Violets. Shadows of the past flattened by sun of the present moment—

No. For fuck's sake. *This is not an idyllic love story.*

I want to look at how things are remembered. How they are memorialized. How Florence fits Will into her history.

At the beginning she and Claire walk in the raw garden that will become one of the classic graveyards of the First World War. That raw graveyard will become manicured. It will become beautiful because so many crosses stand in line and make different patterns depending from which angle you come upon them. Fifty years later, fifty-seven years later, ninety years. It will be set aside forever as a place for people to come and remember in a certain way.

Florence remembers Will but her life goes on, forward, into Claire. Will's wife gives birth to a boy and tells him stories about his father. They are good stories and they present Will in a favorable light. There's no one to contradict them and because Will is dead he won't stand in the way of the version she chooses. And slowly, year by year, she forgets how they sat at the same table and slept in the same bed and became strangers to each other. Instead, she remembers odd moments: sponging him down when he had measles, two months after they were married. "Imagine a grown man getting measles!" he whispered, and his cracked lips smiled at her. The first time he flew solo, when he flew low over the house and she ran out, thinking the noise of the engine was the end of the world.

"And do you know, the shadow of that plane ran right over me," she'll say to Will's child.

Will and Florence together in Florence's attic bed. Whispering. Clasped together after Florence's nightmare. Complete intimacy, like an intimacy after death. Against this moment he will judge all other moments. But she will not.

Will confides in Florence. He wants to tell her all the stories of his life. He tells Florence the story of the rip and his father underground. He talks to Florence about flying. For once he is not angry with Florence because of the sexual failure between them. In the dark he talks and she listens. They are like brother and sister, the same information flowing through both of them.

He understands her withdrawal and her weariness. He clasps her.

The next day, Will's flight. He's afraid. Frizell has gone down in a flamer.

(By now it's clear that Will's relationship with Florence doesn't and can never include sexual happiness. That's been arrested in her, if not destroyed. Everything happened prematurely to Florence. Her first blundering, half-wanted and completely unenjoyable sexual experience gave birth to Claire. Since then she's traded sex for Claire's survival. Because of the sex Florence sells, Claire is warm, clothed, cherished. She has her mother close to her. She drinks chicken soup and eats fruit from the orchard. She's surrounded by flowers, chickens, animals. Florence believes that her daughter doesn't even notice the sound of the guns.

Will knows what has happened to Florence. But he thinks, maybe, that she'll change. Given enough time, warmed and cherished, she'll become again what she might have been. It's too frightening to contemplate that she can't change, that life at Madame Blanche's has destroyed something in her—and that it can't be undone—)

—So Will dies before he has to know it fully? But there has been that moment of perfect intimacy between them. He has held her and they have exchanged their stories. He loves her. He loves what she is in his life.

The graveyard. It comes back to that at the end of the story, as it was in the beginning. Claire and Florence hand in hand again, just the two of them. Will inside the ground. They walk above him but he doesn't know it.

Claire and Florence, hand in hand. The sensation of Claire's hand inside Florence's, in the field of the dead. (Ruby's hand.)

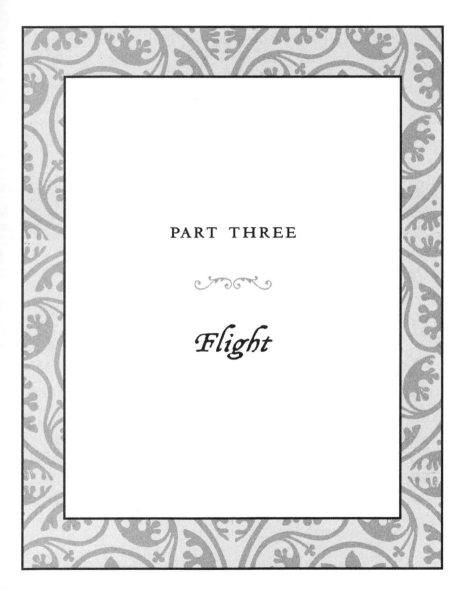

PART THREE

Flight

By the time I finish reading Joe's story, it's dark. Late and dark. I put the manuscript on the bed and lie back.

It's too frightening to contemplate that she can't change.

I think about this for a long time, and about all the stories that cover us—me and Adam and Joe—and weigh us down. I think about Florence and Will lying together, whispering. *Like an intimacy after death.* Yes, that's possible. I know what it means. Me and Adam in bed, when so much sex had washed through us that it seemed to leave us sexless, beyond ourselves. The night that Ruby was conceived.

She had her life and it was her own life.

Hours seem to pass but it's still only eleven-thirty when I look at the clock. I get up, and take the piece of blue and yellow silk that Mr. Damiano gave me. I spread it over the bed. I want to sleep on it to-night. I spread it out carefully, and lie down again, on the piece of fairground silk that's been traveling with Mr. Damiano all his life. I think about the first time the tent went up, and Bella's eyes watching it billow.

There are footsteps on the stairs. It'll be Marie. I snap out my light and Joe's manuscript rustles as I roll over onto it. If Marie hears no sound and sees no light she'll go away. She'll be wanting to talk to me about her daughter's marriage again. Day and night mean nothing to Marie. She's as likely to clean the house at midnight as at midmorning. I lie still.

The footsteps stop outside my door. There's a knock. I don't answer or move a muscle. Another knock. I still do nothing, but suddenly, all over my body, my skin starts to burn. I know with every cell of myself that it's not Marie.

And then his voice says my name.

Painted Lady

When shall we meet again, sweetheart?
　　When shall we meet again?
When the oaken leaves that fall from the trees
　　Are green and spring up again,
　　Are green and spring up again.

The room is high up, at the top of the house. A gull lands, spreads its wings in balance against the force of the wind, folds them. It begins to strut but the wind is too strong and the gull takes off, back into the current. It beats its way upward on oiled, powerful wings.

The window is small and high, the light strong. It's one of those wild, white days of the first autumn gales. No rain yet, but the wind is still rising.

There are no curtains. There's no need for blinds or curtains, since nothing overlooks this window. Below it there's a spread of slate roofs, some of them silvery with age, some with sagging, broken tiles, others smooth and new. Orange lichen has colonized the slate and put a bloom over all the roofs. There are sea glimpses in the distance, and this morning the sea is white with turbulence.

Two bodies rest on the narrow bed. The woman lies on her stomach, her face sideways, pressed into the man's shoulder. Her fist hangs loose over the edge of the bed. They are both naked. His skin is pale, hers darker. The duvet has slipped off both of them onto the floor by the bed. The man lies on his back, deeply asleep. There are no pillows, or maybe these have fallen off the bed, too, and lie tumbled under the duvet on the floor. The man sleeps, his face stern and distant. The woman's face is hidden by the spread of her hair, and there's a crumpled rag of blue and yellow silk between her thighs. They both lie quite still, as if they have fallen from a great height together, onto this mattress in a small attic room in a little town by the sea. They look as if they may never move again. The wind bangs, the frame of the window creaks and a draft sucks at the door. Nobody stirs.

We sit cross-legged on my bed, facing each other.

Outside there are gulls riding on the wind, into the frame of the window and then out of sight. The house creaks and booms with the coming storm.

We stare at each other. I think of him as he was when he came up the narrow staircase to the flat where I lived with Joe. His hair was red then, and now it is gray. His face is more deeply scored, and this time I know what has put the lines there.

He's here now, within touch. He is with me. I can see him, touch him, taste him. I am printing him back onto me, dot by dot by dot. It will take me a lifetime and that's what I want.

Marie is banging about two floors down, cleaning the hallway. You can hear her thumping the broom against the skirting boards, even through the noise of the wind. She's got a vacuum cleaner but she prefers to suffer. She sweats proudly over brooms and buckets. She's an odd kind of landlady, but maybe there's no other kind, and so far we've got on.

"She takes her underwear off when she does the cleaning," I say. Adam smiles. He lifts my wrist and kisses the inside skin. It's a light kiss at first and then more hungry. He runs his lips up my arm.

There's an explosion that buffets the air, and then another. I don't know what it is.

"It's the maroons," says Adam.

A yell from downstairs. "RebeccA! RebeccA! Lifeboat's going out! You coming down the harbor?"

"Shall we?" asks Adam.

"I've never seen it."

"Get your clothes on. We'll have to be quick."

"You go on down, Marie, I'll come in a minute," I call. "I'm not dressed."

The doors of the lifeboat station are open. The edge of the harbor bulges with people as the boat comes down the slipway. Tide's high enough that she won't need the tractor to get out. Water's slopping up the slipway. Even inside the harbor the sea is chopped up, gray and white and wild.

"It's a yacht off Godrevy. She's lost her engine and she's drifting."

The way the lifeboat goes out, she makes your eyes sting, even if you know nothing about her. We are pressed tight together by the crowd. She falls to the water and cuts into it and at once she's off, her engines gunning for the harbor mouth.

And she's gone. All round the harbor the lining of people breaks into clots and begins to disperse. The old man beside us is holding a child's hand. Indicating the child, he says, "He's never seen her go out for real. Only on Lifeboat Day."

People are pushing around us, trying to bear us away as he goes on to tell his tale. It was the lifeboat disaster of 1939. He remembers it. He was a boy then but he remembers all the women going down to the harbor in the black of the night. All of them afraid, the night was so bad. The worst he can remember. And waiting for the boat but she didn't come back, she broke up. One man lived, he was swept over to Gwithian and he was the only one to survive. Some farm people found him when he crawled out of the water. It was morning by then and his wife already thought he was dead, then she got a message. Among all those widows she still had her living man.

"I was eight years old when the lifeboat was lost."

We listen and say nothing. The tale is told and the boy tugs at his grandfather's hand because it's raining now and they're getting wet. And so we part. Adam and I walk close, arms linked against the rush of wind. Suddenly everyone's melted away, back indoors. The old man and the child have vanished. We never even saw Marie.

The wind shoves us along the bare gray streets, around corners, uphill. Rain streams on us now. Uphill, clinging close, catching my breath.

We are at the top. We walk heads down, buffeted. There's a skinny, ripped Tesco bag whirling along the road. Man's Head crouches to our left with the sea blowing up on it. Porthmeor below is buried in white waves.

"There are surfers out," says Adam. "Look."

There are two worlds, I think. In one of them the surfers put on their wetsuits in the car park and take up their boards. The wild sea is their playground. They call the inside of the waves the green room. In the green room they rehearse for the next wave, and the next, and the next. The wave goes on until autumn folds into winter, winter to spring, and then the summer comes again. They ride the sea and the sea lets them.

It's a dreamworld, I think. It's like the places Mr. Damiano makes.

If he saw Porthmeor he would re-create it as a Dreamworld. He would make a tent fashioned like the inside of a wave. It would teem with bubbles and there would be the noise of surf in your ears, and the taste of salt.

❦

In the other world we are opening the iron gate that leads into Barnoon Cemetery. There is a notice saying that dogs are forbidden here. The gate whines as it opens. Adam holds it for me, in case the wind catches it.

I am baffled. I cannot get my bearings or my breath in all this wind. There's a place in my mind I can't get to. I can't remember where Ruby lies.

Adam guides me along the grassy path. We turn downhill, between a line of graves. Ruby used to watch the lugger's brown sails from here, as it came around the Island.

This isn't a graveyard where only dead people and mourners come. We used to walk through it in our shorts and sun cream. We would go down to the beach this way, with rolled-up towels and Ruby's wetsuit. We would stop hereabouts to name what we saw. Over to Clodgy, Man's Head, Porthmeor, the Island, St. Nicholas Chapel, the fishing boats and then the lugger, the *Dolly Pentreath* with her brown sails, bucking as she passed the Island. Ruby could name them all. I would pick her up, smelling sweetly of Ambre Solaire and baby sweat. She would ride in the crook of my arm and name the places. White sand, black rocks.

"Here she is," says Adam. We kneel at the side of the grave, on the wet ground. The grass grows thick around the headstone, where Ruby's name is printed more sharply than the name of Adam's grandmother.

Rain pelts on our backs.

"No, don't go, let's stay here," I say, although Adam hasn't spoken.

"It's all right," he says. "I'm not going."

Rain blows in white gusts from the sea. I clutch the grass that grows by Ruby's grave. We don't want to shelter ourselves. Ruby's here, and we are here with her.

⁓

I see her. We are walking on the field path north of Zennor Head. The sun is brilliant on her dark red curls, making them shine blue. It's late June and we are walking through the foxgloves. Ruby's ahead, with Adam. Where the furze pushes out over the path, he lifts her so that the prickles won't scratch her legs, then he sets her down.

She runs ahead in a sharp spurt of running. She's seen something we haven't seen. She runs ahead, then stops. As I come up behind her she turns, her face astonished, her fist held up. A Painted Lady has settled on her hand.

There is Ruby. The Painted Lady flirts its wings, then spreads them. In a minute it will fly off. Ruby stands neck-high in foxgloves, and the butterfly stays on her hand. Sun strikes on the thick warm dust under the foxgloves. We stand in its cupped heat.

We gave her a box of compressed cardboard because we didn't want to crib her in a wooden box with brass fittings.

They dissolve, they don't last long.

Rain pelts on our backs. We are joined, side to side, as if we'd been made that way.

"Come away now," says Adam, and I do. I let him lift me up from the soaked earth.

Final Chapter: Heaven's Gate

Have you tumbled from the sky until your wires were shrilly screaming
    And watched the earth go spinning round about?
Have you felt the hard air beat your face until your eyes were streaming
    Have you turned the solar system inside out?

Spit's grooming the Nieuport again. He checks the mounting of the Lewis gun. His repair to the port wingtip is holding up perfectly, where it was shredded three days ago.

Will is vomiting into a zinc bucket behind the Mess tent. That's what he does before a contact patrol. It's quite routine and the best way of dealing with things. By the light of his hurricane lamp he sees that the inside of the bucket is spattered with orange and beige particles of the food he ate last night. It seems not to have been digested at all. Will's stomach heaves again and releases a last jet of vomit.

That's it. Done.

He picks up the bucket and walks to the far end of the field, where the stream runs away from the camp. He empties the zinc bucket, sluices it, sluices it again and listens to the water splash away.

Dawn's coming. Dawn is approximately twenty-three minutes off.

Now he is on the earth with his boots in dew-wet long grass. He bends down and wipes his hands on the wetness, then cups his hands together, dips them into the stream and lifts clean water to his mouth. He rinses his mouth, spits into the grass, dips his hands again and drinks. The water tastes cold and fresh. The feel and taste of the water is startlingly clear, as if separate from every other experience he's ever had. His head aches slightly and his diaphragm is sore from vomiting.

On his left the hedge is a gray bulk. It's a hawthorn hedge. Will stretches his hand and brushes it against the leaves. They have lost the skin-softness of early spring, when they burst out of their packed buds.

He thinks of the granite hedges at home, on a gray morning with the cows moving to be milked. At this season the granite is swallowed up in fuchsia, foxgloves and young bracken. The fields slope toward the sea and there he is, walking the lane between them, hidden, with a switch of bracken in his hand.

But this hawthorn hedge is gray. When the sun rises it will be green, and he'll be gone. A blackbird calls, then falls silent as if she might have made a mistake. But she hasn't. Another day's coming, nearly here now.

That sound that the stream makes: it really is babbling. Quick water over small pebbles. Twenty-one minutes.

Will walks back across the field, swinging the bucket. He's empty now but he won't eat anything. Once you're in the sky there's too much adrenaline: you can't digest. He takes out a flask and opens it. Two silver capfuls of brandy-and-water, that's the measure. You have to know these things and not drink blindly or too much. Just enough to help you to know what you're doing.

There is a letter in his breast pocket, from his wife. Why did he put that letter there? It was a lie to make it lie over his heart. She was anxious in her letter. She hadn't heard from him and she'd wanted to know that he was well. She always wants to know that he is well, as if the war is an illness that he might catch.

How the minutes jump. He's in the Nieuport now and Spit's telling him to take the engine up to full rev. Spit listens. He hears things in the texture of the engine's roar that Will can't hear.

Six hours ago he was in bed with Florence. They lay side by side. Claire woke up and Florence disappeared. When she came back and slid her cold feet into bed he said to her, "Make a mark on me."

"What do you mean?"

"A mark. Haven't you got a little pair of scissors, Florence? Or a knife?"

"I can't do that."

"You can. You can. I want it to be there when you're not. When I'm up at eight thousand feet. When I think that this isn't real."

She was silent for a long time, lying beside him so quietly that he thought she'd fallen asleep. He was on the edge of anger with her for leaving him alone, awake, when she said quietly, "Very well."

She got out of bed and lit the candle. He watched her rummage in a drawer with her back to him and the nightdress fallen around her again.

"They're in here somewhere—"

She showed him a pair of ornamental scissors with mother-of-pearl handles. He couldn't fit his fingers into them, but Florence could. Her long hair made a shadow but under it her face was intent.

"Make a mark, Florence," he said.

"Where?"

He thought for a few seconds. "Where I can see it but no one else can. On my hand. No. On the underside of my arm."

"We'll have to be careful," she said.

He turned his arm over. The skin was pale and the veins clear.

"There," he said, pointing to a place on the inside of his wrist, to the right of the tendon.

"There," she repeated. The scissors jerked nervously in her hand. "Are you sure?"

"It's perfectly safe."

The scissors wavered. "I can't do it," said Florence.

"Why not?"

"It'll hurt you. I don't want to hurt you. It's stupid."

He almost felt how stupid it was. The candle flame was trembling too.

"Let's go back to bed," said Florence.

Suddenly he leaned across her and took the scissors.

"You're right," he said. "Listen, Florence, tomorrow—"

"What?"

"If I'm late—or if I can't come—it's because there's another show."

"Come however late it is," said Florence. "You've got the key."

"Yes, I've got it," he said, and he took hold of her and the thick bunch of her nightdress.

It wasn't right. She pressed her body the length of his, but awkwardly. He fumbled with her nightdress. Their bodies moved clumsily together, then apart.

"We want a little house to ourselves," he said.

"Yes," she said, but not as if it was a possible thing. He knew what was in her mind. The rooms and rooms beneath them. The bedrooms where men had come. Officers. It made him want to spit, though he was one of them. He'd come here and sat in the salon downstairs and eaten cake with the rest of them.

She was clumsy with him, like a girl with no experience at all. He wondered again if he had the power to seem something different to her, separate from the men who had rooted in her body for satisfaction.

If we had a place of our own to go, he thought. In his mind he saw a house with Florence sitting at the window, looking out.

And where will the war be then, you fool, he thought. One more enemy advance and they'd evacuate the aerodrome. Madame Blanche's house would be shelled until it looked like all those other houses he flew over at four hundred feet. Part of a chimney sticking up from the collapse of the roof. A crater of mud where the carp pond was. It would all be obliterated.

"Would you be glad, if this house was shelled?" he murmured.

He heard her sharp draw of breath.

"All of it gone," he said, "and everything that's happened here. Should you like that?"

⌘

She'd put her scissors away without them touching his skin. He's got no mark of her on him, he thinks, as the Nieuport judders, trembles all over, begins to climb.

Up, up through the wet white softness of cloud. Mist. Whiteness closing in and making him dizzy. Only the angle of the Nieuport's nose makes him believe he's climbing at all. He's in a tunnel of blankness and his heart pounds with the terror it gives him each time, as unfailing as the vomit in the zinc bucket. He counts the seconds. One-and-two-and-three-and-four-and—

So soon may I follow
When friendships decay,
And from love's shining circle
The gems drop away . . .

Frizell by the piano, singing while Will played. Frizell's red mouth open and shining. A beery, swaying hush as Frizell sang.

He went down in a flamer. All that way down, seven thousand feet of it. Are you conscious all the way down?

"Fact of it is, old man, (yes, he really did talk like that) *you're scared every second and you love every second. But that's it. That's flying."*

Bastards don't give us parachutes. Why don't they? Do they think we'll jump out over the German lines?

There's cloud in his throat. Maybe he's falling. Six-and-seven-and-eight-and-nine-and—

This is flying, thinks Will, as his plane shoots out of the white like a cork from the bottle. And here he is. Beneath him the choking white fog has resolved itself into fleecy cloud. The sky is blue. The clouds are tipped with dawn pink. He is flooded with light as he turns to head east.

And the sky is empty. He has it all to himself. He is himself, alone, as he likes it.

But what am I doing here? For a second he blanks. He cannot remember his mission at all.

⁊

He volunteered, that was it. There's a Fokker that keeps coming over at dawn on bombing raids. Three times this week already. The squadron could spare a plane to deal with it. Why he volunteered he cannot now imagine. Maybe for a sensible reason—to avoid something worse?

Everything was breaking up. Soon they'd be retreating to another aerodrome. No one has said it yet but everyone knows. The camp that looked so sure and permanent when he arrived will be packed up in a few hours. As soon as you tried to put your hand on the war's tail it twisted inside its skin and became another animal.

⁊

No sign of the Fokker. The fleece of cloud below him is beginning to break. Beneath it, showing through the holes, there's the scar of the front. But what he can see, can also see him. White puffs blow at him like dandelion clocks.

He wants that Fokker. He wants the bastard to appear before it has laid its eggs, heavy and lumbery with bombs.

⁊

"*What do you mean?*"

"*A mark. Haven't you got a little pair of scissors, Florence? Or a knife?*"

"*I can't do that.*"

"*You can. You can. I want it to be there when you're not. When I'm up at eight thousand feet. When I think that this isn't real.*"

⟶

Florence stirs in her sleep. Is it Claire? No. Stickily she opens her eyes to a square of dawn in the window. There are streaks of red. A bad sign. Already the guns are firing. So close now, closer than they've ever been before.

But the house will stand. Florence believes in it. The cherry tree, the orchard, the pond with the carp. Even the bedrooms. She hates them and yet she's afraid to be without them. The big kitchen where Solange used to make chicken broth for Claire. All the rooms are empty now. The girls left a week ago.

The guns sound. The noise of them vibrates in the floorboards and the frame of her bed. The door of the attic bedroom opens and Madame Blanche stands there in her gray linen traveling dress.

"Get up, Florence," she says. "Pack everything of value into a basket that you can carry. There's a cart waiting in the yard. We must leave."

"But we can't leave," says Florence.

"But of course we can," says Madame Blanche, and her face breaks into a curious, ironic smile.

⟶

It comes at him out of the blue. An Albatros, diving from the east. It got behind him and caught him. It's onto him, emptying its drum.

⟶

Florence scoops Claire out of bed. She presses the child close to her, telling her it's time to get up, they've got to get dressed and go out early today. Claire's heavy head lolls. There's a red crease on her cheek where the pillow has marked it. Florence sets her upright on the bed and Claire staggers drunkenly. Her eyes are open but really she's still asleep. Florence lifts her again and Claire burrows her head into her mother's shoulder. She's damp with sweat and sleep.

"You must wake up now, Claire. We've got to go."

There's Madame Blanche out in the road, in the dust, gesturing to Petit Paul to hurry. But Petit Paul is having trouble with the mare. The guns are firing too close for her. The thump of shells makes the earth tremble. The mare throws up her head and her long yellow teeth show as she whinnies in terror of the earth that's betrayed her. Petit Paul struggles with her bridle. He hauls her forward but she won't come to be harnessed to the cart. She shudders all over and throws back her head again, spitting the froth of her mouth at him.

Petit Paul has got to get her forward, into position, and then back her into the traces. How will he do it with his lean, scant strength? Florence knows he will not. He's lost the heart for it. He's afraid of the mare now, and afraid of Madame Blanche and of the sounding of the guns he thought he'd got away from, working in this house. He looks a long way off in the dust that the mare's hooves kick up.

But Madame Blanche won't take no for an answer. She catches up her skirt and runs at the mare. The mare sees her coming and backs, blundering into the cart shafts. Madame Blanche raises her strong arm in triumph, to beat the mare about the eyes and then to beat Petit Paul. No one, nothing, will get away from her like that. Florence, clutching Claire in her arms, moves backward.

A zip of bullet catches the fuel tank. Will understands it almost faster than it happens. The tank will leak and a few drops of benzine on the red-hot engine will start a flamer.

The plane comes in low. Florence neither sees it nor hears it: it is too close for that. Every fiber of her flesh vibrates to it. She throws herself facedown in the dust, covering Claire with her body, as the plane swoops the length of the dusty road, spitting out bullets. She doesn't look and she sees nothing. Only the dust and small stones beneath her face where she strains to cover every inch of Claire's flesh with her own.

The tank will leak and a few drops of benzine on the red-hot engine will start a flamer. He knows what to do. The Albatros is coming in again, sure of its kill now and careless of its approach. He sees pilot and gun coming at him. He fires until his drum is empty and the Albatros sheers away, as if falling off a shelf of air.

Florence looks up from the dust. The plane has passed over. At eye level she sees the bulk of the mare down on her back. Her hooves thresh the air. Petit Paul and Madame Blanche are invisible. They do not speak or get up or scream. The engine's noise is in the distance. It will come back again, thinks Florence. It will turn and finish what it's begun. Already she hears the engine note changing, beginning to bulge again in the distance.

Florence scrambles to her feet. She hears for the first time the sound of Claire's screams. She is not hurt, no. The grip of her legs winding around Florence's waist is too strong for that. Her fingers dig into her mother's flesh. Florence runs to the side of the road but the ditch is too shallow to hide in. There's a gate. But she cannot climb with Claire in her arms. She peels the child off her while Claire's screams rise to a frenzy. She lifts her daughter and drops her into the soft long grass on the other side of the gate, then clambers after her.

Florence runs bent forward over Claire, so that her body shields the child. Her breath comes harsh as she runs the length of the field, in the shadow of the hedge, hidden from the road. She runs parallel to the road, westward, to where England is.

He must switch off the engine, quick, before a drop of benzine hits the red-hot metal. Will switches off the engine and sudden quiet rocks him. The Albatros has gone, somersaulting into the cloud below. Maybe the pilot will pull out of the spin, but if he does Will won't see it. Now he is really flying, eerie, solitary, up in the blue.

If your fuel tank's pierced, switch off your engine immediately. No, Ackroyd, you won't fall out of the air. You're not sitting on a bloody tin tray, are you? Another one who wasn't listening in my lecture yesterday. Can any of you gentlemen tell Ackroyd what will happen if he switches off his engine?

Wind rushes through the ailerons. Without the engine the sky is huge and it bulges with all the silence his engine has kept away from him. A white vapor streams behind Will's machine as he descends, and as the vapor spreads across the blue it seems to form itself first into letters, then words. The words hold steady in the sky for a second, but there is no one to read them.

Epilogue

A field is enough to spend a life in.
Harrow, granite and mattress springs,
shards and bones, turquoise droppings
from pigeons that gorge on nightshade berries,
a charm of goldfinch, a flight of linnets,
fieldfare and January redwing
venturing westward in the dusk,
all are folded in the dark of the field,

all are folded into the dark of the field
and need more days
to paint them, than life gives.

We've been walking side by side for a long time. I've said so much: too much, maybe. Joe was right, we are brother and sister, reader and writer. If you only knew how much I've wanted to keep your presence, and your attention. But sometimes you've smiled, or nodded, and I've had the feeling that you're accompanying me. Or that your imagination is accompanying mine.

I am grateful for it. Without your imagination the story would die.

Maybe you know this stretch of the coast path. It's very beautiful.

Far below there is white sand under deep water, and it produces a shade of turquoise which you see nowhere else. The power of these colors brings me to a standstill.

There's a farm collie running in front of me. Sometimes he stops and waits for me to catch up. His body quivers, tense with willingness. He's shepherding me. He does it to everyone who walks this way, if they let him.

You can go two ways here. One path continues along the coast, following the sculpt of the cliffs. The other forks right and leads you back across the fields.

This is where we'll separate. You'll frown or smile for the last time. Maybe you'll even say something, though I'm beyond imagining what those words might be. And then you'll go your way and I'll go mine.

Epigraph Sources

Prologue: "A car comes up, with lamps full-glare..." from "Nobody Comes" by Thomas Hardy

PART ONE

Chapter One: "She was a good-looking girl, too..." from Chapter One of *Oliver Twist* by Charles Dickens

Chapter Two: "the wife wants a child..." from "The Farmer's in His Den" (Traditional)

Chapter Six: "For the sword outwears its sheath..." from "So, We'll Go No More a–Roving" by George Gordon, Lord Byron

Chapter Nine: "I have mislaid the key. I sniff the spray..." from "Old Man" by Edward Thomas

Chapter Ten: "But never met this Fellow/Attended, or alone..." from "A Narrow Fellow in the Grass" by Emily Dickinson

Chapter Twelve: "Life has become better, Comrades, life has become more cheerful!" Slogan taken from a speech made by Stalin in December 1935

Chapter Thirteen: "beautiful today the surf on Porthkidney sands/ and the standing out of the lighthouse, sheer..." from "beautiful today the" by Helen Dunmore

Chapter Fourteen: "After great pain, a formal feeling comes./ The nerves sit ceremonious, like tombs..." from "After Great Pain, a Formal Feeling Comes" by Emily Dickinson

Epigraph Sources

Chapter Fifteen: "We wove a web in childhood,/ A web of sunny air..." from "Retrospection" by Charlotte Brontë

Chapter Sixteen: "Out of the wood of thoughts that grows by night..." from "Cock-Crow" by Edward Thomas

Chapter Seventeen: "To know the change and feel it,/ When there is none to heal it..." from "In a Drear-nighted December" by John Keats

Chapter Twenty: "If ever I forget your name, let me forget home and Heaven!" from *The Woodlanders* by Thomas Hardy, Chapter XLVIII

Chapter Twenty-one: "And to get to him—to his very heart..." from the second Voronezh notebook of Osip Mandelstam, translated by HD

Chapter Twenty-two: "Golden fleece, where are you, golden fleece?" from *Tristia* by Osip Mandelstam, translated by HD

Chapter Twenty-three: "We dip our heads in the deep blue sea..." from "The Big Ship Sails on the Alley-Alley-O" (Traditional)

PART TWO

"Have you left the ground in murkiness, all clammy, grey and soaking..." from "The Call of the Air" by Jeffrey Day

PART THREE

Chapter Twenty-five: "When shall we meet again, sweetheart?/When shall we meet again?..." from "The Unquiet Grave" (Traditional)

Final Chapter: Heaven's Gate: "Have you tumbled from the sky until your wires were shrilly screaming..." from "The Call of the Air" by Jeffrey Day

Epilogue: "A field is enough to spend a life in..." from "Crossing the Field" by Helen Dunmore. A line from this poem also heads the Prologue to the "Boomdiara" section of the novel.

The hymn that Florence teaches to Claire is by Mary Howitt.

The song that Will sings in his bath, "Boomdiara," is a traditional campfire song which occurs in many variants.

"How many miles to Babylon" is a traditional rhyme.

The song that Frizell sings in the Mess is "The Last Rose of Summer" by Thomas Moore.

About the Author

Helen Dunmore is the author of seven novels, including *A Spell of Winter, With Your Crooked Heart* and *Talking to the Dead,* and has been published in fifteen countries. She is also a children's novelist, short-story writer, prize-winning poet and the first-ever winner of England's prestigious Orange Prize.